Five interesting things about Janet Mullany:

1. My favourite books are *Wives and Daughters* by Mrs Gaskell, because it's so lush and romantic; *Villette* by Charlotte Brontë for its passion and subversiveness; and *Emma* by Jane Austen, for its perfect plotting.

2. On the other hand, my commuter reading tends to be the same sort of stuff everyone reads, and my rating system for good reads includes missed stops (very good) and wrong lines (very, very good).

3. Once, staying overnight in an old house, I woke up and heard someone breathing. I was alone in the room. I got out fast.

4. I like tea. I mean, really like tea. I get mean if I don't get enough.

5. When I was five my brother pushed me into a tadpole pond. To this day he denies it.

Find out more about Janet at www.janetmullany.com and riskyregencies.blogspot.com.

By Janet Mullany

The Rules of Gentility
A Most Lamentable Comedy

A Most Lamentable Comedy

Janet Mullany

**little
black
dress**

First published in 2009
by LITTLE BLACK DRESS
An imprint of HEADLINE PUBLISHING GROUP

A LITTLE BLACK DRESS paperback

1

Cataloguing in Publication Data is available from the British Library

ISBN 978 0 7553 4779 7

Typeset in Transit511BT by Avon DataSet Ltd,
Bidford-on-Avon, Warwickshire

Printed and bound in Great Britain by Clays Ltd, St Ives plc

HEADLINE PUBLISHING GROUP
An Hachette UK Company
338 Euston Road
London NW1 3BH

www.littleblackdressbooks.com
www.headline.co.uk
www.hachette.co.uk

To Rosie Mullany, with love and admiration

Acknowledgements

Many thanks to a bunch of people, and my apologies if you should be mentioned here but aren't: The design and editorial teams at Little Black Dress, in particular Catherine Cobain and Leah Woodburn; my agent, Lucienne Diver; Charles Dickens for the beginning of the beginning of the story; my brother Martin, who has the photograph to prove it, for the button-eating pig; Elena Greene for the dancing bear; ROMNA for the last-minute answers on the view from Hampstead Heath; the Risky Regencies and History Hoydens blogs; the ladies of the Beau Monde; Maryland Romance Writers; the Wet Noodle Posse; the Bad Girls Critique Group; the staff and volunteers at Riversdale House Museum; writing friends Anna Campbell, Julie Cohen, Kate Dolan, Colleen Gleason, Delle Jacobs, Christie Kelley, Kathy Love, Pam Rosenthal, Robin L. Rotham and Leanne Shawler; non-writing friends Gail, Lucy and Maureen; my daughter Alison (sorry, there's sex in this one, but it's mercifully fast); and my husband Steve, to whom I must offer apologies for the omission of the chapter where a huge structure is built and then exploded in slow motion and from many angles.

London, 1822

Lady Caroline Elmhurst

Devil take it. I have seen this done a hundred times on the stage and read it a hundred more in novels, yet tying my sheets together proves almost impossible in real life.

'Milady, they'll break the door down,' my maid whimpers.

'Don't be a fool. Here, put these on.' I throw some petticoats at her. We have been unable to stuff all my possessions into my trunk and bags, and I am determined to leave nothing behind for that rapacious cow of a landlady to take. I wrench at the sheets and break a nail. 'Oh, don't stand there snivelling. Come and help me.'

Mary shuffles across the room, half in and half out of a petticoat.

Outside, the thunderous knocks on the door

resume. 'Open up, madam. We know you're in there,' bellows one of the seething mob of creditors. Heavens, it is like the French Revolution! How dare they!

'I am unwell, sirs,' I call in a quavering voice, tightening a monstrous knot that takes up half the length of the sheets.

'She's a dreadful liar and a whore to boot,' says a female voice, that of my landlady, Mrs Dinsdale. I can imagine how she stands there, mottled arms cradling one of her infernal cats, snuff sprinkled over her shoulders and grubby shawl. My shawl, my precious blue Kashmir, that I gave her in lieu of rent, the dirty, fat, ungrateful thing.

'Send your maid out, then.' The door shudders under their blows, and the tallboy we have pulled in front of it shifts a little on the floor.

'She is very poorly too, sir. Why, she is covered with stinking sores – oh horrors, I believe it is the smallpox.'

Is there a pause for reflection? If there is, it lasts but a few seconds. I loop the sheet around the bedpost, tie it in another hefty knot, and sling my rope out of the window. The trunk and bags follow. 'Out!' I hiss to Mary. 'Oh, sir,' I call out, 'I am too ill to move. I beg of you, come back another day.'

'Enough, Lady Elmhurst. We've had enough of your tricks and lies. Open the door, if you please.'

'Sir, I cannot. Have pity on a poor widow.' I shove Mary towards the window.

'I can't. I'm afraid of heights.' She clings to me like a limpet.

I shake her off.

'Oh, don't ask me to do it, milady.'

'Would you rather I leave you here? Get down that rope, girl.' I long to slap sense into her, but she is my only ally. I peer out of the window. There is a good six feet or so below the knotted sheets, but if she lands on one of the bags, she'll have a good soft landing. 'Come on, Mary. We'll laugh about this later, I promise you. I'll give you my blue-spotted muslin.'

'Very well. And an inside seat in the coach.'

'Yes, yes, but *go*.' I shove her out of the window. 'I fear I shall swoon,' I add loudly, for the benefit of the creditors outside the door, hoping it explains the silence that results when we have flown the coop.

Mary's face, like a piteous white flower in the dark, gazes up at me. Her mouth opens. If she is to scream, we are lost, and she seems set to dangle indefinitely in mid-air like some ridiculous spider. I look around the room for something to inspire her descent, and dart back to the window with it. She does scream a little as cold water hits her – doubtless she thinks it is the chamber pot, but even I am not so hardened – and then swears horribly as she lands. The china jug rolls from my hand as I fling myself on to the rope, there is a loud scraping sound as the bed moves, and I find myself catapulted on top of Mrs Dinsdale's cabbages.

I scramble to my feet. It is raining, of course, and pitch dark, and Mary sobs as she gathers our bags. 'I am giving notice, Lady Elmhurst.'

'Very well, but I shall not pay you a penny.'

She mutters something under her breath, probably a prediction that she will not get paid anyway, and I am sorry to say it is all too likely.

If my hands were not full of my worldly goods, I swear I would box her ears, but she has stuck with me so far, and I need her help. 'Come along. You're a good, brave girl, and remember the blue-spotted muslin. It looks far better on you than it does on me.'

More whimpers from Mary as we haul our belongings through Mrs Dinsdale's vegetable bed, have a brief fight with the laundry on the line and escape into the alley at the back of the lodging house. Stumbling in the dark, we make our way to the street, where I send Mary to find a hackney carriage – I am reluctant to show my face too near the lodgings, lest other creditors are on the prowl. My shoes are quite ruined – I have trodden in some most unpleasant substances – and, oh heavens, is that rustling sound a rat?

Just as I am about to give up on Mary and deciding

which of my bags I should take, for I cannot carry them all myself, a hackney carriage draws up. The driver and I have an acrimonious exchange about the justice of extra charges for the luggage. I am happy to say I win, but then Mary and I must load all the things ourselves, while he snickers and makes comments about bedraggled slatterns. And indeed, from Mary's appearance, that is what we probably both look like. I treat his comments with the contempt they deserve, and we set off, finally, for the early-morning coach that will take us out of London and away from my creditors.

There, another unpleasant surprise awaits. As we are so late, there are only two seats left, but only one of them is inside.

'You promised,' Mary says, and there is mutiny in her voice.

'So I did. Come, fair's fair. We'll cut for the inside seat.' I pull my pack of cards from the capacious reticule with which I travel. 'High I go inside, low you go outside.'

She cuts a king, and cackles with glee as I pull a four. 'High I go inside, low you go outside,' I repeat, and push her towards the coach as she opens her mouth to howl protest. 'And if you don't keep quiet, I'll tell everyone you stole my petticoats – why else would you be wearing four?'

I help her on to the roof of the coach with a

vigorous shove to the arse, hand her the umbrella (I am not totally without feelings) and settle myself inside, opening the book of sermons I carry to repel male attention.

Oh, that I have come to such a pass. I, that diamond of the first water, the former Miss Caroline Duncan, the catch of the season only seven short years ago, and now . . . twice widowed, down on my luck, forced to fight off unkind creditors; and it is true, I did allow the gallant Colonel Rotherhithe to assist in the payment of the rent. He was so very insistent. He even offered to pay my milliner, although I found out later he had not. But then I have always been gracious enough to accept gifts from admirers; why, even Mr Linsley, the gentleman with whom I had a brief *affaire de coeur* before I succumbed to Elmhurst, brought me a basket of mushrooms from the country. I remember their earthy scent and rich, meaty lobes and my stomach growls louder than the carriage rattling over the cobbles.

As for Elmhurst, God damn him and rot him in hell for squandering the money I inherited from dear Bludge, and for dying in such an unnecessary and absurd way, and what a fool I was to love him so. I miss Elmhurst quite dreadfully despite his faults. How degrading it was to have his brother snatch back the family diamonds and sapphires before I could sell them. It is true, though, that his family never liked me, and said very unpleasant things in my hearing about women of little breeding (meaning me) marrying rich gentlemen with one foot in the grave (meaning my first husband, Viscount Bludge, who was indeed several decades older than me).

And they have continued to say the most dreadful things about me as I have grieved and suffered this past year. There is no family loyalty towards me at all (the stupid fools).

I am most sadly put upon by all, and indeed, if I cannot find some gullible fool with a great deal of money to marry soon, all shall be lost.

I can only hope my latest dark cloud has a silver lining. Perhaps this most recent venture will have a happy outcome for me – no, it *must* have a happy outcome, for things could not get much worse than they are now, as I flee with my possessions and a sulky maid my only (unwilling) companion.

I find the letter from Lady Otterwell in my reticule and read it again. Yes, I have accepted the invitation to their house in the country – I doubt my creditors will follow – but what I have agreed to is worse than anything I envisioned even in my darkest hours.

Lord Otterwell has a longing for theatricals, and so I shall become – oh, the horror – that most vile and depraved of creatures, an *actress*!

Venice, a few weeks earlier

Colonel Maximilian Franklin alias *the Reverend Tarquin Biddle* alias *Vicomte St Germain-d'Aubussy* alias *Lord Francis Bartholemew* alias *Sir Rowland Weston* alias *Viscount Glenadder* alias *Mr Sebastian Fitzhugh-Churchill* alias *Count Mikhail Orchovsky* alias *the Earl of Ballyglenleary*, et cetera, et cetera.

Upon other occasions I have appreciated the Contessa's choice of spontaneity over finesse, but when her irate husband's servants throw me into the canal, I regret I did not remove my boots.

I'm dying, sinking into hell, my breath going, dragged down to a dark, noisome abyss, and my last thoughts are of mist and the sun rising like a new copper penny; green fields and the song of a lark against a glittering hazy sky.

God or the devil knows where I am going, but I want to go home.

I am surprised to find that hell is a warm, noisy sort of place where a lot of people, many with high piping voices, chatter incessantly, and I am destined to vomit for all eternity.

'That's it, sir. You'll feel better for it.'

The voice is familiar. Barton, my manservant, is

here too? And those dark eyes ranged around me must belong to imps or devils or some such, with the flicker of firelight in the background. But it's a gentle golden light, not the raging fires I anticipated. As the most recent paroxysm dies away, I become aware that I'm not in fact dead, but I am stark naked beneath some sort of rough blanket, and lying on a – a *table*? Surrounded by Italian children?

Barton, concern on his ugly face, nudges the basin beneath my chin. 'You want to get it all up, sir. You know what's in them canals.'

I do indeed, and am inspired to do as he says.

Later, and after several attempts to sip wine, I take note of my surroundings. There are indeed a fair number of children, ranging in age from a small child barely walking to a girl of about sixteen, who looks vaguely familiar. They gaze at me with unabashed curiosity; apparently I am the evening's entertainment. The room is low-ceilinged, and firelight dances off copper pots and low dark beams, pinkish plastered walls with a saint in an alcove. The air is scented with wood-smoke, tobacco and garlic. Someone, the mother of the brood, I presume, clatters around at the hearth, and a male figure is slumped in a chair, puffing on a pipe.

The oldest girl approaches me and shyly asks in Italian how I am doing.

'It's Maria from the piazza,' Barton says. 'The one you always buy flowers from.'

Flowers for the Contessa – bought with her money. Ah, yes, Maria. Of course I barely noticed her, as generally I only notice women who are rich and beddable, but she apparently saved my life. I clasp her hand and thank her. She giggles and tells me how she was riding home in her brother Giovanni's gondola when they found milord in the water, apparently dead, but I puked as soon as he pulled me aboard. Encouraged by this sign of life, they brought me to their home. Maria then sent Giovanni for Barton, suspecting that something untoward had happened for the English milord to end up fully bare-arsed and three-quarters drowned. She giggles mightily at this point. And now, if milord is feeling better, dinner is to be served and the family needs the table. Milord's servant has brought trousers for milord. Barton, enterprising and capable man that he is, has packed our things, suspecting that Venice and I have outworn each other's welcome.

Later that evening, with the family asleep around us, Barton and I confer in whispers by the fireplace. Indeed, so sore is my throat that I can barely talk.

'Paris, then, sir? Or how about Vienna?'

I look up from my writing case, tossing billets-doux into the fire. 'No. It's been too long. I want to go home.' My fingers search for the hidden spring in the writing case, and with a quiet click the secret compartment opens.

Barton raises his scarred eyebrows as gold glints in the firelight. 'Ireland?'

'No. England.' England. It must be the damn weakness from nearly drowning that makes me want to weep.

He shakes his head. 'Well, I suppose no one knows you in England. It's as good a place as any. Near twenty years since I was there, too. What shall we do there? The usual?'

I nod and lay a handful of coins on the table for the family who have saved my life and shared their meagre food with us. It is the least I can do, for I plan to steal away before dawn.

'And your name this time, sir?'

My name.

'My own name.'

He looks at me blankly.

'My name is Nicholas Congrevance.' It is a stranger's name on my tongue.

'Yes, sir. Of course it is, sir.' He winks at me.

Guildford, Surrey

Lady Caroline Elmhurst

'And did you have a comfortable journey, milady?' Mary asks. She has just alighted from the roof of the coach from London, showing, in my opinion, an unnecessary amount of ankle and petticoat. Now we both stand in the courtyard of the King's Head, the nearest stop to Elmhurst's house, surrounded by our luggage, while around us fellow travellers arrive and depart.

'Quite delightful and refreshing,' I reply. 'And you?'

She has the look of a cat that has been in the cream. 'The gentlemen on the roof were most attentive, and, lord, I ate like a pig. Pie, cake, bread and ham – why, it was a regular feast.' From the pink spots on her cheeks, she has also consumed a fair amount of gin. She turns to smile at her admirers who have plied her so willingly with food and drink.

Since the rain let up an hour from London, she is dried out, whereas my clothes are quite creased and soggy still. I had but one meagre cup of tea along the way (for I could not afford more), and I was crammed in between a fat woman who ate seven hard-boiled eggs and two raw onions (how they stank!) and a man with a runny nose who sniffed regularly – I timed him – once to a count of ten. The gentleman – I use the term loosely – who sat opposite me gazed at my bosom and tried to press my knee between his for almost the entire journey.

I suppose I should only be grateful that I was not forced into the even more vulgar company of those who travelled outside, but as I reflect upon this small comfort, my stomach gives a low, menacing growl.

Another coach pulls into the courtyard, the horses sweating and their hoofs striking sparks from the cobbles. Servants rush forward to change the horses and greet the passengers.

'Oh.' Mary now stares at a gentleman who steps down from the coach, hatless and pulling on a pair of gloves. 'Now *that's* what I call a man.'

Oh, indeed. Tall and lithe, long muscles I can imagine only too well beneath that tailoring (not up to London standards, and cut a little loose for the highest of fashion, but who cares), tawny gold hair, an aristocratic slash of long nose beneath straight, dark brows – and that mouth. Good God. The sort of lips that make a woman—

'That's enough. Mind your place,' I snap at Mary, afraid that I too am standing there with my mouth hanging open. The gentleman – do I know him? I don't believe so – disappears to the other side of the coach, doubtless to direct his servant.

At my side, a man wearing a linen apron bows obsequiously, to my relief. A canny innkeeper must know the presumed value of his customers, and if I have passed his test, I may yet preserve my reputation as a wealthy and respectable widow at Otterwell's.

'Would you care for some refreshments, milady?'

'I think not, sir. I should like to hire a trap to take me to Lord Otterwell's.'

'A gentleman has just hired it, milady, and is about to leave, though the driver should be back in an hour or so. If you'd care to step inside . . .'

Oh, certainly. Caught like a fly in some squalid private parlour where I shall be charged an inordinate amount of money for some weak tea and other refreshment. 'You have no other means of conveyance, sir?'

'I'm afraid not, milady.'

The innkeeper bows again, and opens a door, inviting me and my dwindling funds inside. A gust of cooking smells, roasting meat, fresh bread, assails me – oh heavens, I am so hungry I think I shall die. I wonder at what hour Otterwell dines.

Beside me, Mary, the greedy thing, smacks her lips. 'A cup of tea would be just the thing. Wouldn't it, milady?'

My hunger is followed by a wave of nausea. Oh, good heavens, I fear I am about to swoon. And not the swoon I have perfected (have not all ladies? A graceful sinking at the knee with a heartfelt sigh on to the closest piece of comfortable furniture, certain to inspire the nearest gentleman to besotted acts of gallantry). No, this is the real thing – a helpless and sickening plunge into darkness (and the filthy cobbles of the courtyard).

Mr Nicholas Congrevance

I've forgotten how lovely Englishwomen can be, and she's entrancing, this stranded beauty surrounded by the flotsam and jetsam of her belongings – surely that can't be a porcelain candlestick peeping out from the large basket? Maybe this is how English ladies travel. Her maid, a cheeky, pretty piece, has already given me the eye and now flutters her lashes at Barton, so she is not able to see her mistress stagger and sway, but I do, and cross the courtyard in a few swift strides. She slumps into my arms, somewhat damp – she must have been caught in the rain – and her bonnet falls from her head and rolls on to the cobbles.

She is entirely without colour, her eyes and mouth half open, and I hoist her into my arms.

'Why, she don't usually faint like that, sir,' her maid offers, swinging her mistress' hat by the ribbons, and brushing a fleck of horse dung from it.

'She's ill? Should we send for a doctor?' I peer into the woman's face, a perfect oval, long dark lashes on her pale skin, and a mouth a little wide for fashion. A curl of dusky hair, dark brown, tumbles on to my arm.

'No, sir, she'll be right as rain. I think the journey has been too much for her, poor lady.'

The obsequious innkeeper bows, holding the door open, and I carry my fragrant armful – moist with a hint of lavender – into a private parlour.

'We'd best loosen her clothing,' the maid says with great cheerfulness, and unfastens the lady's spencer and plucks a muslin fichu from her bosom as I deposit her on to a settle.

Good God.

Barton, behind me, gives an appreciative grunt.

'Out!' I push him and the innkeeper out of the door, and order tea and toast for the lady.

'That's a prime piece, sir,' Barton says with a chuckle, when I join him outside. 'A good big arse on her, too.'

'Mind your place,' I snap at him.

'The maid, sir.'

'Indeed.' I couldn't help but notice that myself.

After a discreet interval of some ten minutes or so, I enter the parlour, where my rescued lady sits, still a trifle pale, before a plate of crumbs and with a teacup in her hand, in an interesting altercation with her maid.

'Did you have to tell them in London I was covered with stinking sores, milady?' the servant demands, elbow deep in grubby linen. She folds the items and smacks them on top of the candlestick. Her arse seems much reduced, and I suspect she has removed some half-dozen petticoats. Barton will be disappointed.

'Don't be a fool. It worked— Why, sir, I am much obliged for your kindness.' Her voice is warm and throaty. 'May I have the honour of knowing who my rescuer is?'

'Congrevance, madam. Nicholas Congrevance. I trust you're recovered?'

'I am Lady Caroline Elmhurst.' She pauses and looks for a reaction. Obviously her name should mean something to me. 'Have we met in London, sir?'

Her maid mutters something, curtsies and leaves the room, banging the door behind her.

I take Lady Elmhurst's outstretched hand, her fingers warm and supple in mine. 'No, madam, I'm but lately come back to England.'

'You have been on the Continent, then, Mr Congrevance?'

'Yes, I have. Do you travel alone, madam?'

She lowers those long eyelashes and sighs. 'I am a widow. And you, sir?'

Well, well. She wears no mourning jewellery that I can see, so this cannot be a recent bereavement.

'I travel only with my man, Barton. I am a bachelor, madam.'

She nods and gives me a discreet, appraising glance as she offers a chair and tea. I accept for the pleasure of seeing the grace of her arms and bosom as she wields the teapot, lashes still modestly lowered.

'I'm bound for Otterwell's place, as I believe you to be,' I tell her. 'Might I offer you and your maid a place in the trap, Lady Elmhurst?'

'You are too kind, sir.' She raises her eyes to mine – large, blue-grey and enchanting. An extraordinary sensation comes over me; I fall into their depths as surely as I was lost when I sank into the canal.

Lady Caroline Elmhurst

I am tempted to lick the crumbs from my plate, but I really feel I do not know Congrevance sufficiently to do so before him. In the interests of propriety, or its appearance, I suggest we leave for Otterwell's house. I am not so much of a fool, or a hypocrite, to deny the carnal interest that hums between me and Congrevance. He has done nothing but sum up my various parts since we met, and I must admit I have given him every opportunity to do so. My lawn scarf is too creased to wear at my neckline, and I cannot help if my skirt pulls up a little as I enter the trap. I study him with equal interest. I was not entirely unconscious when he carried me inside the inn; I heard the pleasing thud of a man's heartbeat close to mine, and had the opportunity to examine the cloth of his coat (a very fine wool). An excellent sign, as is his absence from London, for chances are he has had little opportunity to squander his money there, or to know the most sordid details of my fall from grace.

Being pressed against his warm, hard person (his chest, that is) almost made up for the distressing weakness and sickness that assailed me, but happily that was dispelled shortly after by toast and tea (paid for by Congrevance), and now I feel quite restored to health.

He travels simply, but the quality of his clothes, his air, speak of breeding and undoubted fortune. He is accompanied by a manservant whose ugly face and squat build I find repulsive, but with whom Mary, the shameless slut, flirts and giggles as the trap bowls along the country lanes.

'I have missed this,' Congrevance says, gesturing in a foreign sort of way.

'Cows, sir?'

'No.' He shakes his head, smiling. 'The countryside. It is so very green and soft.'

'You are a great traveller, then?'

'I was most recently in Italy.'

He doesn't seem inclined to chat, which is as well – for gentlemen, I find, gnaw upon topics that are of no interest whatsoever, like a dog upon a bone: politics (Bludge), horseflesh (Elmhurst), cricket, surely the worst of the lot (Linsley) and military manoeuvres, a close second (Rotherhithe). So I am quite content to watch Congrevance, and a beautiful creature he is, with his long elegance of bone and his dark grey eyes – a surprise, for I should have thought he would have blue eyes. However, I do not wish to appear a mindless ninny who cannot carry on a conversation, and I like to watch his mouth when he speaks.

'Do you know which part is yours in Otterwell's play, Mr Congrevance?'

'His play?'

'Yes. Has he not invited you to be an actor in his, or rather Shakespeare's, *A Midsummer Night's Dream*?'

'Ah. He did not mention anything of the sort to me when we met in Italy earlier this year, although one cannot help but notice how much he admires Shakespeare. And you, Lady Elmhurst? What part is yours?'

'I am to play Hermia.' Hermia, in my opinion, is something of a tediously virtuous ninny, but she fits quite well into the impression I intend to make on

Congrevance – that of a respectable and modest widow. How very fortunate that he has been abroad, and how relieved I am to find that my reputation has not crossed the Channel. If he had been in London, it would be an entirely different story. Indeed, it is a miraculous stroke of luck that he is a blank slate upon which I can rewrite myself, provided he does not listen to vulgar gossip from his fellow guests.

'You enjoy the theatre, Lady Elmhurst?'

'Oh, I adore it.' I clasp my hands to my bosom (he watches) and sigh deeply (he blinks). 'It is tremendously diverting. It is one of the great pleasures of town.' I do not mention that cards and flirting and activities well beyond flirting behind closed doors are what I really prefer. 'And of course I enjoy music; I play a little upon the pianoforte – my friends say I am not totally devoid of taste – and I have a very small skill with watercolours.'

'Otterwell has some very pleasing prospects on his estate. I expect you will wish to sketch them. Perhaps I might be permitted to accompany you, Lady Elmhurst.'

'That would be delightful, Mr Congrevance.'

The question, of course, is whether I should take him as protector or husband. As enamoured as he seems to be of the countryside, there is a good chance he will want to settle on some tedious estate and commune with his cows. He might expect a wife to slop around there with straw in her hair and breed! But I am sure that if Congrevance wished to amuse himself in town, he could keep me in the manner to which I am accustomed (or, to be honest, *unaccustomed* of late). Mary, whose knee is now pressed firmly against that of that ruffian of a manservant, can find out the extent of Congrevance's fortune well enough.

However, there is no great rush to entrap him. I should wait and see who else Otterwell has invited; for although I cannot deny the attraction I feel to Congrevance, it would not do to sell myself short. How would I feel if, for instance, I missed a duke?

Mr Nicholas Congrevance

Now I am not the sort of fellow to ponder much on philosophies or languish around thinking poetic thoughts of love, life and death – in my life, I have had to deal with more practical issues. But I cannot help but reflect that I emerged from that canal a changed man, and a stranger to myself.

Would the Nicholas Congrevance of only a few weeks ago be content to look at trees and meadows and hardly bother to respond when a pretty and undoubtedly available widow tries to engage him in conversation? Barton, of course, will find out the extent of her wealth from that saucy maid, with whom he is getting on famously. And I – well, glib reports of my doings abroad, adventures and the hint of a love affair gone sour (a broken heart in a man rouses a competitive spirit in a woman, I find) – these should have flowed from me as naturally as water. But my wits are quite softened, and while this is not unpleasing – for Lady Caroline Elmhurst is certainly good to look at (particularly around the bosom), and her husky voice most attractive – I must rally myself for my meeting with Lord and Lady Otterwell.

The trap turns off the road; a boy runs from the gatehouse to open finely wrought-iron gates and the wheels and the horse's hoofs crunch on gravel. The drive curves to an open vista with an avenue of lime trees leading to Otterwell's house, a handsome structure of honey-coloured stone. It is precisely the sort of house that I am denied by both birth and fortune; the sort of house that I might, with luck, lease for a quarter or so, before I leave to seek my riches again.

The trap draws up at the front of the house, where two symmetrical sweeps of stairs lead to an imposing front door. I take Lady Elmhurst's hand and assist her down from the trap; it is a pity indeed that we are both decently gloved.

The trap leaves to go to the servants' entrance, and the crunch of feet on gravel announces the approach of Lady Otterwell, carrying a basket of flowers. Less pink in the face than in Rome, she is still pretty in a plump, petulant sort of way. She sees me, drops the flowers, and sinks into a curtsy so deep I wonder if she will be able to get up again without assistance.

'Monsieur le Vicomte!' she cries. She wobbles and regains her vertical state as the front door opens and Otterwell emerges from the house, bald head gleaming, wearing one of his colourful waistcoats. 'Oh, Otterwell, my dear, look who is here! It is St Germain-d'Aubussy! Oh, the honour. I am quite overcome . . .'

Otterwell sweeps a courtly bow and I wonder for a moment if he will topple down his marble stairs, before he makes the journey safely and grips my hand. 'Why, sir, this is an unexpected and delightful surprise. It is, let me see, but six months since we met in Rome, and I am delighted you should condescend to visit. I—'

'I beg of you, Lord Otterwell, not a word more. It is not safe.' I glance around as though foreign conspirators lurk in the neatly trimmed bushes. 'A *nom de guerre* – or of peace, rather. I regret I had to deceive you, but when king and country . . .' I shrug. 'I am Nicholas Congrevance.'

'You . . . Good lord. Well, of course you are welcome, Congrevance.' He wrings my hand with the greatest of affability, while clearly believing he has a (possibly French) aristocrat spy in disguise under his roof. 'We must call the gentleman *Mr Congrevance*, my dear.'

'Oh, how . . . how romantic,' Lady Otterwell sighs. 'I always said, did I not, Otterwell, that the dear Vicomte had hidden depths. I assure you, *Mr Congrevance*, you shall be safe under our roof. I wish . . . although of course you probably cannot . . . but it would be so exciting if you could tell us . . .'

A loud sneeze interrupts us as Lady Elmhurst simultaneously stuffs the gathered flowers back into their basket and curtsies to her host and hostess.

Otterwell bows and looks into her bosom. I can hardly blame him.

'How charming that you should be able to join us, Lady Elmhurst,' Lady Otterwell says with deep loathing. 'Do come and meet the other guests.'

'I am delighted that you were kind enough to invite me,' Lady Elmhurst replies with equal insincerity as she takes her hostess' arm. 'You are looking very well, Lady Otterwell.'

'I see you have made the acquaintance of Lady Elmhurst,' Otterwell says, winking heavily at me.

'But recently, sir. We met in Guildford, and shared the trap.' I wonder about the relationship of these three; clearly there is no love lost between Lady Otterwell and Lady Elmhurst, in whose person Lord Otterwell takes a far too obvious interest. I suspect it was he who invited her, possibly with ungentlemanly intentions, a thought that makes me uncomfortable, although I am not sure why.

Lady Otterwell hands her dishevelled basket of flowers to a servant, and then the four of us proceed around the side of the house. Beneath the spreading branches of a cedar tree ladies take tea, while on the lawn in the sunlight some gentlemen and a small boy play cricket. I notice that at Lady Elmhurst's approach most of the women busy themselves with their conversation, turning their shoulders away from her. It is done quite deliberately to snub her, and I wonder why she is so very unpopular.

She, however, extricates herself from Otterwell's arm with a puff of annoyance, looks longingly at the cakes – I wonder whether she fainted from hunger at the inn – and wanders towards the game. As she does so, the batsman hits the ball vigorously and it flies high in the air towards her – a good hit for a little fellow, for he can only be about six years of age.

I step forward to warn her, but another fellow dashes towards her, and at the same time she turns and sees the ball hurtling at her like a comet. To my astonishment she leaps, arms outstretched – someone has taught her how to catch – colliding with the gentleman in mid-air, and the two of them crash to the ground.

The gentleman, who has landed half on top of her, extricates himself from her skirts, revealing her shapely ankles as he does so. 'Good God, Caro, what are you doing here?'

She gasps, and I realise she has had the wind knocked out of her before she growls, 'And what the devil are you doing, Linsley? Get off me!'

He does so, grinning, and offers a hand to help her up. Apparently they know each other quite well, well enough for him to swipe grass off her backside as she stands. A small, pretty woman with a mass of curly hair approaches, glaring, and Linsley puts his hand behind his back, stepping away.

Caroline, while still clutching the ball to her chest, curtsies in a minimally polite way to the woman. 'Mrs Linsley.'

She curtsies back in similar fashion, still glowering at her husband.

The youthful batsman, meanwhile, comes to join us, dragging the bat behind him. 'Papa, am I out?'

'You are indeed. I caught you fair and square,' Lady Caroline says. She picks up her unfortunate bonnet, now looking much the worse for wear, and gives it a hearty shake.

'You're a girl. Papa, girls cannot play cricket.'

'I can, sir. Did I not just catch you out?' She hands the ball to him.

'Caroline, this is my son Will,' Linsley says with easy familiarity. 'And Will, I'm afraid she did catch you out, and if she had not done so, then I would have.'

'It's not *fair*,' the child says, his face reddening.

Another woman, tall, and with short reddish hair caught in a bandeau, taps the child on the shoulder. 'Will, please bow to the lady and gentleman. Have you forgotten your manners altogether?'

I think at first she is a nursemaid, although very well dressed for one, until the child replies, 'Yes, Mama,' hands the bat over to his father and obeys.

As Master Will makes his bow, Caroline and the child's mother stare at each other with obvious dislike, while Linsley turns to me and introduces himself, and the short, pretty woman as his wife. The other woman, Will's mother, is Mrs Fanny Gibbons. 'And before I cause you further embarrassment,' he says, 'Will is Mrs Gibbons' son, and this one, Master James Linsley, is mine also.'

'Woof.' I look down. A small child in petticoats barks at me.

'Woof,' says Caroline, and the child regards her gravely, then turns to Mrs Linsley and holds out his arms to be picked up.

Mrs Linsley smiles at her son, and then at me. 'He is to play Moonshine's dog and the Indian child,' she says. 'And Mrs Gibbons is to direct us and play the part of Helena herself.'

I would have thought there might be animosity between Mrs Linsley and her husband's mistress, but they move closer together, much in the same way that ships of the line engage for battle, and I realise that they are united against Caroline. Lady Otterwell, too, raises sail and joins them, and I wonder who will be the first to send a warning shot across Caroline's bows.

'I regret I never saw you on stage, Mrs Gibbons,' I say to her, for of course I recognise her name. 'I've been abroad for some time.'

'I'm retired from acting for the most part of six years now,' she says. 'But what part is yours, Mr Congrevance?'

'He shall play Lysander,' Otterwell says. He rubs his hands together, apparently enthusiastic at the prospect of squabbling actresses. 'I received a letter today from the gentleman who was to play that part that he is detained by some business with a horse and a beehive, and I was quite at my wits' end until Congrevance arrived.'

'So I shall have to be in love with this gentleman, Otterwell?' Caroline looks at me with a challenge in her eyes.

'Aye, madam,' I say, and meet her gaze while shivers run down my spine, and heat rushes to other parts of my anatomy. 'So you shall.'

Lady Caroline Elmhurst

It is just my luck. I should never have come had I known Linsley and his harem were to be in attendance. It is bad enough that he flaunts his bastard in public, but that slut the actress, my former rival, is accepted in society, too! It is quite scandalous. I hear he keeps her in a cottage not half a mile from his house. As for his wife, that common little thing who was after Elmhurst and any other titled gentleman she could get her hands on, there was a great deal of talk when she married Linsley. He is of a good family after all, his brother being the Earl of Terrant, whereas she is from trade. In fact I believe her family owns a coal mine or some such.

And the look in Linsley's eyes when he realised he had bedded all three of the women within arm's reach – oh, the mortification, and in front of Congrevance, after all my hard work to convince him of my respectability! Or to be exact, as much hard work as I could reasonably fit in during the half-hour of our acquaintance.

At least there is nothing scandalous in my dealings with Otterwell, although he probably wishes there was; he is one of those people one is forever running into at this party or rout or ball or that. Possibly he flatters himself that the frequency of chance meetings is fortuitous, although I am sure Lady Otterwell keeps him on a tight rein. I don't believe the Otterwells are aware of my dire financial straits, and of course the others spend most of their time in the country.

I can only hope Mary smoothes things over in her dealing downstairs with Barton – and I hope she has finally forgiven me for the remark about the stinking sores. It was, after all, the inspiration of the moment and I did not realise she was so offended by it.

Otterwell has given me a good room – it has wallpaper of pagodas and a vaguely Chinese air about it, old fashioned but comfortable, with a view of some rosebeds and a lake. It is all pleasant enough in the evening light, although I wish there were one soul in the house who actually seemed glad to see me. Otterwell is pleased to see my bosom, and that is about all.

The door opens and Mary enters, carrying my freshly ironed dress for the evening. She appears in good spirits, to my relief, and chatters on about the room she is to share and what the servants have had for dinner as she helps me into the dress. Otterwell keeps country hours, with dinner at six. I am still starving, having been prevented from reaching the cake by a bastion of female disapproval that afternoon.

'Don't you gobble at dinner, milady. It's not genteel. After them foreign ladies, he won't like it.' Mary reaches into her pocket and hands me a hunk of bread and butter. No need to say who *he* is, of course. I hate to tell her that my new reputation is ruined already. My foolish comment that I should fall in love with him stings, as I know the only fall he had in mind for me was backwards with my skirts up. And, his comment implied, I was only too ready to do so, thanks to Linsley's appalling familiarity. I finish the bread, brush crumbs from the gown, and allow Mary the pick of my ribbons as thanks for her good service.

'And how is your friend Mr Barton?' I ask as she rummages among the ribbons.

She giggles. 'Oh, he's a fine one, milady. He and his master have been all over Europe and now Mr Congrevance has a fancy to return home, so they're back in England.'

'Home? Where is that exactly?'

'He didn't say rightly, milady. Some castle in Ireland and lands in the north somewhere. Beautiful shirts he has, milady. All silk.'

I think of them at their ironing, elbow to elbow,

gossiping about their master and mistress. It has a certain appeal. 'And what did you tell him of me?'

'Why, that you're in no hurry to marry, as you're comfortably off.' Mary says it without a trace of irony. She adds, 'And that you miss Lord Elmhurst.'

I stand up so fast my chair tips over backwards. 'That was completely unnecessary!'

'Well, milady, I thought it might spur on him if—'

'Pray do not make things up.' A ludicrous command if ever there was one.

She shrugs, not offended, and rights the chair. 'And Mr Barton says he'll take me to see a ferret.'

'Very well. You be careful it is not a ferret he keeps in his trousers.' I catch a sight of myself in the mirror. 'Can we make this neckline higher?'

'Higher?' She stares at me as though I am mad. It is certainly a request I have never made before.

'Never mind. It will do.' I adjust my turban, fiddle around changing my earrings and putting the original pair on and leave for the drawing room.

Another lady is headed in the same direction, tall, grey-haired and with a familiar look to her. She turns, hearing me behind her, and I sink into a curtsy as my heart sinks even lower. It's Inigo Linsley's terrifying mother, the Dowager Countess, given to odd outspoken bursts – she is never afraid to speak her mind. 'Good evening, Lady Terrant.'

'Ha. Lady Elmhurst.' I haven't seen her for some

years, after she left London under a cloud, so I heard, while I was on honeymoon with Elmhurst. I know Linsley was frightened to death of her, although she liked him above all of her sons. She gives me a good inspection, and comments, 'You're ageing well.'

Since I admit to three and twenty I do not take this as a compliment. She, however, is as handsome and bright-eyed as ever. I know she married very young, and she must now be well over fifty. Then she says, 'I am Mrs Riley now. I married again, to an Admiral Riley. When you are my age one may do as one pleases.'

'Oh. My felicitations, madam.'

'I was sorry to hear of Elmhurst's death. He was a handsome rogue.' Before I can say anything, as taken aback as I am, she adds, 'I shall have to talk to Otterwell about his gardeners. They should all be hanged.'

Indeed, yes, the lady has a passion for gardening, I remember, and doubtless intends to make good use of her stay stuffing her pockets full of purloined cuttings from Otterwell's garden. She turns on her heel and marches down the stairs ahead of me, and I am glad I have her preceding my entry into the drawing room. She may be a commoner now but the guests part before her like the Red Sea, bowing and scraping, and then almost fall over themselves in their haste to get away from her without seeming rude.

Ignoring them, Mrs Riley makes a beeline for a white-haired, jovial-looking fellow, who must be her new husband, while I express an interest in the pictures on the walls. This gives me the chance to observe my fellow guests.

A tall, brown-haired man I have not seen before escorts Mrs Gibbons, and they are both in lively conversation with Congrevance, who looks devastatingly handsome in his black coat and breeches. Lady Otterwell flutters around him with an inappropriate girlishness. I wonder about the extent of their acquaintance in Rome (surely he was not her lover?), and, not for the first time, why he pretended to be a French nobleman. Was he truly a spy? It is most romantic and exciting, if true, but I have found so many gentlemen claim they have been involved in espionage abroad that they might as well have donned uniforms and made themselves into a regiment.

We are led into dinner, and there is a minor whirlwind as the guests, torn between avoiding Mrs Riley and myself, choose their seats, with the consequence that I find myself next to her and with Mrs Gibbons' companion on the other. He introduces himself in a most friendly way (obviously not someone who partakes of London gossip) as Mr Thomas Darrowby, Otterwell's secretary. I flirt a little with him purely to annoy Fanny Gibbons who sits opposite, but she smiles with great serenity and converses with her neighbours. Mrs Riley throws in an odd comment as the fancy takes her.

'And what is your part in the play?' I ask Darrowby.

'I play Demetrius, Lady Elmhurst. Lord Otterwell is most gratified that Mr Congrevance has joined us, having lost his Lysander. He and Lady Otterwell, of course, are to play both Oberon and Titania and Theseus and Hippolyta.'

I try not to giggle, for the plump Lady Otterwell is a most unlikely queen of the fairies, let alone of the Amazons, but then it is a most silly play, as I remember, with two sets of lovers lost in the woods, and fairies and enchantments and so on.

'And Philomena Linsley is our wardrobe mistress.' He smiles down the table at her with great affection. 'Of course, she's more interested in the costumes than in acting. I know her well, Lady Elmhurst. She is like a sister to me. Our families have been friends for years, and I was secretary to her brother-in-law for a time.'

Indeed. I wonder what Mr Linsley thinks of Darrowby following his wife around. Linsley, it appears, is stage manager, and his son, Will, a youthful Puck.

'And the rude mechanicals?' I ask.

'Otterwell's servants,' Mrs Riley says. 'His butler fancies himself a thespian, and so plays Bottom and takes charge of their rehearsals. Of course Otterwell plans to cut out all the business with the ass's head so his butler does not make love to her ladyship. And your audience will be Otterwell's friends and neighbours from miles around, with a ball following, and too much strong beer and a roast ox for his tenants.'

After dinner – we dined early, as Otterwell has announced that since we have but two weeks to perfect our play, we start rehearsals the next day at ten of the morning (is he mad?) – there are cards, so I play whist in a boring and ladylike sort of way, winning a few shillings. I feel quite satisfied with myself – everyone has drunk enough wine from Otterwell's excellent cellar to be cordial (and Mrs Gibbons, most gratifyingly, plucked Mr Darrowby from my side with a proprietorial air and a cool smile). It seems the evening is about to end, as people yawn and exclaim at the time, the women gathering fans and shawls.

I should know, surely by now, that when things appear to be progressing well, disaster is about to strike.

'So, Lady Elmhurst.' A hand brushes against the back of my chair, and thereby against my bare shoulder. 'I hear you are a great card player. What say you to a hand of piquet?'

Congrevance.

'Why, sir, I was thinking of my bed.'

Moving round to sit opposite me, he smiles in a predatory sort of way. 'A pleasant thought indeed,

Lady Elmhurst. I could spend a great deal of time thinking of you in your bed. But before you retire . . .'

He is already picking the low numbers from a pack of cards.

I watch, fascinated, as he indulges in some fancy shuffling, sweeping the cards face down into a sinuous curve on the table, tipping them over, and gathering the pack together with those long, elegant hands. He has beautiful hands and I find myself torn between watching them and his lips.

'Very well.' The words tumble from my foolish mouth before I can stop them. 'I trust a shilling a point is satisfactory?'

'Of course.'

There is a slight stir around as the other guests, bedtimes postponed, gather round to watch this new entertainment for the evening. Otterwell calls for candelabra to be moved closer to our table so that all may see.

We cut for who should deal, and although Congrevance picks the higher card, he bows towards me and indicates that I should be younger hand, with the privilege of dealing first. It's most gentlemanly of him, indeed, as it gives me an advantage in the game, but I am not sure I trust him.

So I shuffle and deal, and find myself possessed of a miserable hand.

Congrevance, lounging opposite me, smiles,

discards five cards and picks five new from the *talon*. Quite as I would expect. I do the same, hoping to replace my incoherent dozen cards with something better – but no, they are only incoherent in a different way, with a meagre pair of kings and a run of hearts in my favour.

He raises an eyebrow, waiting for my declaration.

Good heavens, the man is distraction itself, and it crosses my mind that I am being played as surely as his hand.

Someone places a glass of wine at my side, and I take a sip, while reflecting that I have had a considerable amount to drink already, and this will not help my game. But it seems I am beyond help or luck. In fact, and to make short work of misery, I am trounced, defeated, trampled and, despite my initial advantage as younger hand, at the end of the *partie* some three hundred and eighteen points in debt.

There is a slight smattering of applause. The fools. Where do they think they are, at the play? And I – I am not the heroine of a tragedy; rather, I am the clown in the farce who's just landed on her backside. Damn them all.

'Oh, well played, sir, well played indeed!' Otterwell crows. 'Not to worry, Lady Elmhurst, the luck will turn, you know.'

'Another *partie*, Lady Elmhurst?' Congrevance asks, as smooth as silk, as deadly as sin. He rises to his feet and stretches, and I look away, fearing I drool, even as humiliated as I am.

I force a smile to my lips. 'I regret not, sir.'

Now that the entertainment is over, the others resume their leisurely progression from the room. A footman enters and snuffs the candles, but when he approaches the table, Congrevance gestures to him to leave us.

'You owe me, madam.'

'I regret I am at somewhat of a disadvantage, Mr Congrevance.' A disadvantage puts it mildly, indeed. I, who have but a couple of guineas to my name, am now in debt to the tune of fifteen guineas and three shillings.

The last person to leave the room hesitates, drawing his breath in sharply. I see it is Linsley, and shake my head. God knows he is in trouble enough with his wife after this afternoon's blunders. He nods, bows and leaves the room, and Congrevance and I are left alone.

A nearby clock strikes midnight as I unhook my earrings, and toss them on to the table. They land with a slight metallic sound, diamonds and sapphires winking in the candlelight; the last of my good jewels, a gift from Elmhurst, the pieces I swore I would never sell. 'I trust these will satisfy my debt, sir.' I add, in as careless a way as I can, 'Until I return to London, that is.'

'Of course.' He turns the earrings over in his hand. 'Very pretty, Lady Elmhurst, but not worth more than ten guineas, in my estimation.'

'I believe you are wrong, sir.'

He dangles the earrings between forefinger and thumb, eyes dark and wicked, and leans forward, his elbow on the table among the discarded cards.

'I believe, Lady Elmhurst, we can come to an . . . arrangement.'

'An arrangement?' I try to sound offended, but fear my voice reveals only breathless anticipation. I rise in an attempt to regain my wounded dignity.

'Yes, madam.' He has taken one swift step, meeting me at the side of the table. 'If you are willing.'

My legs almost give way. 'Why, sir, what can you mean?'

He inclines his head towards mine, his voice low and caressing. 'A kiss, madam, but one kiss, and honour will be satisfied.'

Mr Nicholas Congrevance

My behaviour alarms me. This is not how I conduct myself.

Never.

I am not one of those hair-raking, pacing, heroic fellows who charge into the amorous fray like a ram into a field of ewes, and sweep defenceless women into bed. My success is due entirely to my good manners, my ability to listen to women talk, to sympathise; to behave, as one lady said, 'like a sister with a cock'. (A most troubling definition, I realised later. At the time, my mind was on other matters.)

I certainly did not leave a string of happy, satisfied women in my wake by thrashing them at cards and then asking them to sell themselves.

And now I've done it and I have no idea of the course I should take. I can barely think, not with Caroline so close. I wonder for a moment if she will storm out in disgust, but she gazes at me, her lips parted in voiceless assent, an invitation no man can resist. I am not made of stone. I can rethink my tactics later.

I shall not be ungentlemanly about it.

Definitely not.

With what is left of my common sense, I prepare to brush my lips against hers in moderately chaste fashion, and determine that none of the following shall occur:

1. Interplay of tongues.
2. Unseemly groping or rubbing.
3. Moving lips from mouth to lobe of ear, neck or any other regions.
4. Groaning or other lewd sounds.
5. Loosening of any articles of clothing.
6. Any of the above that will prompt her to respond in kind.

She is the first to disengage. 'Do you usually kiss ladies for a quarter-hour at a time?' she asks.

'Do you usually time such activities?' I respond, feeling like a fool as, sure enough, the last chimes of the quarter-hour fade away. I pluck at my disordered neckcloth. I have broken every single resolution regarding the nature of the kiss. I want to toss her on to the card table and finish what we have started, I want to run from Otterwell's house before I am in deeper trouble than I am now – and I am duty bound to report to Barton that a successful campaign is under way, although I have never felt so at a loss, such a fool, after one kiss.

She sets the bodice of her gown to rights and reaches past me for her fan, discarded on the table among the cards, murmuring something in which I catch one word: *bed*.

She is inviting me to bed? Already? I have made a conquest in half an hour's bullying and a quarter of an hour's kiss?

She looks at me expectantly.

'I . . . I am most deeply honoured, madam. Should it be, well, that is to say, I, ah, do you wish your maid to . . .'

'Congrevance,' she says, in the sort of clear, kind voice one would use to a very young child, 'I do not need my maid to open the door. I am going to bed now. Good night, sir.'

She walks past me, opens the door herself and leaves.

Wonderfully well done, I tell myself, and after a decent interval – God knows I do not want her to think I follow behind her with my tongue hanging out – I trudge upstairs to report to Barton.

'Going well, I see, sir,' he says with a broad smile, taking in my dishevelled appearance, the shirt outside my breeches, the wrecked neckcloth.

I don't have the heart to contradict him.

Lady Caroline Elmhurst

Well, the man can certainly kiss, even if he does turn into a rambling fool thereafter. I am actually glad of it – it made me appear less of a rambling fool myself, for I was afraid I should push him on to the card table or the floor to finish the business. I drag myself upstairs on weak and trembling legs, taking deep breaths to steady myself; it is like climbing the Alps. I have not been kissed like that in an age; I am thrown into a turmoil. I must not, shall not, do it again. He has taken unpardonable liberties with my person (a quarter-hour! *A quarter-hour!* Oh heavens!), and I cannot have him think me a trollop, even if I wish to behave like one. No, I am a chaste and respectable widow, unless one of the other guests takes it upon him- or herself to tell him otherwise, and I can do little about that. (He carries the scents of citrus and bay on his person. I shall never look upon a lemon in the same way again.)

I push open my bedchamber door, imagining the absolute horror of finding no one but Congrevance stretched naked upon the bed (*Oh! Sir! What are you about? I shall scream!* And so I should, I am sure. Without a doubt he would make me do so.)

Mary springs to her feet from her seat by the fire,

blinking and pretending she has been wide awake all this while. 'Have you had a pleasant evening, milady?'

'Oh yes.' (I wonder what colour the hair on his chest is. And how much he has. I saw the hairs on his wrists glint coppery brown in the candlelight.)

Mary moves behind me to unfasten my gown. 'Why, you've a button undone already, here.' (That was when he pulled my gown down and bit my shoulder. Not too gently. I did not want gentleness.) 'I think you've had a bit too much to drink, milady.'

I don't argue. I am indeed drunk; intoxicated by Congrevance.

I shall have to be very careful indeed.

And, damn him, he still has my earrings.

Nine in the morning! It is quite hideous. I am surprised the sun is up (true, we left London in a rainy dawn, but we had stayed up all night). I barely have time to snatch a cup of coffee and slice of seed cake before running to Otterwell's theatre. For yes, he has a theatre in his house, albeit a small one, built below a musicians' gallery in the old part of his house – little more than a platform with curtains. Chairs are arranged on the worn flagstones of the room, and sunlight slants in through mullioned windows.

I am the last to arrive, and can only take a chair in the front row. Otterwell, spectacles perched on the end of his nose, and Mrs Gibbons stand on the stage, while behind them two aproned servants paint scenery. I stifle a yawn and sit.

'Delighted you could join us, Lady Elmhurst,' Otterwell says. 'And now our company is all gathered together' – he smirks knowingly at us as he quotes from the play – 'I shall yield the stage to my fair colleague, Mrs Gibbons. But first allow me to welcome you all to this theatre, our wooden O, where we shall pay tribute to the Bard; a poor thing, but mine own. You see Geoffrey and Stephen hard at work here, and they are also to play Snug and Peter Quince. They have been at it for some weeks now, is not that right, sirs?'

The two of them, paintbrushes in their hands, bow and mutter something obsequious to their master. From their expressions, they do not seem to be nearly as excited by their extra duties as Otterwell is.

'And now,' Otterwell proclaims, 'we shall become actors and actresses!' He trots down the stairs at the side of his stage and proceeds to hand out pencils and prompt books, small, roughly bound and printed copies of the play, interspersed with blank pages.

Fanny Gibbons steps forward. 'We have but two weeks to rehearse,' she announces, 'and so I trust all have learned their parts? Except for Mr Congrevance, of course, who only just yesterday arrived – a fortunate accident, indeed, for otherwise we would have no Lysander.' She smiles, presumably at him. I am too well bred to twist in my seat and look at him. Her gaze shifts to me. 'You know your part, Lady Elmhurst? It will help him a great deal.'

I nod in a responsible fashion.

She narrows her eyes a fraction, and her stance becomes masculine – for sure, I do not know how she does it.

'The course of true love never did run smooth; But either it was different in blood . . .'

Oh heavens, she quotes from the play – or at least so I suppose – and I am expected to respond.

Someone mutters from behind me, and I repeat his words. 'O cross! too high to be enthrall'd to low!' (What all this means I have no idea.)

'Very good, Lady Elmhurst.' She pauses for one moment. 'I regret that is a scene we shall cut. Ladies and gentlemen, if you will follow me, we shall mark together the rest of the cuts on which Lord Otterwell and I have agreed.'

And so we do, and a tedious job it is, as we reduce the play down to little more than some scenes in the woods and the mechanics' play at the end. There are some grumbles from the few who have actually memorized their part (or are bold enough to make that claim), while Otterwell beams and smirks, and announces that we are to picnic in the grounds this afternoon while we polish our lines.

Excellent, I am starved.

But dues must be paid. I turn to the person who so obligingly whispered my lines to me. 'Sir, I am much indebted to you. How may I repay you?'

Mr Nicholas Congrevance

A sumptuous picnic has been set up for us in a pretty little Greek temple, but there's no sign of Caroline. I wander back towards the house, thinking that she might be seeking out a hat or scarf or some other sort of female frippery. I plan to escort her to join the others, and to my great satisfaction I catch sight of her walking across the lawn in front of the house, curls floating in the breeze that forms her muslin gown to her figure. Her bonnet is cradled in the crook of one arm, and I wonder if she has raided Otterwell's strawberry beds like a mischievous bird.

I certainly made a fool of myself last night. I can only hope that today I may redeem myself; the first thing I should do is return those damned earrings, which burn a hole in my waistcoat pocket, and indeed, in my recently acquired conscience. Nicholas Congrevance with a conscience! How has this happened?

She smiles and my mouth becomes dry. Extraordinary.

I clear my throat and bow. 'Lady Elmhurst, may I offer myself as an escort? Otterwell and the others are gathering for the picnic.'

'How very kind of you, Mr Congrevance.'

I offer my arm.

'Regrettably, I have an assignation with another gentleman.'

An assignation? What can this mean? Linsley? Darrowby? Surely not Otterwell himself, under Lady Otterwell's nose? 'Who the devil— I mean, may I ask who?'

She smiles, looking beyond me. 'Ah, here he is. Have a pleasant afternoon, Mr Congrevance.'

I turn, full of murderous rage, ready to throttle my rival, and see, to my absolute surprise, young Will Gibbons, carrying a fishing rod and a large basket.

'Lord Otterwell's cook gave me bread and cheese and cider,' the child says. 'Good afternoon, sir. Did you get some bait, Lady Caro?'

She allows this boy who barely knows her to address her in such an appallingly familiar fashion?

'Indeed I did.' She lowers her bonnet, the crown of which I now see is lined with rhubarb leaves, and inside – a mass of grey and pink wriggling things – worms!

'Oh, capital!' Will exclaims, jumping from one foot to the other. 'We are to go fishing, Mr Congrevance. Did not Lady Caro choose some excellent worms for us? Would you like to come too, sir?'

'Mr Congrevance has another engagement,'

Caroline says with a polite smile. 'Come, Will, let me help you with that basket.'

She hands him her bonnetful of bait, takes the basket, and the two of them walk across the lawn away from me.

I go to join the other guests. Jilted for a six year old! I am losing my touch for sure.

Lady Caroline Elmhurst

Young Master Gibbons proves excellent company, and to my surprise I am quite glad that he asked me to take him fishing in return for those lines he whispered to me. I am touched that he should decide on the spur of the moment that I am a friend, for God knows I have few enough here; and also much gratified that Congrevance was jealous – yes, jealous! I don't think he's used to women saying him nay.

Will is interested in everything, pointing out birds and insects, and chattering away most agreeably without expecting much effort in return. He leads me through Otterwell's grounds to a pleasant spot by a small lake with a minuscule island in its centre, and we set up our fishing stance in the shade of a large willow tree. It is, as we both know, the worst time of day to fish, but we agree that maybe the fish will be obliging enough to gather in our shady spot.

I compliment him on his mastery of the play.

'Oh, that is easy,' he says. 'Mama can look at a page and memorise it, and I can too. She says it is useful for an actor to be able to do so.'

'And do you wish to go on the stage when you are grown?'

He selects a worm from my bonnet with great care. 'Yes. Or I shall be a soldier or a coachman, for then I will not have to go away to school as Papa wishes.'

'And what does your mama say?'

He wrinkles his nose and casts his line on to the water. 'She wants me to be an educated man like Mr Darrowby, or a lawyer. But she doesn't want me to go away to school.'

'Lots of boys like school. My brother did.'

'Did he teach you to play cricket?'

'Yes. He taught me about worms and fishing, too. He's in India now.'

'I should like to go to foreign lands,' Will says. 'Does your brother ride on elephants?'

We chat about India, and I try to remember something from my brother's infrequent letters other than complaints about the climate, his digestion and his servants.

While Will fishes, I apply myself to learning my part – now reduced almost to the point of incomprehensibility, although Otterwell claims he plans to write any supplemental lines to explain exactly why the lovers are in the wood. Doubtless it is

Oberon who will intone these amendments to the Bard. I wonder how long it will take for him and Mrs Gibbons to make enemies of each other (I cannot help it; I have a natural inclination towards mischief). Occasionally Will exclaims that he is sure a fish is biting, and we both hold our breath, watching the line, until we decide that it must have become bored and gone elsewhere, or that we need fresh bait. He seems quite content to concentrate on the fishing itself rather than be concerned about the catch.

We dine on bread and cheese, and after a while Will yawns and rub his eyes. 'You will look after my line, won't you, Lady Caro, if I go to sleep? I don't think I shall, though. But if I did, you would wake me if we got a bite?'

'Certainly.'

Will yawns again, and settles down to sleep, his curly head in my lap.

It is very pleasant beneath this tree, green and gold light filtering through the trees from the blue sky above. Fairly sure there are no fish to be had, I reel in Will's line and throw some crumbs into the water. The ducks are cautious at first, then peck greedily at them, and circle, expecting more. There is a flash of azure as a kingfisher flies past.

The weight of the sleeping child on my lap is surprisingly comforting. I cannot say I am one of those women who dote, or claim to dote, on children, but I find them refreshingly short on guile and prejudice. I had always expected to breed, but the honour was denied me in matrimony (and fortunately outside of it, too). However, if I had been so careless as to bear Linsley's child, he or she would have been of almost Will's age, a thought that makes me unaccountably melancholy.

My reverie is interrupted by the crack of a foot on a branch, and an irate voice.

'What are you doing, Lady Elmhurst?'

Lady Caroline Elmhurst

I don't bother to turn my head. 'Fishing, Mrs Gibbons. Pray calm yourself.'

She moves into my line of vision. 'I beg your pardon, I did not mean to be rude, but when I found Will was not in the nursery with his brother, I was worried. Mr Congrevance mentioned you and he were to go fishing, so I thought I should make sure all was well.'

'I do not eat children, Mrs Gibbons.'

'Of course not. I thought you might find his company irksome after a while. You cannot be used to the ways of small boys.'

'On the contrary, he is a good companion.'

She looks pleased at my words – not my intent, it is true – and smiles at her son, leaning down to stroke his hair. 'I think so too, but then, as his mother, I am prejudiced.'

I wonder if she will wake Will and take him away,

but instead she peers across the lake and waves. 'There's Philomena and James. Over here!' she calls.

Mrs Gibbons leaves me to confer with Mrs Linsley, and I hear a (mostly) whispered conversation. The parts I do hear are not encouraging.

'I assure you, Fanny, that if Lady Elmhurst takes your son fishing, it can be with no good intentions.'

'Oh come, let us try to be a little more charitable towards her. What on earth could she possibly hope to gain from such an act? In anyone else I would think it exceedingly kind.'

'Kind! You don't know her as I do. In London, when first I met Linsley . . .'

Eventually Mrs Linsley approaches and drops a barely civil stiff half-curtsy to me.

I acknowledge her with a nod of my head. Heavens, it is like a pair of cats circling each other, tails fluffed out, and I wait to see which of us will yowl first.

It is James who breaks up the frigid atmosphere by barking at his half-brother, and then tugging at his hair in an attempt to wake him. Will whimpers and bats him off, falling back into sleep again and drooling on my skirts.

'Have a care,' Philomena Linsley scolds, pulling her son away. 'I am sure Lady Elmhurst does not want you climbing over her.'

'It is no matter, Mrs Linsley.'

An uncomfortable silence ensues, broken by Mrs Linsley. 'Lady Elmhurst, I do not mean to be impertinent, but what have you done to your bonnet?'

'I used it to carry the bait,' I say.

'Oh. I think your maid should be able to clean it.' She hesitates. 'I have a silk flower that would look very pretty on the crown, if you would care to have it.'

'Why, thank you, Mrs Linsley. You are very kind.' I take it as a friendly gesture. If I ruin a bonnet I generally buy another. I suppose Mrs. Linsley is one of those women who enjoys picking things apart and retrimming them; and I may have to become one of those women from necessity if I cannot succeed with Congrevance.

I invite the two women to sit and offer them some cider. It is weak enough stuff, but I wonder if it contributed to Will's sleepiness; and if so, whether it will make Mrs Gibbons and Mrs Linsley unbend a little.

'Lord, it's hot,' Mrs Gibbons says after a while, and strips off her stockings to dangle her feet in the water. 'Lady Elmhurst, give me that child so you may take your stockings off, if you wish.'

I hoist the sleeping Will on to her lap and remove my stockings, rolling them fast so the other women cannot see how darned they are. The water is cool and delightful, and tiny fishes dart around our toes.

'What an excellent idea!' As Mrs Linsley takes off her stockings I notice her garters are red ribbons with seed pearls and silver thread – surprisingly expensive and whorish for a respectable married lady. Mr Linsley's tastes have not changed much, it seems. 'Oh look, there are the gentlemen.'

Sure enough, on the other side of the lake, Linsley, Darrowby and Congrevance stroll, coats unbuttoned and neckcloths loosened, and each carrying a stone bottle like the one that holds our cider. They wave back and in a few moments have joined us.

'Water nymphs, I declare,' Darrowby says.

'The three graces.' Congrevance bows.

'Six ankles.' Inigo Linsley. No, he has not changed much.

At the sound of his voice, Will stirs and jumps to his feet. 'Papa! Papa, may we swim? Lady Caro and I have had such fun. She and I have been fishing, but we didn't catch anything, and Papa, Lady Caro's brother is in India and sticks pigs.'

'A swim? What do you think, gentlemen?'

'I swim too, Papa,' says James from his mother's lap, proving he has the power of speech as well as that of barking.

'Very well,' Mrs Linsley says. 'Inigo, you must be very careful. Hold on to him all the time, and—'

'Don't fret, my love.' Inigo grabs his younger son as he scrambles towards the water, eager to immerse himself. 'Come here, James. Will, don't take your trousers off in front of the ladies; it's not polite.'

'We don't have any towels,' Mrs Linsley says in a worried tone.

'Oh, they'll just have to sun themselves,' Mrs Gibbons murmurs. 'It is fortunate indeed that it is so warm.'

The gentlemen and boys meanwhile have modestly removed themselves behind another tree to disrobe, and I must admit that I await with happy anticipation the sight of Congrevance stripped. The subject has been on my mind ever since last night, if not since I first met him.

'Lady Elmhurst,' Mrs Linsley says, 'I should be most honoured if you would address me by my Christian name.'

'I too,' says Mrs Gibbons.

'Oh. Thank you. And I am Caroline.' Of course we know each other's names, but we must go through this curious bit of formality; besides, it passes the time until we can ogle the gentlemen. By now we have appropriated their bottles of cider, which have been laced with brandy and are quite potent.

There is a splash as the first gentleman dives into the water. He emerges shaking water from his head, then swims with slow, strong strokes towards the tiny island, little more than a willow tree clinging to a speck of land. It is Darrowby, followed by Inigo with

James clinging to his shoulders, and Will, who shrieks with joy, paddling beside his father.

'Watch me swim, Mama and Mrs Philomena!'

Congrevance surfaces a little ahead of them, sleek as a seal in the water, and to my disappointment swims to the side of the island and disappears from sight. Linsley and Darrowby arrive at the willow that hangs over the water, where Linsley unloads his son, who joins Will in playing with stones and sticks on a tiny, gravelled sort of beach.

We ladies modestly avert our eyes – not daring to meet each other's gaze in case we burst out laughing – until the two gentlemen are landed, their backs turned to us with the utmost modesty before they take shelter behind the willow. I am happy to say that when I look again, Congrevance has rounded the island and is wading towards dry land.

Goodness!

I almost drop my bottle of cider.

'Well, well,' Fanny Gibbons says. 'There's proof of the theory that a big nose portends size elsewhere. And in cool water, too.'

'He has big hands too,' I say, swigging cider. I should know. 'Big, beautiful hands. I daresay big feet as well.'

'You mean that . . . ?' Philomena asks.

Fanny whispers in her ear, and she giggles.

I do find unclothed men interesting, I must admit.

'Which one do you think has the best arse?' I ask before I can stop myself. Oh, horrors. Surely, even after their overtures of friendship, they will cut me for the duration of the visit.

'Oh, that's obvious. Little James, of course,' Philomena says fondly. 'Look at him – he's like a little peach.'

'I used to nibble on Will's arse when he was a baby, it was so round and sweet,' Fanny says. She sounds quite foxed. 'Darrowby's is most . . . handsome,' she continues. 'It's a pity he can't afford a better tailor.'

So she's not his mistress after all – or not yet, although there's something between them. But I stare at the island, hoping the men – or, to be honest, Congrevance – will find a reason to emerge from their leafy bower. We can see them vaguely through the greenery, and they seem to be having a spirited conversation, gesturing towards the far shore of the lake. The occasional word reaches my ears . . . *barley . . . oats . . . manure . . .*

'Bah,' says Philomena, 'they're talking about crop rotation again. Congrevance and Inigo bored us to death about it at the picnic. I was surprised how much Congrevance knows about land stewardship, for all he's been abroad so long.'

Meanwhile, Will and James splash and giggle at the water's edge like a couple of little otters. At one point Linsley emerges to settle some dispute about the ownership of a particular stone, and we three hypocrites avert our eyes, talking of the weather with great interest in loud voices for the gentlemen's benefit.

'Mr Congrevance is a very pleasant gentleman,' Philomena says when it is safe again. 'He knows a lot about bonnets and Paris fashions.'

'No, he doesn't, dear heart,' says Fanny. 'He knows a lot about pretty women, which is why he talked to you in the first place.'

'I was not flirting with him!' Philomena takes an indignant swig from her bottle and chokes a little. 'I am a married woman.'

'You were flirting,' Fanny says, patting her hand. 'It doesn't matter. You're allowed to flirt with a gentleman as handsome as Congrevance.'

Congrevance was flirting with her? After kissing me for fifteen minutes – that quarter-hour of vice – the night before? How dare he!

'He flirted with me too, under the guise of sensible talk about the theatre,' Fanny adds. 'And helped me most gallantly with my shawl when it caught on a branch. Don't you think he's a dreadful flirt, Caroline?'

'I—' And at that moment, the gentleman in question steps from behind the willow and plunges into the water, allowing me to confirm once more the theory of matching large extremities. In addition, his skin has a faint golden hue, his chest sports a delightful dense curl of hair in the centre, and he has long shapely legs and is as lean and muscled all over as a greyhound. 'Oh!'

'We may possibly have a shower of rain in the next few days.' Fanny almost chokes with laughter.

'Avert your eyes, ladies,' Linsley calls out with great good cheer. 'We're coming back.'

'Indeed, this good weather cannot hold for much longer.' Philomena dissolves into giggles. 'What do you think, Caroline?'

'Oh. I think – I think there will be big . . . big . . . clouds,' I gasp, mortified, as I hear some male chuckles.

I may be overcome with hopeless lust, and half foxed on the fortified cider, but there is one thing I have noticed about Congrevance that has me puzzled – on the pale gold of his skin, the sunlight picked up the gleam of thin silver lines across his back. It's something I should never expect to see on a gentleman, for such scars can only be from a flogging.

I am aware that Congrevance may not be all – or he may be more than – he has allowed. And I wish to find out more.

Mr Nicholas Congrevance

Having been thoroughly ogled by the three ladies, we gentlemen return to civilised manners and our clothes, although the two little boys are allowed to run around naked, squealing and laughing. I must admit that I am surprised at how well the three women seem to get on together now – part of it must be attributed to the empty bottles, of course – and take the matter up with Linsley as we stroll back towards the house.

He is more discreet than I would have suspected. 'Well, Fanny will like anyone who is kind to Will, for some look down on him because he's a bastard. And Philomena is the sweetest woman in the world.' He's quite genuine in his expression, even though they have been married some years.

'But why was Lady Caroline so coldly received when she arrived?'

'Some blame her for Elmhurst's death, and she has

a . . . certain reputation. Much of it is vicious gossip, for she has been wrongly accused of everything from murder to adultery—'

'*Murder?*'

'Good God, no. The circumstances of Elmhurst's death were unfortunate, but Caro held no blame. However, now I think of it, I'm not too sure about the adultery, for she is of the *ton*, but . . .' He stops and taps me on the shoulder in a friendly sort of way. 'Listen, Congrevance. I'm fond of her in a way, although I found her a great deal of trouble during our liaison. I wouldn't like to see her injured or slandered.'

'Sir, am I to believe you are warning me to behave in an honourable fashion towards your former mistress?'

'Precisely, sir.' We resume walking. 'Both of them. If you flirt too much with Fanny, you'll have Darrowby to reckon with as well, although I'm inclined to think a little competition would do no harm. The two of them have put up obstacles in each other's path for almost six years, and Philomena and I are finding it tedious, as fond as we are of both of them. Good God, Otterwell should take better care of his hedges – they are like forests. I suppose in the north you have more dry-stone walls than hedges?'

I wonder at the sudden change of topic, but it is explained by the appearance of Mrs Linsley, who has left the other two women to join her husband.

'You're gossiping about us all,' she says with great affection, taking Linsley's arm. 'Gentlemen are such gossips, aren't they, Mr Congrevance?'

'Guilty as charged, madam.'

'And what have you been saying about me?'

'That you are a paragon of womanhood,' I say.

'Oh fie, you are a dreadful flirt, just as Fanny said. What is it, James?'

The small, persistent presence tugs at Mrs Linsley's skirts. 'Carry me, Mama.'

He's a solid child, and she is such a small thing. I grab him by the skirts and swing him on to my shoulders, where he tugs my hair and squeals with pleasure. The Linsleys look upon me with great approval. Well, I have never objected to small children (other than six-year-olds who snatch pretty women from under my nose).

'I suppose you intend to seek a wife now you have come back to England,' Mrs Linsley says with the enthusiasm of a married person seeking to enrol all in that happy state.

'Possibly. To tell the truth, Mrs Linsley, I haven't given the matter much thought.' Since I have usually sought other men's wives, this is only too true.

'Oh, sir. You should. Look how happy little James is with you.' She laughs and lays one hand on my sleeve. 'Nay, I will not tell you of the virtues of my sisters, for one is married and the other two fend very well indeed for themselves in society. I daresay we will find you someone at the ball after the play, unless you—'

'Now, Philomena, leave the man alone. Don't interfere,' Linsley says.

'Or perhaps even tomorrow,' she continues. 'Some of Otterwell's neighbours are to dine with us, and doubtless there will be some eligible ladies.'

I mumble something non-committal, with little James's feet kicking against my chest, and resolve to stop acting like a fool with Caroline. She is, after all, only a woman of little breeding, attractive fortune and passable looks, and her hoydenish streak and idiosyncratic fondness for small boys are of no consequence. It is her fortune I must bear in mind. I shall not need to associate with her for long, once I have what I need. My campaign begins in earnest tonight.

Thus it is that I make a point that evening of ignoring Caroline altogether, but flirt with Mrs Gibbons while Darrowby glowers. Bearing in mind Linsley's theory, I assume it can only benefit the couple, as well as my own interests.

My campaign with, or rather against, Caroline continues in the drawing room, but I find it harder than I imagined not to watch her, her face animated and beautiful as she slaps cards on the table and rails at Otterwell for his bad play. Or as she performs some piece on the pianoforte, quite badly, to tell the truth. After producing a fistful of wrong notes, she stops, announces that she will not take the repeat as it bores her and surely will bore us all, and bangs out some concluding chords. For some reason her lack of accomplishment, and her honesty about it, is quite charming. I find myself looking forward to the rehearsal of our play the next day with great eagerness.

Lady Caroline Elmhurst

Another rude awakening at the crack of dawn – how I shall survive these next few days I do not know – another hastily grabbed breakfast, and so we gather at Otterwell's theatre for our first proper rehearsal. I do, however, still feel sustained by the triumphs of the previous day: Congrevance in all his unclothed glory, and my successful effort to ignore him at dinner, for every woman knows the way to attract a gentleman is to pretend indifference. The only problem was that he seemed to be ignoring me too, which was not my intent. Today, possibly, I shall unbend a little, and heavens, I shall have to pretend he is my lover (in the play, that is).

I have spent some little care on my appearance – a cotton gown, almost totally devoid of ornament, save for some pretty tucks at the hem, in a peach and white stripe, and a lawn fichu tucked around the neck. I look almost . . . virginal; the sort of woman a gentleman retired from foreign adventures might very well choose as a wife. I debate on whether I should wear a coral cross, but not wishing a thunderbolt to strike me, decide against it. The only ornament I wear is a pair of pearl bobs that would not look out of place on a miss fresh from a schoolroom. I can only hope I sustain the appropriate behaviour to match my appearance.

Fanny Gibbons is most correct, addressing us all formally, and after a mild tussle with Otterwell about who is to lead the rehearsal, she takes over. With a polite yet firm smile, she sends Otterwell to his library to finish his improvement on Shakespeare, since the whole first scene in the Athenian court has been cut. And so, since Oberon is busy chewing his quill in the library, Titania takes advantage of her consort's absence to consult with her cook about dinner, and we begin at the scene where Hermia and Lysander are lost in the woods.

Fanny allows us to read from our prompt books, in which we may mark our directions on the stage. Congrevance is not half a dozen words into his speech before she stops him.

'Mr Congrevance, please remember you are weary. You too, Lady Elmhurst. Start again, if you please.'

After three attempts, in which Mrs Gibbons tries to stop Congrevance striding on to the stage as though he were a lord surveying his estate, and orders me not to smile – I am sure she is wrong, all actresses smile – I actually manage to say the lines I drummed into my head yesterday.

'*Be it so, Lysander: find you out a bed; For I upon this bank will rest my head.*'

'Lie down, Lady Elmhurst.'

I dutifully write it in my prompt book.

'Very good, Lady Elmhurst. Now lie down, if you please.'

'I am afraid my stays do not allow me to do so, Mrs Gibbons.'

She rolls her eyes. 'Short stays in future, please. Mr Congrevance, if you could be so kind.'

I look at the floor. 'But it's dirty!'

Congrevance removes his coat and lays it on the floor.

'Very good, Mr Congrevance. We shall keep that, although you will wear a cloak in the play. Please make a note of it. Now, if you could help Lady Elmhurst lie down.'

His arm snakes around my waist, and his other hand grips mine. Goodness, how strong he is. He gazes into my eyes and, as he lowers me to the floor, murmurs, 'Would I were my coat, madam.'

I giggle.

Fanny frowns at me. 'On one knee, Mr Congrevance, for your next line.'

Still holding my hand, he kneels beside me, and I feel quite dizzy with longing.

'One turf shall serve as pillow for us both; One heart, one bed, two bosoms, and one troth.'

Oh heavens. My mind is a complete blank. It is as if no one in the room, the house, the world exists except we two. I swear the spiders pause on their cobwebs, a bee buzzing at the window stills, and we gaze into each other's eyes as time slows and stops.

'Nay, good Lysander . . .' pipes up Master Gibbons, our Puck, who has been appointed prompt for the moment.

My voice is breathless and wobbly.

'Nay, good Lysander; for my sake, my dear, Lie further off yet, do not lie so near.'

'If we were in London, and you a more experienced actress, I believe you could read the line that way,' Fanny says with great kindness after a short, embarrassing pause. I am glad Otterwell is out of the room. It is bad enough that Linsley is there, smirking away, but I am glad to see Philomena kick him quite hard. What Fanny really means is that I apparently sound as abandoned as I feel at the moment. She continues, 'However, Lady Elmhurst, Lord Otterwell and his neighbours would be shocked. Could you endeavour to sound more like an Athenian maiden?'

'I thought I did,' I say, thoroughly confused. Congrevance holds my hand still, and smiles at me –

that rare smile that somehow hurts me and pleases me at the same time.

'Watch,' Fanny says. She runs up the stairs that lead on to the stage and sinks to her knees. There, she gazes at Congrevance and repeats the line with the touching innocence of a debutante who has received an invitation from a rake to waltz.

'I'd feel a fool to say it that way,' I say. Was I ever that young and stupid?

'Try for something halfway between,' Fanny says as she rises, brushing dirt from her dress. 'We don't want Mr Congrevance to forget himself, do we? Continue, please.'

With much stopping and restarting, we continue the scene. Master Will as Puck, word perfect and with very little encouragement from his mother, abandons his post as prompt and pretends to squeeze the juice from the magic flower into Congrevance's eyes. And then Fanny and Darrowby join us on the stage, and things become quite different.

Helena's first few lines remind me rather uncomfortably of my state of mind when Mary and I escaped from London – that everyone else was better off than me, and I wandered lost in an unfriendly world.

Congrevance awakes – or pretends to – and hurls himself on his knees towards Fanny.

'*And run through fire I will for thy sweet sake,*' he

declaims with great ardour, and he sounds absolutely convincing. At that moment I hate Fanny Gibbons as passionately as I ever did. Painful memories overwhelm me as I remember how seven years ago in London I was in love with Linsley and believed that Fanny was attempting to lure him back into her bed. Even though the play demands that Congrevance declare passionate love for her, I am furious that he sounds so convincing.

Congrevance continues. *'Transparent Helena! Nature shows art, That through thy bosom makes me see thy heart.'*

Fanny utters a strangled shriek and crosses her arms over her bosom, and were I not so angry and sad I should have laughed. As it is, I have to pretend to sleep still, until the two of them have left the stage, when I wake and find myself alone. I speak my lines, of how I have had a nightmare, which when I memorised them seemed as silly as the rest of the play, but now have a new meaning. Hermia has dreamed of her imminent betrayal by her lover, and I realise how fragile is my connection to this man I barely know.

'Very well done, Lady Elmhurst,' Fanny says. She scribbles a note in her prompt book. 'Would one of you gentlemen help Lady Elmhurst to her feet?'

I truly believe that if Congrevance had stepped forward I would have murdered him, so it is just as well Darrowby is the one to come to my rescue.

I know Congrevance is watching. I contrive to show a lot of ankle on my return to the vertical, and my lawn scarf drops carelessly away. Naturally Darrowby can see into my bosom. 'Thank you, sir,' I breathe, brushing up against him, my hand resting lightly on his sleeve.

He clears his throat and steps back.

Fanny looks furious; Congrevance's face is like stone, and I have the great satisfaction of knowing I have made them both jealous.

Altogether it is a satisfying morning's work and I have worked up quite an appetite for luncheon.

Mr Nicholas Congrevance

I cannot help but notice during our rehearsals that Caroline does her best to make me jealous by flirting with Darrowby. I tell myself I should ignore it, but I cannot, and flirt with Fanny Gibbons. Shortly after luncheon we are let go for the day, most of us in poor spirits except for Otterwell, who returned triumphant with his verse after a couple of hours summoning up the spirit of Shakespeare. Even I can tell it is poor stuff. I am much in sympathy with Master Will, who sits, wriggling and screwing up his face, occasionally mouthing some gibberish in the manner of da-*dum*-da-*dum*-da-*dum*-da-*dum*.

Given the tensions between the players, we are all relieved to go our own ways thereafter. I stroll around the grounds, taking care to avoid any of the others, and eyeing various spots that might be useful for the art of seduction (the maze, certain secluded paths and so on).

One thing I have learned about Caroline is that she does not like a rival, so that evening I set out to charm the daughters of Otterwell's guests. They are a group of toothy gigglers, overdressed and overcurled, Miss Clark and Miss Julia Clark, and Miss Eggham. I cannot tell one from the other. Neither do I care. I produce the same tired compliments that have served me well in the past, forcing the shallow words out; they giggle; and so on. After dinner (following some sensible male conversation) we join the ladies in the drawing room, where I make a point of helping the three misses choose music to play and assisting them with their shawls.

I am heartily sick of it and bored almost to death.

I have sworn once again I shall not look at Caroline. So I find myself Orpheus to her Euridice, although naturally she does not call to me, or follow behind me, but every atom of my being is aware that she is nearby. I am also aware that at some point I must make the first sortie in my campaign, and I have no idea how to go about it.

Nicholas Congrevance seems to be an entirely clumsy oaf, as incompetent as he ever was at the age of sixteen, the last time I used the name. I regret ever having brought him to life again. My other manifestations would have handled the situation far better.

The Reverend Tarquin Biddle: Madam, as a

younger son I am in no position to offer you anything other than my heart, which will be yours for eternity. Alas, my meagre allowance is spent on my ministry among the poor of Naples . . .

Count Mikhail Orchovsky: When those *muzhiki* at the bank are finished robbing me, I will take you to the steppes, where we shall ride in my troika, naked beneath the skins of bears I have killed with my bare hands, and I shall make love to you like a tiger . . .

The Earl of Ballyglenleary: Och, ma'am, we're an ancient family, and I the last of our clan, and under an ancient curse. 'Tis said only a bonnie lass bearing gold can break the curse, but I dinna ken the meaning of that. I canna offer for your hand, for I own only a crumbling romantic ruin, and now even my heart isna mine own . . .

In retrospect, I'm amazed any of the women believed me, particularly as the foreign accents of Orchovsky, Ballyglenleary, St Germain-d'Aubussy et al. tended to slip during amorous encounters. Did those women, who squandered their husband's money on me as easily as they might patronise a milliner or jeweller, know they were dealing with a scoundrel – and not care? The best that can be said is that I did not leave a trail of broken hearts or bastards behind me. And, without boasting overmuch, I gave the ladies value for money – which brings me to another troubling thought about Caroline. I might be able to kiss her for fifteen minutes, but I doubt whether I could last as long in more intimate circumstances.

'Oh, how delightful,' trills one of the Misses Clark, interrupting my unhappy reflections. 'Mrs Gibbons is to sing for us.'

Fanny Gibbons moves into the bright candlelight around the pianoforte. She looks particularly handsome tonight, and I can well believe she captured hearts and theatre audiences in London. Mrs Linsley seats herself at the pianoforte, removes a few bracelets and flexes her fingers. The two of them confer briefly, and then they begin.

I know the music, and Mrs Gibbons sings in the original Italian. It is as though she has read my mind.

'Che farò senza Euridice?

Dove andrò senza il mio ben?

Euridice! Euridice!'

Her voice is remarkable, strong and clear, supremely eloquent. Something strange is happening to me, a tightness in the throat, a pricking sensation around my eyes. The golden light and Mrs Gibbons' tawny-coloured gown blur before me.

Good God, I am about to burst into tears.

I stand, muttering an apology to my neighbours as the legs of my chair scrape on the floor. The drawing room has doors that stand open to the garden, and I flee outside, taking deep breaths of the air, fragrant with stock and wallflowers. I had forgotten the scents of an English garden, the long-shadowed clarity of an English summer evening. The sun has barely set and the air is soft and warm.

Behind me, Mrs Gibbons continues to sing of love, loss and despair.

I find my handkerchief and blow my nose.

There is an answering snort as someone else does the same.

I turn warily, hoping whoever it is has not observed my excessively emotional state.

'Damned grass,' says Lady Caroline Elmhurst. 'It's the same every time I come into the country. What are you doing here, Congrevance? Did the Misses Clark and Miss Egg-whatever-her-name-is tire of your charms?'

'They bored me.' I offer her my arm. 'I'd rather be with you.'

She lays her fingertips on my arm and we stroll across the lawn. 'Oh, certainly. Very pretty, sir. As I'm the only woman out here, of course you can make that claim.'

'However, I feel it is only correct to tell you, Lady Caroline . . .'

She plucks a handkerchief from her sleeve and blows her nose in a long, protracted sort of way.

I clear my throat and continue, 'I do not believe I shall ever fall in love again. You see, my heart was broken . . .'

She gives a final snort into the handkerchief and tucks it away. 'I beg your pardon. I did not hear all you said.'

'I was saying that as much as I enjoy female company, I regret I shall never love again, having known only one woman, an incomparable member of her sex, who . . .' I pause, so she can ask me about my broken heart. No woman, in my experience, can pass up such a challenge.

She gives a loud sniff, but not one inspired by sentiment.

Guessing that her handkerchief must be flooded, I offer her mine.

'Thank you. I daresay you'll get over her. One tends to.' She blows her nose. 'And you seem to amuse yourself quite well in the meantime. Why does your handkerchief have these initials?'

'I shall have to reprimand my manservant. We stayed at a sorry sort of inn on the way here, where our linens were washed.' I resolve not to lend any of my collection of mismatched handkerchiefs to this sharp-eyed woman again.

'My maid does my linens when we travel. She's very skilled with stains.'

While I would be quite happy to discuss the lady's underlinen, this conversation is not proceeding exactly as I would have wished.

'Have you visited Otterwell's maze?' I ask.

'Not yet. I shall ask Will to take me, as he can find his way to the centre and back again.'

'Ah, Lady Caroline, I should quite like to take you there myself.'

'I'm sure you would.' She flicks the handkerchief in my direction, a flirtatious gesture that loses its impact with the soggy nature of the item.

'Call me Nick,' I blurt out. No one has called me that in years.

She loosens her hand from my arm. 'I don't believe we should be on such intimate terms, Mr Congrevance. I shall return to the house now.'

I bow. 'Very well, Lady Elmhurst.'

She nods in a dignified fashion, an effect spoiled immediately after by another wetly unabashed nose-blow, and stuffs the handkerchief, now somewhat the worse for wear, back into my hand.

I watch her walk away, feeling confused and not altogether happy. She wears a gown much the same colour as the evening sky, a soft grey-mauve – I wonder if she wore it during her period of mourning, although I doubt it had a neckline then low enough to show her charms in such a spectacular manner. Rosettes and a line of ruffles around the hem produce a soft, intimate rustle as she moves.

The first star of the evening, Venus, has appeared. Apparently she does not shine on me.

I wander through the garden, which is cultivated

by Otterwell in old-fashioned Elizabethan style – stiff formal hedges, paths and beds; no romantic vistas or wildernesses here – until the light begins to fail. As I turn back (it would not be courteous to be gone for too long), I see a woman leaning against a plinth in the centre of a rose garden, so still I think she is a statue. In the fading light her gown is a tawny russet, a shade or two darker than her hair. She turns as I approach, one hand resting against the plinth, on which is set a sundial. Fallen petals scent the air, lying pale on the ground.

'Mrs Gibbons.' I bow. 'Do you contemplate the passing of time?'

She smiles, but there is something melancholy in her face. 'Something of the sort, Mr Congrevance. Do you return to the house now?'

'I should be happy to escort you.' I offer my arm.

She slips her hand into the crook of my elbow. 'I should be angry with you, sir. You left when I sang.'

'Yes, I did. I beg your forgiveness. Your singing moved me greatly.'

'Ah, of course, you understood the Italian.'

'I would have understood whatever language you sang in, Mrs Gibbons.'

'Very pretty,' she says, much as Caroline did.

'That may be, but it is the truth. Why were you out alone?'

'Oh, the others are somewhere near. To tell the

truth, Mr Congrevance, I craved solitude. Sometimes singing makes me sad. I miss the stage and wonder whether I made a mistake in retiring when I did.'

'Do you think you'd return to the theatre?'

'I don't know. It is . . . complicated.' She stops and looks at me. 'I find you interesting, Mr Congrevance. I've known a great many people playing roles of one sort or another, and I suspect you are not what you seem. Oh, you're very good at it – I was quite surprised by your talents as an actor today – but . . .'

And then I do something foolish. She is the wrong woman, and God knows I have no designs on her. At the same time I am unhappy and unsettled and I have spent several hours of the day flirting with her. Above all, there is also the issue of stopping her mouth and distracting her before she produces further revelations. I bend my head and kiss her. She tenses in surprise and kisses me back – not the frenzied grappling I experienced with Caroline, but the curious, intimate exploration of strangers, our arms slipping around each other; strangers who have played with a slight attraction to each other and have each been alone for too long.

A roar of anger interrupts us.

Mr Nicholas Congrevance

The mild and scholarly Mr Thomas Darrowby hauls me away by the shoulders and aims a wild blow in my direction. 'You scoundrel, sir!'

I duck to avoid his blow, and he almost falls over.

'For Christ's sake, Tom!' Fanny Gibbons says, blushing deep red.

'Tell me, for God's sake, he did not . . . did not . . .' He makes a grab for her hands, and she swats him away as though he were a particularly annoying sort of fly.

'It was a *kiss*, Tom. That was all.' She pats his arm. 'Calm yourself.'

He looks even angrier, as any man would if a woman spoke to him in that way and under such circumstances, and turns back to me, fists clenched. We're about the same height – he carries a little more weight, but I think I'm faster on my feet. 'You have insulted the lady, sir.'

'Then I beg her pardon, sir.' I bow to Fanny. 'Forgive me, madam.'

'Fanny, did he force his attentions on you?'

She hesitates and looks at me. I remember Linsley saying Fanny and Darrowby had found every excuse in the world not to resolve their relationship, and that the two of them needed a push in the right direction.

In a split second, I decide what I must do.

'Of course not!' I say in a loud, blustering tone. 'She's only an *actress*, after all. You saw how she flung herself at me at the rehearsal today.'

'Oh!' Fanny looks at me, uncertain, and then at Darrowby. 'Tom, I—'

'You – you foreign bastard!'

I'm tempted to laugh, but another of Darrowby's wild swings catches me in the ribs and I drop to one knee, clutching my side. I lurch back to my feet again.

My gaze meets that of Caroline, who stands a few feet away. Apparently she did not go indoors as I thought. Is she jealous?

'It really doesn't mean anything to Congrevance,' Caroline says. 'He was inviting me into the maze but a quarter-hour ago, Darrowby.'

'You blackguard!' Darrowby rushes at me again, but this time I step aside and he blunders into a shrub. As he extricates himself, picking leaves from his waistcoat, he splutters, 'I demand satisfaction, sir!'

Excellent. Now Fanny will see him as a hero.

Instead she takes Caroline's arm, and the two ladies regard me with contempt and Darrowby with what appears to be kindly pity.

'I suppose men can't help it,' Caroline says.

'Probably not. Caro, I rather fancy some of the little cakes we had with tea in the drawing room. Shall we see if there are any left?'

I have never been so embarrassed in my life, and Darrowby blushes bright red at Fanny's indifference. She gives us one last amused glance. 'I trust neither of you will do anything foolish.'

'Hit me!' I mutter to Darrowby.

'What?'

'Hit me. You're losing her interest.' I brace myself. 'Thumb outside your fist, Darrowby, you'll break a bone else.' I'm not thinking too clearly, but my reasoning goes something like this: Fanny will be impressed by Darrowby's manly strength and his ardent defence of her honour; Caroline will dart forward with a cry of distress as I fall.

Stars burst at the side of my head, and the gardens and evening sky wheel in a crazy spiral.

'A beefsteak should do the trick nicely, sir.'

To my disappointment, the face that leans over mine as I regain my senses is that of Barton. He helps me to my feet, brushing grass from my coat. My eye is rapidly tightening and closing, my cheekbone throbbing.

'Where are they?'

My question is answered as I see that Darrowby stands nearby. Of the two women there is no sign.

'I'm dreadfully sorry,' I say to Darrowby. 'Maybe I should have hit you. In any case, I had no business kissing Mrs Gibbons. My apologies, sir.'

He utters a long sigh. 'Possibly I should kiss her more myself. Women are so difficult, aren't they? You never really know what they want you to do. But what went wrong? I shouldn't be asking for your advice. I was about to challenge you to a duel.'

'You may still do so if you wish.'

'Not much point, Congrevance, if the women aren't to know about it. Besides, we have no disinterested parties for seconds.' He examines his knuckles and flexes his fingers. 'I hope I can still write.'

'I'll set you right up, sir, if you come along with us,' Barton offers. 'Or, if you wish, I'll get out the false beard . . .'

I shake my head. Not the false beard of which Barton is so fond and that he has assumed for a number of roles – seconds in duels, doctors, priests, et cetera.

What a failure. Not only have we subverted the code of honour, but we have lost the two ladies to dessert – Darrowby's timing was not of the best, as by the time he struck his blow they had turned away, arm in arm. Doubtless, if they discussed us at all, it was only to comment on what fools we were.

She doesn't care. I should abandon the pursuit, I'll leave tomorrow.

Beside me, Darrowby sighs. 'Congrevance, tell me. Do you think Mrs Gibbons is entirely indifferent to me?'

'Of course not.' My words ring with false heartiness.

At rehearsal the next morning, further humiliation awaits.

Otterwell sweeps into the hall, clad in a long flowing garment and crowned with peacock feathers that nod above his bald head. 'Costumes, gentlemen!'

He ushers us into the chamber assigned as the gentlemen's tiring room and gestures to a large chest. 'You shall be dressed in the ancient classical style. Mr Linsley will advise you on the fitting of the costumes.' After Otterwell has left – doubtless he intends to visit the ladies' tiring room on some pretext – with some trepidation we pick through the garments in the chest, which emits a musty smell; I suspect mice have made their homes in it at some point.

'What the devil . . .' Linsley holds up a pink knitted item.

'Tights!' says Darrowby.

'I fear so. And tunics.'

We gaze at each other in horror.

So this is the punishment the gods have devised for men who do not fight each other properly.

Skirts.

With much grumbling we pull the garments out of the chest and determine that the musty smell comes mainly from the tights; they are knitted silk, and the thought strikes us that possibly they have not been washed since Otterwell's last theatrical extravaganza. We undress with our backs turned to each other – not from modesty, but from a reluctance to see how hideous these costumes are.

I tie a belt, some sort of shiny gold rope, around my tunic and shove my feet into leather sandals that curl up at the toes, badly in need of cleaning. Barton would not approve.

'Well, it's not so bad.' I take a step towards the pier glass that stands in the corner. A strange downward movement accompanies me. Another few steps and the waist of the damned tights is halfway down my thighs and I am reduced to a waddle.

'You can't do that on stage,' Darrowby says as I hoist my skirts and heave the pink monstrosities to their original position. He too takes a turn around the room, his manly stride deteriorating to tiny mincing steps as his tights collapse in folds around his knees.

'Impossible!' Linsley declares. He leaves the room, to return brandishing a large pair of scissors. 'Gentlemen, I have the solution. You shall retain both modesty and comfort.'

A few minutes later, self-conscious and hampered by our skirts, which swish around our knees and get in the way of our normal stride, we make our way on to the stage. Mrs Linsley, seated and surrounded by a great length of stuff on to which she sews some trim, giggles.

At the same time, Linsley's mother, the formidable Mrs Riley, tall, silver-haired and imperious, strides into the hall like a warrior queen, accompanied by Otterwell and several housemaids. She comes to a halt and stares at us, eyes narrowed.

'Inigo,' she booms, 'pray, what do your associates wear beneath their skirts?'

He wriggles with embarrassment and mutters, 'Linen, ma'am.'

The housemaids, retrieving threaded needles from their apron pockets, giggle.

'Speak up, Inigo.' She frowns at the housemaids. 'You, Susan, Kate and Meg, pay no attention to the gentlemen and get on with your sewing. I ask you again, gentlemen, what do you wear beneath your skirts?'

Linsley wriggles like an embarrassed schoolboy and Darrowby is in an equal state of red-faced shame.

I step forward. 'Drawers, ma'am. Cut off above the knee.' I grasp the hem of my tunic in demonstration, and Mrs Linsley and her assistants turn scarlet, overcome with mirth.

'There is no need for that sort of thing, Congrevance. At least one of you has some sense.' She gives her son a pointed look.

'I must insist you wear the tights, sirs,' Otterwell cries.

The word *tights* sends the women into a fresh fit of laughter.

'Regrettably, my lord, we cannot walk in them.'

'But they were borrowed from Drury Lane. I trust you did not cut them too.'

At this point we are joined on stage by Caroline, who arrives in a rush, bosom heaving, and I at least notice that the bosom continues to heave even after she comes to a stop.

'This is intolerable, Otterwell!' she cries.

She is magnificent, hair loosened, her arms bare to the shoulder and much of her bosom revealed by thin draperies. She turns her head to catch we three staring at the revealed flesh. 'Pray avert your eyes! You too, Otterwell.'

Fanny Gibbons comes on to the stage too, similarly clad, although the results, particularly around the bosom, are not nearly so spectacular. 'Caroline, you cannot tell the audience to avert their eyes.'

'I think you look lovely,' Mrs Linsley says, glancing up from her sewing. 'Don't you think so, Congrevance?'

Some strange sort of noise emerges from my throat.

'Oh. Do you? Do I?' Caroline gazes down at herself with what appears to be indecison, then fixes Otterwell with a fearsome glare. 'Can you explain, sir, why I am dressed so, and the other ladies are almost decent?'

'Ma'am, they did not have stays in ancient Greece—'

'Nonsense, Otterwell. I am made to look like a . . . like a . . .'

'Like a goddess,' I say, to my extreme embarrassment once the words are out.

'Oh. Do you think so indeed?' She gives we bare-legged gentlemen a close inspection. 'What are you wearing under your skirts?'

'Cut-down drawers,' Mrs Riley interjects. 'They are quite decent, ma'am, I assure you.'

'More decent than I.' She tosses her mane of hair and crosses her arms over her bared bosom. 'I insist I have a scarf or some such, Otterwell, otherwise *I shall not play*.'

Lady Caroline Elmhurst

For sure, it is my trump card. Once the words are out of my mouth, Otterwell becomes almost obsequious, discussing suitable wraps with Philomena – after all, as she sweetly points out, we are in an Athenian wood and surely any sensible woman would wear a pelisse or spencer or some such. Lady Otterwell, clad in regal purple and huge silk flowers with a tottering crown, joins us, and Otterwell makes a great effort not to look at my bosom. Lady Otterwell sends a maid for a hefty brown woollen shawl that looks as though it was borrowed from a horse, and the rehearsal begins.

And Congrevance thinks I look like a goddess! I am mightily pleased and almost forgive him for the male perfidy of the night before. I am glad to see the shadow of a bruise on that handsome cheekbone. He deserves it – I wish I had planted it there myself. After his maudlin ramblings of lost love and broken hearts (or whatever he was talking about) and his attempts to lure me into the maze, the vile seducer, he had the audacity to kiss another woman, my former rival (although I suppose he does not know that, unless Linsley has blabbed to him of it).

However, I am happy that my hay fever has abated this morning, and it is a pleasure to not sneeze continually.

And I very much enjoy the sight of Congrevance in

a skirt, or rather, his tunic. At first the men are awkward, but then some strutting and posturing occurs, and their skirts swish with great assurance, the peacocks.

'Gentlemen, gentlemen,' cries Fanny. 'Pray have a care when you sit. The audience does not wish to see your unmentionables!'

'But they'll be wondering,' Linsley says. 'We might as well let the audience know what we have beneath to avoid vulgar speculation.' The other two nod in agreement; they do not refer, I believe, to the linen, which in truth may cover all but has a certain transparent quality.

'Knees together, gentlemen,' Fanny snaps, sounding remarkably like Mrs Riley, and meekly they obey.

Otherwise the rehearsal is frustrating and tempers grow short. We no longer have pockets for our prompt books and we stumble over our lines. Otterwell makes the mistake of advising Fanny on some point of stagecraft, and the atmosphere becomes unpleasantly chilly. (That is, unpleasantly chilly for the others, maybe, but highly diverting to me.)

Today Otterwell has decided we shall enjoy an expedition and a picnic luncheon on a grand scale. Outside the sun blazes down, and open carriages await us in the driveway, the horses dozing and twitching flies from their flanks. It is quite a relief to be decently laced into stays and a great joy to have Congrevance look at my bosom again (Otterwell and Linsley too, although I must say it is mere habit with them, as a dog may cock its leg against a tree). I remember only just in time that Congrevance behaved exceedingly badly the previous evening (I do hope Fanny enjoyed it, for the man can kiss, but I did not feel it proper to question her about it), and moreover has disposed himself shamelessly in his tunic and lack of tights (delicious). I must remember to treat him with disdain, for I do not want to be an easy catch. I may masquerade as an actress, but that does not mean I adopt the low morals associated with the profession, unless of course I should receive an offer I could not refuse (in fact it would be simpler all round if Congrevance were to offer marriage and my conscience remain untroubled. I am much pleased with my firm moral stance).

I arrange my muslin shawl carefully over my shoulders. I do not wish to burn, and neither do I wish to be driven into a ditch, as Otterwell has the reins.

We trot through the dappled golden and green light of woodlands before emerging into the bright sunlight of a dusty track leading between fields. Ahead is our destination, Puck's Hill (doubtless named by Otterwell), where we are to picnic. The horses strain forward as the ground slopes uphill, harness creaking, the air heavy with their sweat.

'There's no need to punish your cattle, Otterwell,' Congrevance says from behind me. 'We shall walk. You'll join me, Lady Caroline?'

Well, heaven forfend I should appear indifferent to the plight of the sweating horses. Otterwell applies the brake – even so, the horses snort and slither on the dusty track, worn smooth in the heat. Congrevance vaults over the side of the carriage and offers his hand as I alight. Behind us, the other carriage halts to discharge its occupants.

Lord, it's hot, and the air smells of horse (and also of Congrevance, delightfully so, who assists me with opening my parasol).

'Caro – Lady Elmhurst – tell me you are not indifferent to me,' he murmurs in my ear.

'Lord, Congrevance, you have such a practised air. You must have said that to dozens of women.'

He gives me a rueful crooked smile. 'Hundreds, ma'am.'

Then he is gone from my side, to assist Mrs Linsley with her armful of young Master James, shawl, parasol, toy wooden horse and various other necessities. She smiles up at him with a friendly ease that I envy. If only I were indifferent to Congrevance, for then we could be as comfortable together. But as it is, I must be on my guard until he has declared himself.

In the bright sunshine I shiver as I remember the mob of creditors in London and the threat of debtors' prison. And I wonder if it is possible to be both comfortable and yet full of desire for a gentleman at the same time. I admit I have never had both; comfort with Bludge, desire for Linsley and Elmhurst and Rotherhithe (and a few other gentlemen, but they hardly count). Maybe it is why people marry when they do not have to (that is, with no expectation of a happy event, or for pressing financial need, or to satisfy family expectations). Indeed, it is a mystery. I sigh so loudly that Fanny, who walks by my side, asks if the heat is too much for me.

When we come to the crown of the hill, an extraordinary sight awaits us. Otterwell's servants, in livery and with hair powder running in sweaty rivulets down their faces, stand outside a pavilion with a distinctly Eastern air – a silk pennant at its peaked top and ochre and scarlet fringes hang limp in the still air. Even as we approach, one of the footmen sways and collapses full length on the ground, overcome by the heat. A couple of others drag his recumbent body into the shade of a clump of gorse bushes so our appetites will not be spoiled by his suffering.

Otterwell mops at his sweaty face with a large handkerchief and ushers us into the shade of the pavilion. A few flies rise from the food and buzz away with weary indolence, as overcome by the heat as we. We ladies sink on to the pillows and carpets spread on the floor and fan ourselves.

Oh, thank heavens Otterwell has brought ice for the lemonade and champagne. I press a handful to my throat and groan aloud with pleasure as cold water trickles into my bodice.

Behind me, someone, Congrevance I believe, clears his throat.

And the devil of it is that he is the only one who is not red-faced and sweating; in fact the warmth makes him quite brisk, fetching us platefuls of food and filling our glasses. He must be used to the heat from Italy, I suppose. He takes little Will outside and plays catch with him for a time.

Even Otterwell is subdued for once. Instead of boring us to death with his eternal Shakespeare quotations, he drinks a lot of wine and falls asleep with his head on Lady Otterwell's lap, Titania's very own ass, as I remark to Philomena.

She giggles. 'Oh, you are so wicked, Caroline.'

Little James totters towards her and collapses on to her lap. She smoothes the sweaty curls on his forehead.

'What a sweet child,' I say, hoping it sounds sincere, for I am grateful to Philomena for her friendliness. And to be sure, although I can enjoy the company of a rational child like Will for a time, one who mostly only barks is something of a mystery to me.

'My sister expects her next confinement any day,'

Philomena says. I assume she means the one who is married. 'I do so enjoy being an aunt. Do you have nieces and nephews, Caroline?'

'Oh yes. I dote upon them.' I rack my wine-befuddled brain to remember how many children my fecund sister has produced. 'They are the most lovely children.'

I expect they are. The last one I saw, when I was in my sister's good graces, was at his christening, a red-faced, shrieking creature I was frightened to hold.

'And how about you, Mr Congrevance?'

He has dropped down beside us on to his elbow, coat discarded and in his shirtsleeves and waistcoat. He rests one wrist on his raised knee – it was most enjoyable when he posed so in his tunic. A little, a very little sweat stands on his forehead, darkening the hair that springs forward. As I watch, a bead trickles from his temple. Were we alone, I should lean forward and touch my tongue . . .

'Ma'am?'

Philomena repeats her question about nieces and nephews.

'Several, ma'am.' He springs to his feet. 'If you'll excuse me, ladies.'

'Oh dear.' Philomena bites her lip as he walks away, his back stiff. 'I do hope I have not offended him. It would be a shame if our plan were to go awry.'

I yawn. 'Oh, I wouldn't worry about him. He's

probably gone to look for a tree or a furze bush or something. What plan?'

'Why, Linsley has decided we should bring Fanny and Tom together, and you and Congrevance are to help us.'

'What? How?' I glance towards Congrevance, who stands with his back to us – not in the way of a gentleman who has found a bush or tree to his liking, but in a most elegant way, gazing out poetically, I suppose, at the view, which is quite striking. We ladies have failed to gush sufficiently over the fine prospect, as we are made quite limp and stupid by the heat.

'Oh, it's simple,' Philomena says. 'Congrevance will invite you to walk through the woods on the way home, and since it would be improper for you to be alone with him, I shall encourage Fanny to accompany you, and it is almost certain Tom will want to walk also. Then all you and Congrevance have to do is walk ahead and let nature take its course.'

'But—'

'Please, Caroline. He must propose to her.'

I consider this idiocy. It is unlikely any of us will go to sleep, and even more unlikely that Will or anyone will else will drop a magic potion into our eyes, or give any one of us an ass's head, but Congrevance may well have some ideas of his own once we are in the woods. I cannot afford to have my virtue assailed – but I certainly don't want him kissing Fanny any more, and if she is engaged to Darrowby, possibly he will leave her alone.

'What if they fight again?'

'Oh, I am so sorry I missed that.' Philomena smiles. 'It must have been so amusing. But you must not let them, Caroline. It is up to you to distract Congrevance, so Fanny and Tom may be alone.'

A dozen ways of distracting Congrevance flash through my mind. I take another gulp of cold wine.

'Of course. It will be my pleasure.'

Lady Caroline Elmhurst

The heat does not give up and the sun continues to blaze down.

Lady Otterwell reads some dreadful poetry she has written, and we are all too enervated to make the admiring comments she expects – all except Congrevance, that is, who enters into a grave discussion of rhyme and metre with her. To my disgust, she becomes girlish and flirtatious in a pink, wobbly sort of way.

Otterwell's servants have packed drawing instruments and watercolours, and we ladies are obliged to venture outside the shade of the pavilion – although it is not much of a relief, since the air is so still – and demonstrate our ladylike artistic accomplishments. Remembering my fatuous boast to Congrevance, made to impress upon him what a virtuous sort of marriageable ninny I was, I grit my teeth, and pick a view of Otterwell's house and the lake. I proceed to produce my usual sort of in-different mess, the paintbrush slipping in my sweaty fingers.

The footman who set up the easel and stool and carried the paints and board stands behind me, holding my parasol over my head. I can hear his heavy breathing and he stinks like a sweating horse. 'Pray take off your wig.'

'Milord wouldn't like it, milady.'

'I insist. What part do you have in the play? For sure, Lord Otterwell will be most put out if you are sick with the sun and cannot act. Good. Your gloves too, and your coat.' To my relief, he obeys – I would not want a footman swooning on top of me; it would do my reputation no good at all.

A scent of citrus indicates that Congrevance is nearby, looking over my shoulder. 'An interesting use of perspective, Lady Elmhurst.'

'Nonsense, sir. It is rubbish.'

He laughs and strolls across the hillside to where Philomena sits. I watch as his head disappears beneath her parasol, held by another sweating footman, who has followed the example of mine, wig, gloves and coat discarded. Congrevance and Philomena appear to be deep in conversation. Well, of course it is acceptable for an unmarried gentleman to flirt with a respectable matron, but I see Linsley stride towards them with a scowl on his face and James following behind, petticoats stained with grass and food.

Heavens, I now understand why so many horrid novels are set abroad, where sun and heat make people behave in most peculiar ways.

After our artistic pursuits – mine is the worst, but only slightly so – Otterwell announces that it is time to leave, and the servants set to dismantling the pavilion and packing china and silver. We walk down the hill, not wanting to strain the horses again, and enter the cool of the woods.

'Why, this is most pleasant,' Congrevance says as we are about to board the carriage. 'Would you care to continue the rest of the journey on foot, Lady Elmhurst? It can't be more than a mile or so to the house.'

'Oh, sir.' I cast down my eyes. 'As much as I should like to, it would not be proper for me to accompany you.'

Someone – I shall kill them when I find the culprit – gives a muffled snigger.

'Oh, you are quite correct, Caroline,' says Philomena. 'I would accompany you, but alas, I fear James may vomit, for he ate too much cake. Fanny, would you be so good as to accompany Lady Elmhurst?'

'Oh, very well.' She does not sound very pleased at the prospect. She glances at Will, who is asleep on his father's lap.

'Why don't you go with them, Tom,' Philomena continues relentlessly.

'Well, I—'

'Oh, do, Tom.' She turns the full force of her smile on him. 'You and Congrevance can make up your quarrel of yesterday.'

'Quarrel? What quarrel? Why, our guests must all be the best of friends . . .' Linsley leads Otterwell and Lady Otterwell into a frenzy of nosiness, and Darrowby jumps down from the carriage before the embarrassments of last night can be revealed. With the threat of a vomiting child, it is a wonder all the occupants do not choose to disembark.

Congrevance offers me his arm and tucks my hand into the crook of his elbow. His coat is slung over the other shoulder, for he is still in his shirtsleeves, and my hand encounters fine fabric and, beneath, the warmth and strength of his arm. As we stand back to allow the carriages to pass us, he murmurs, 'We must endeavour to lose the happy couple, Lady Elmhurst.'

'You mean we should become separated from them?'

'Precisely. We shall leave the path as soon as we can.'

Now I had thought we might walk ahead of them, leaving a good distance, so Darrowby might fling himself at her bosom, or sink to his knees, or do whatever he must, but this suggestion is a little unnerving.

First, I am sure we shall get lost. And second, that that is exactly what Congrevance intends – all the better to frolic with me in the woods! And of course I cannot let him have his wicked way with me yet. I must behave as the most virtuous of women until he is panting at my feet, ready to do exactly as I wish. My attempts to be cool towards him have not been particularly successful, and I am sure he is aware of the heated imaginings that run through my mind; on the other hand, his mask as a rakish seducer frequently slips and shows . . . what, I am not quite sure.

Men do not marry their mistresses. I must keep that in mind. Although I am not sure of the proprieties, if you will, between a gentleman and his future mistress, I am fairly sure an agreement should be drawn up, preferably by a lawyer, before intimacies take place. A cold-hearted approach, to be sure, but not that much difference from the alliances of the great families of the *ton*.

The carriages disappear around a bend in the track, and we four are left alone in the woods.

'How delightfully cool it is!' I cry. Not the most original of remarks, to be sure, but no one else seems inclined to make conversation.

'I am sure the weather will break soon,' Darrowby

replies. 'I hope it remains fine for the play.'

Obviously talk of the weather will not do. Congrevance tugs me forward. 'Look for a path to the side or some such,' he murmurs into my ear. We set off at so fast a clip I am almost running to keep up.

We are out of their sight now, and Congrevance points to a gap in the trees. 'There!'

He urges me forward – I grab at my bonnet as it catches in a tree branch, and then he pushes me down to the ground, one hand over my mouth.

I regret that although I should be terrified, I am thrilled by his proximity as we lie in the bracken – it is a pity indeed that so many small flies buzz around us. He is half on top of me and I can feel his heartbeat; his citrus scent and the feel of that wonderful masculine body against mine makes my head swim.

He lowers his head, and his hair and breath tickle my ear. 'Listen,' he whispers.

'. . . the disappointment, Fanny, could scarce be borne. It is my fault, I know, that I have not spoken before. I am mad with jealousy that you should even look upon another man.'

'I told you it was nothing. For God's sake, Tom, ask me to marry you and have done with it.'

'Oh, Fanny . . .'

'Do not kneel there, sir, a horse has passed by. May we not keep walking while you propose? These flies are driving me mad.'

Congrevance raises his head. His eyes dance with amusement and we both shake with silent laughter.

Darrowby and Fanny's voices fade away as they continue along the path. I think they are unaware of our absence.

I, however, am only aware of Congrevance, who takes his hand from my mouth – or almost so. His thumb trails along my lip.

'This is most improper,' I say.

'Exceedingly so.' He makes no effort to move.

'What if I were to scream for help?'

'Do you think it likely?'

'You are compromising me.'

'And you are enjoying it.'

'I am not, I assure you. I have a paintbrush in my pocket I could use as a weapon.' Two wicked lies in one.

'Ah, but you see, I shall immobilise you.' He grasps my wrists and holds them above my head, pressing against me even closer. (I am quite sure, by the way, that what I feel at this moment is not a paintbrush, and neither is it in his pocket.)

'Oh!' How wicked and delightful this man is. But I shall not succumb this easily. Or shall I? His head lowers to mine. He will kiss me. *Oh*. Oh heavens, his mouth—

Something crashes through the bracken towards

us, and Congrevance twists away from me as a small furry presence yips at us.

The terrier, for that is what it is, worries at Congrevance's coat, growling, tail wagging, delighted with our company. It releases the coat, rushes at me and licks my face.

'Damnation, I was just about to do that myself,' Congrevance says with a grin, and hands me his handkerchief. He stands and shakes out his coat. 'Down! Good dog.'

The dog sits, tail sweeping the bracken, eyes bright as it waits for the game to be resumed. Congrevance reaches a hand to me and we brush bracken debris from ourselves.

'Let's see where this path leads,' Congrevance says. 'I am pretty sure it will take us to Otterwell's house; besides, we should take this dog home.'

'How do you know he has a home?'

'He's well mannered. I expect he belongs to one of Otterwell's tenants.' He sets off along the narrow path, the dog scampering after him, and I follow them, half relieved and half disappointed that the seduction was interrupted in such an undignified way. It strikes me how very much Congrevance looks at home striding through the bracken with a dog at his heels.

'Do you have many dogs on your estate?' I ask.

'I've been out of the country for some time. But yes, I like dogs.'

'And what sort of land do you have? Is it like Otterwell's estate?'

'Hilly. With sheep.' He picks up a stick and throws it for the dog, which is delighted to be set to work and streaks off after it.

This is interesting. He doesn't want to talk about his family or his land, and I wonder why. I shall have to make Mary ask some questions of that rogue Barton, who I am sure is up her skirts already, but I am hardly in a position to give moral advice.

A walk of several minutes takes us to a clearing where a small house stands, and a man in rough clothing works at a bench outside, turning over various pieces of metal. Chickens cluck and scratch around the house. A small child rushes inside, and emerges with a woman, who wipes her hand on her apron and drops a curtsy.

'Milord, milady, welcome. We'd be most honoured if you'd take refreshment with us, wouldn't we, husband?'

Her husband grunts, makes a minimal bow and returns his attention to his work.

The woman, whose name she tells us is Betty Culver, leads us into the house, apologising profusely for its condition, and shoos a chicken and several children out of the way. 'You'll take a dish of tea, milady?'

I open my mouth to accept, but Congrevance

interrupts. 'Thank you, mistress, but some ale would serve us well enough on such a hot day.'

I am surprised he knows how expensive tea is – a rude shock recently to me – and am impressed with his tact. She pours spruce beer from a jug into horn cups, and Congrevance takes two, saying he'll go to talk to her husband outside.

We are in a large room that is both kitchen and parlour, with a hearth at one end. An iron pot sits in the embers and the air is scented with woodsmoke and cooking bacon. As Mrs Culver chats, I learn that Mr Culver is under-gamekeeper to Otterwell. His present task, that of mending someone called Jack, is mystifying to me, and I suppose it shows on my face, for Mrs Culver laughs.

'No, no, mistress, I mean the jack for cooking. You know what men are, they take something to pieces to improve it and it turns out worse. Maybe milord can help him, for I'd dearly like to cook something other than bacon boiled with vegetables. He's a good man, Mr Culver, but helpless as a babe with machines. Our old clock has never been the same since he took it apart to clean it.'

She indicates a clock in the corner, a fine ancient piece with a face painted with suns and stars. As I look, the hands shift to the hour of four o'clock, and it whirrs and strikes. And strikes. At seventeen, it stops.

If it is indeed four o'clock, we shall probably miss

dinner at Otterwell's, something that does not worry me unduly. I sip my beer, content to be inside in the shady cool of this pleasant house, where I am unknown and do not have to act any part.

A child rushes in with a handful of green stuff, some sort of cabbage, drops it on to the table and runs out again.

'If you'll excuse me, milady.' Mrs Culver takes the cabbage from the table, shakes it dry and grasps a large wooden spoon. With it she lifts the lid of the pot, releasing a gust of bacon-scented steam, and then adds the cabbage to whatever else is cooking there, stirring vigorously.

Something squawks and then gives a tentative wail from the corner – the latest addition to the Culver family. Mrs Culver looks up from her cooking, and I see that were we of equal rank, she would ask me to take the baby.

I usually try to avoid infants, but brace myself to pick up the warm, damp, squirming thing, which opens its mouth and eyes wide at the sight of me.

'Don't scream,' I tell it in a whisper.

Its face creases in preparation for a howl.

Oh God. I set it on my lap and jiggle it around, hoping it does not leave a damp patch on my skirts. It sets up a low sort of crooning, humming sound that reminds me of a hen on its nest. Its mouth opens again into a huge toothless smile, drool falling from its chin.

'Well, look at her, the little poppet, bless her!' Mrs Culver, wiping her hands on her apron, comes back to the table. 'She's taken such a fancy to your ladyship!'

For one awful moment I wonder if she's about to try and sell me her child – they live in very modest circumstances and there seem to be quite a lot of children underfoot – but the unpinning of her bodice indicates that I should probably have to buy the mother too. Frankly, I would rather buy the terrier that led us here.

'We have repaired your jack, Mrs Culver. Caroline, I think we should take our leave now.' Congrevance, one shoulder propped against the doorway, smiles at us. Good God, I hope he did not see me handle the infant – he will think I am some sort of dreadful broody creature.

Mr Culver lurks behind Congrevance, the jack in his hand, and smaller Culvers arrive, sniffing the fragrant air. It is dinner time at the Culvers' house, and we must go; besides, I am afraid Congrevance may be invited to repair the clock if we stay. I drain the last of my beer and shake hands with Mrs Culver. I wonder whether we should offer to pay for the spruce beer somehow without insulting her; Congrevance, with the greatest of tact, hands the children pennies from his pockets, and lays a sixpence on the table, explaining it is for the baby. I, of course, have no money on my person anyway.

The air is deepening a little as we leave – not dusk, precisely, it is still far too early for that, but in the dimness of the woods a few fireflies appear. We walk in silence along a rutted track that Mr Culver told us would lead straight to Otterwell's house. Now and again our hands brush. I have rarely felt so at ease with a gentleman and I do not believe the Culvers' excellent spruce beer has anything to do with it.

The air is sweet and holds the lingering scent of honeysuckle. Once, Congrevance places his hand on my arm and points with the other; a doe and her spotted fawn stand motionless like statues, regarding us. We stand still too, until the deer bound away, disappearing into the light and shade.

Congrevance is silent – not that he is a particularly garrulous man, but I have become accustomed to conversation with him, even if it is of a suggestive or flirtatious nature. I wonder if he is thinking what I am – that in only a few more days our play will be performed, after which the party will disperse, and everything between us is unresolved.

We arrive at Otterwell's house near some outbuildings and the kitchen gardens, and stroll round to the front of the house. If anyone notices our arrival, they will immediately jump to improper conclusions.

Let them.

What I do next surprises me and I am sure it surprises him. I turn to Congrevance and lay my hand on his chest, his waistcoat to be exact, as he still carries his coat over one shoulder.

'Thank you,' I say. I am not sure what I am thanking him for – for the peace of the woods, for his kindness to the Culvers. Maybe, in some strange sort of way, for allowing me silence as we walked back to the house.

I rise on my toes and kiss his cheek, slightly rough under my lips. Warm. *Him*.

Mr Nicholas Congrevance

'It's not like you,' Barton says. 'Sir.'

'I know.'

'Just the other day you were saying we should leave, and we're still here. You haven't got under her skirts for all you were out with her for hours the other afternoon and missed dinner. All downstairs talk of how you favour her. What—'

'That's enough. You haven't found out how much she's worth.'

'Enough to make it worth your while. I told you. Sir.'

I finish pulling my shirt over my head and look at Barton. He stands, razor in one hand, towel over his arm and staring at a basin of soapy water as though he has never seen any such thing in his life before.

'Barton!'

He grunts.

'What is the matter with you?'

He heaves a huge sigh, and the shaving water slops in the basin. 'It's her, sir.'

'Who?'

'Mary.' His lip trembles. For one awful moment I fear he is about to burst into tears. I snatch the razor from him; I certainly don't want Barton, in this fragile state, anywhere near my throat with cold steel. I proceed to lather my face.

'She – she's like a – a flower. So pretty and delicate, like.'

I almost cut myself. *Barton?* Barton, comparing a woman to a flower?

I squint in the mirror to reach that tricky place beneath my ear. 'And your problem, Barton? Not got under her skirts yet?'

In the ominous silence that follows my question, I see Barton's face redden. His large, meaty fists clench.

'I beg your pardon. That was most indelicate.'

He heaves a great sigh. 'Oh yes, sir, of course I did. What do you take me for, sir? Lovely, it was. But – but I want to keep doing it. With her. Only her, if you follow my meaning.' His face takes on a soft, dreamy expression so incongruous with his ugly features that I'm tempted to turn Catholic and cross myself. 'Marry her.'

I drop the razor.

Barton continues to stare into space, doubtless anticipating the pleasures of the marriage bed. I retrieve the razor and wipe dust from it; Otterwell's servants, nearly all of whom have been press-ganged into the play in some way or another, have been neglecting their usual duties. Barton hardly seems to notice as I take the towel from his arm and dry my face.

'I'm sorry,' I say finally.

He nods and hands me a neckcloth.

We don't need to spell out the situation. Without money, Barton cannot marry Mary. With money taken from Mary's mistress, under the usual circumstances, he still cannot marry her, for of course we will disappear soon after. He may have some savings of his own, but I doubt whether he is in the position to make a respectable marriage. And to what trade could he turn his hand to support a wife and family? He is an excellent rogue but an indifferent valet.

With a great dramatic sigh Barton empties the shaving water into the slop bowl.

Having tied my neckcloth, I stroll over to the window. My room looks out over the flower gardens, and I can see a woman there, wandering around the rosebeds.

Caroline, walking and reading – possibly she is perfecting her lines for the play. Yes, she clasps the book to her bosom (would I were the book), recites, looks down to her place again. Most of us spend our time alone muttering to each other, forcing lines into our memories at this point in the preparation for the play. Otterwell has become most impatient with us.

I give one last glance at the woman upon whom I have improper designs and whom I must seduce sometime within the next few days and whose money I must purloin.

I curse myself for my inaction. Damn the play, damn whatever it is about Caroline that makes me want to adore her, make passionate love to her and run from her like the wind, inexplicably all at the same time. In my heart I know I should leave her and Otterwell's house. Yet I have made no move to do so.

I remember again how she sat in a beam of sunlight, a baby on her lap, looking like an Italian Madonna in a church. The baby smiled at her and she smiled back, both of them innocent and unsullied. A painter would have loved that scene, the rough table, scrubbed almost white, where a stoneware bowl and a jug of flowers stood, and the contrast of light and shadow in the room. And surpassing all, the beautiful woman with a child.

The woman who kissed me and thanked me; I am not sure for what. She will probably not thank me in a few days when she realises I have seduced and abandoned her, and left with her guineas in my pocket (which reminds me, those damnable earrings are still in my possession). I doubt whether she will laugh at her adventures, sigh a little, and consider the experience money well spent.

Lady Caroline Elmhurst

At breakfast this morning I am inspired to write to my fecund sister Jane. We quarrelled most violently after Bludge died and I ran with a fast set in London; she disapproved thereafter of my marriage to Elmhurst, which makes no sense at all. Would not she, as the wife of a churchman whose sights are set on a bishopric, rather have me married than not? However, if I am the one to offer the olive branch, she will appear at a moral disadvantage, something she will be aware of and that gives me a small moment of pleasure.

In the breakfast room I sit through as much billing and cooing as I can stand, while Tom caresses jam on to his beloved's toast, and Fanny, fondling the spoon in an indecent way, stirs sugar into his tea. Their feet intertwine beneath the table; they touch hands as often as they can. Every meal has been the same since the announcement of the engagement.

Oh, I admit, I am jealous. I wish Congrevance and I could be as open and as amorous. I want someone to smile on me indulgently and make silly arch comments the way the Otterwells and the Linsleys do, and talk of weddings and honeymoons and new clothes and family members yet to be met. So I write to my sister, and after much crossing out I take my letter and my addled head into the garden, and read through my attempt:

My dear sister,

I trust you and the Reverend Pargeter and ~~Thomas Peter Paul Henry Robert Ann Annabel Catherine Katherine~~ my ~~dearest~~ nieces and nephews are all well. I regret that ~~you acted like a pig-headed fool, chose to disown your own flesh and blood cast me aside~~ our correspondence has been limited of late. Do not excite yourself, ~~dear~~ sister, ~~I am not about to ask you for money, not that you would lend me any~~ that I write with bad news. It is in fact quite the contrary. I am well and ~~not pregnant out of wedlock as doubtless you suspect~~ happy. Currently I visit Lord and Lady Otterwell's house as an honoured guest in their ~~ridiculous~~ theatricals with a most ~~lively~~ respectable group of ~~mostly~~ high-born ladies and gentlemen.

Sister, my news is of the very best kind. I have met a gentleman. He is handsome and rich and ~~I believe~~ returns my affections and ~~I long to bed him~~ I await his proposal, for although he has not yet declared himself I am sure he will. Be happy for me; he is ~~all that is desirable in a man~~ very respectable and ~~beautiful naked~~ of a good family from the north. I trust that next time I write I will ~~have enjoyed his~~ be an engaged woman.

I think often of the time ~~you stole my doll and pulled off all her hair~~ *when we were the most affectionate of sisters and wish we could return to that happy state. Please write to your* ~~most~~ *loving sister,*
    Caroline

Well, it will do, I suppose, once I have made a clean copy.

I wander further into the gardens and see a burly figure bent over a flower bed, carefully plucking Otterwell's choicest blooms in his large fingers. As I watch, he raises a rose to his hairy nostrils and sniffs, his ugly face transformed. Barton, picking flowers for Mary – she has appeared recently with flowers pinned to her bodice.

He sees me and hides the roses behind his back, raising his hat.

'Good morning, milady.'

'Good morning, Barton. I did not know you liked flowers.'

He blushes deep scarlet and mumbles something. Then he smiles. 'I have a part in the play, milady.'

'Indeed?' I do hope Otterwell has not cast him as a fairy.

'Yes, milady, I am one of the rude mechanicals. The footman who was to play the part has a boil on his – he cannot sit down and must have it lanced and stay abed, so I am to play the part of the wall.'

'I am sure you will do wonderfully well.' I speak with sincerity, for his sheer solidity and size must suit the part well.

'Thank you, milady. I will wear the false beard I have for such occasions.'

'You act often, then?'

'No, milady. That is – well, abroad, sometimes, we – the master and I . . .' He stumbles to a stop, obviously reluctant to continue.

I remember that Congrevance has been a spy. Afraid that Barton is about to reveal secrets of the realm, I hasten to reassure him. 'Oh, of course, Barton, you need say no more. I understand.'

He shifts from one foot to the other, crushing a pansy beneath one large boot. 'Yes, milady. Thank you, milady.'

I nod to him and walk on, folding the letter and placing it in my pocket. It is almost time for breakfast, and today we will have rehearsals in the morning and afternoon. It is the first day on which we are to attempt the complete play, without our prompt books and supposedly without interruptions. Time is running short.

So, it appears later, are tempers.

We are at the beginning of the play. Congrevance and I are seated on the chairs in the theatre, the Linsleys and Darrowby are somewhere in our backstage area and Fanny stands before the stage, making notes and occasionally giving directions to the cast.

Master James, hand in hand with Lady Otterwell, makes his appearance as the Indian child fought over by the king and queen of the fairies.

He barks.

Some of us laugh, and pleased by his success, James does it again.

'No, boy!' Lord Otterwell says. 'No barking!'

'What a naughty child!' Lady Otterwell says.

'Carry on, please,' Fanny says. 'James, you shall bark later, but not now. Remember that now you are a little boy.'

'Woof,' says Master James.

'Enough! Off the stage with you!' Otterwell bellows, scarlet with rage – and with heat, too, I imagine, for the room is exceedingly stuffy.

'Sir!' Fanny starts forward, but it is too late. The Indian child bursts into tears, producing, indeed, a torrent of water at both ends, for in his fright he now stands in a puddle of his own making.

Will rushes to his brother's side and puts a protective arm around him. His voice quivers slightly. 'He is only a baby, sir. He does not know—'

'Silence!' Otterwell thunders.

I start from my seat, but to my surprise Congrevance reaches the distressed children before I do and picks James up, wet petticoats and all, soothing him.

Fanny, meanwhile, storms on to the stage and delivers a veritable tirade at Otterwell. 'How dare you treat a child so! Pray remember, Otterwell, it is I who direct this play and I who tell the actors what they should or should not do.'

'On my stage and in my house, ma'am, and I will not have this production be a laughing stock.'

'As it may be anyway, sir, unless you allow me to do as I see fit.'

'I assure you, ma'am, you are not as indispensable as you believe, and neither is this child. My tenants are pleased to produce scores of children who would do as well in the role, nay, indeed, be honoured to assist me. I have presented dozens of theatricals to the delight of the gentry, who have the most discerning taste and education, and—'

'You mean they are dull and polite, sir, and do not wish to give offence. The child remains. Your behaviour is grossly insulting to me and to the Linsley family – you remember, sir, this child is the nephew of an earl.'

I am ashamed to think that I, who foresaw the clash of wills between Fanny and Otterwell at our very first rehearsal, actually looked forward to it with anticipation.

'That's enough!' Congrevance, even with a wet, weeping child in his arms, has an air of authority. He turns to a housemaid, one of the fairies. 'Please fetch

Mrs Linsley to see to her son. Mrs Gibbons, Lord Otterwell, may I suggest we take a half-hour break.'

The actors shuffle off the stage. Fanny storms out of the hall through the doors at the end that open into the gardens. Will steps down from the stage, wide-eyed, and I wonder whether he is about to cry himself, frightened by his mother's rage. I place my arm around his shoulders.

Philomena arrives, and scoops her child into her arms. 'What has happened?'

Congrevance informs her in a few brief words.

'This is intolerable. I shall tell Inigo and we shall leave immediately.' Her lip quivers. 'Oh no. If Tom hears of this, he will give his notice to Otterwell and then he will not be able to marry Fanny until he has found a new position. They are so happy. This is dreadful, Caro. What shall we do?'

Congrevance answers. 'You clean your child up, Mrs Linsley, and perhaps Will can go with you. I'll change my coat and speak with Otterwell. Lady Elmhurst, will you talk with Mrs Gibbons?'

I step outside into the bright sunlight of the garden. It is dreadfully hot again, and a group of Otterwell's gardeners lounge in a patch of shade, not even pretending to work. There is no sign of Fanny, but I do not doubt I shall find her. I am not looking forward to this interview at all. Fanny is friendly enough to me, but that is all, and generally we have the sunny presence of Philomena to maintain civility. I wanted to tell Congrevance that Philomena might have been the better emissary, but she had her hands full with two distressed children; besides, I had absolutely no intention of becoming involved with the matter of James's wet petticoats.

Fanny sits under a large oak tree at the edge of the garden, where it becomes parkland. The air shimmers with heat, and far off a cuckoo calls. She sees me approach, and I believe she tucks away a handkerchief, but she makes no effort to stand or greet me.

'What a pleasant spot. May I join you?'

She shrugs. 'I can hardly stop you, Lady Elmhurst.'

This is not a good sign, that she does not use my Christian name, but I sit a couple of feet away from her and remove my bonnet, smoothing the ribbons out. 'Your son is with Philomena.'

'Thank you. I have decided that – that Will and I shall leave the house as soon as possible,' she says.

'I am most sorry to hear it.'

'Indeed. Are you, Lady Elmhurst?'

'For God's sake, Fanny, are you determined to make enemies of us all?' I speak more sharply than I intended and her eyes flood and spill over.

I hand her a handkerchief and allow her to collect herself.

'I have made a great many mistakes,' she says, wiping her eyes.

I hope she does not mean her engagement to Darrowby – after all, I risked my honour in bringing it about. 'Congrevance has gone to talk to Otterwell.'

'Ah, yes. I fully expect to offer my apologies to Otterwell, which he will accept with the greatest of condescension. I am sure Mr Congrevance will be suitably ambassadorial.'

What does she mean by that? 'I believe there will be no repercussions regarding Darrowby's employment, or at least so Congrevance hopes.'

'It doesn't matter. Tom was to leave soon, to work for a newspaper in London.'

'Well, then, it seems all will be for the best.' I try to keep my voice cheerful. 'Shall we take a walk? I am sure it will do us good.'

She plucks some blades of grass and lets them flutter to the ground. 'Caroline, upon reflection I realise I should not have accepted Tom's proposal. I have known him several years and thought only that I liked him well enough. It is only within the last few days that I have realised I love him most passionately. But I have been afraid for some time that now that Will is older, and particularly now that I am to marry, Inigo will want to bring our son up himself.'

'What would Tom say to that?'

'I think he would be quite agreeable to the plan.

After all, neither Tom nor I can give Will the opportunities Inigo and Philomena can. It makes perfect sense. And neither do I wish to take Will from his father. They are very close, even now he has a son of his own, and of course you know Philomena is expecting again.'

I had no idea, and am disappointed that I should hear it from another, and not Philomena herself. I had hoped we were better friends than that, and I am taken aback by the jealousy that afflicts me. 'No, I didn't know. But surely you cannot deny your own happiness on a supposition? Have you spoken to Inigo about it?'

'Oh, you know Inigo. He is like most men in that he will ignore an unpleasant confrontation. Besides, for all his good humour, he comes from a family that is used to getting its own way.'

'Would you like me to speak to him?'

'Oh, Caroline, no, I cannot impose upon you so.' She grasps my hand and squeezes it, attempting a smile. 'I wish I did not love Tom so. Love complicates things, does it not?'

She stands, brushing grass from her skirts. 'I know we have not always been friends, but since we are speaking to each other so openly, there is something I must talk to you about. Let us walk together as you suggested. I think it might be easier.'

'Very well.' We put our bonnets on against the

fierce heat. In a few minutes we reach a great mass of rhododendrons that give some welcome shade, and neither of us speaks until we are there.

She smiles. 'Don't worry, Caroline, I shall step down from my high horse. The play will go on as planned – I would not disappoint my son, or our friend Barton, who is an accomplished actor despite the hideous false beard he insists on wearing. These things happen all the time in the theatre – we scream at each other and then swear eternal friendship. I had no great liking for Otterwell before he made little James cry, but I shall tolerate him for a few days more.'

'That is most generous of you.' I am quite relieved, thinking this must be the other matter she wishes to talk to me about.

I am mistaken.

'Caroline, I must speak. My conscience does not allow me to do otherwise. I feel it is only right that you and I should talk about our friend Mr Congrevance.'

Lady Caroline Elmhurst

'You must forgive me for what I am about to say,' Fanny continues. 'It is purely supposition. I could well be wrong, but I have worked in the theatre all of my life, and have met some crooks and rogues. I married one when I was too young to know better. He abandoned me and I found out only a year or so ago that he had died in the most miserable of circumstances – but that is not the point. You surely have noticed Mr Congrevance's skill at acting, Caroline. I suspect that he acts when he is off the stage too.'

I pause to pick a rhododendron bloom, as big as my fist, and for all its glorious colour with hardly any scent in the golden centre.

'Fanny, I don't understand what you say.'

'I knew this would be difficult. Are you in love with him?'

'No.' I stare at the flower in my hand, wishing that

this conversation was not taking place and dreading what is to come.

'Forgive me, but are you his mistress yet?'

Oh God. Is it so obvious? We glare at each other and shredded petals float to the ground as I crush the flower between my fingers.

She shakes her head. 'I am sorry. I am not expressing myself well.' She begins walking again, and I hurry to catch up with her, trying to ignore the chill I feel in my heart. What on earth has she found out about Congrevance?

'What do you know of him?' she asks.

'He is rich, respectable and has extensive lands in Ireland and the north. He has been abroad for some years, and Otterwell thinks he worked for the Crown as a spy.' I am not too sure about the respectable part. I add, 'My maid found out about him from his manservant. And if he has been a spy, that would explain his skill in acting.'

She shakes out the handkerchief I lent her, yet another one of Congrevance's. 'This is his, I believe?'

'Why, yes.' Now what? I am beginning to resent this questioning, as though I am a guilty party somehow. My behaviour has been beyond reproach!

She shows me the embroidered initials on the handkerchief. *F. E.* With some misgiving, I recall yet another pair of initials on another handkerchief.

'A laundry mix-up somewhere,' I suggest. That is how Congrevance explained it.

'Of course. And Otterwell, who is not a particularly clever man, knew Congrevance abroad?'

'Yes, in Rome, I think.' I know what she is saying. I think of how Congrevance has evaded questions about his relatives and his land, and of how little generally he talks about himself.

'When he – when he kissed me that evening, Caro, I had tried to ask him who he really was. I must say, the kiss was an effective diversion. And although I think he may be genuinely attached to you—'

'Oh! Do you?' What a fool I am. I sound like a silly schoolgirl.

'I think he may not be all that he appears. He is a very good card player; it's possible that he made his money gambling and is embarrassed to tell you so. He may be from humble beginnings and is intimidated by your title and connections with the *ton*.' She grasps my hand and removes the fragments of deep pink petals from between my fingers. 'Caro, do be careful. Do you owe him any money? Have you told him anything you would not wish others to know?'

This is dreadful, dreadful indeed. I don't want to hear this about Congrevance, I don't want to indulge in idle, vicious speculation about him, but . . .

And then I am angry that she takes it upon herself – an *actress*! – to tell *me*, Lady Caroline Elmhurst, how

I should conduct my business. How dare she! She, with all her alleged worldly knowledge and squalid experiences in the theatre (so far removed from the life of a gentlewoman), has the effrontery to give *me* advice!

A small voice of reason inside me whispers that she may indeed be right about Congrevance. Despite the heat of the day I experience a cold shiver.

I prepare to give a convincing performance. Somehow I produce a patronising smile. 'You have a very active imagination, Fanny, although I suppose your profession requires one. While I am most grateful that you should take an interest in my affairs, I assure you it is unnecessary to do so. Mr Congrevance is excellent company – merely an amusement. I am sure you understand.'

'Caro . . .' She lays a hand on my sleeve.

I raise my eyebrows and she steps back.

I think briefly, and with great pleasure, of steering her into a cowpat.

'I believe I would prefer to walk back to the house alone.' I turn away and after a few steps take a hearty swipe at a buttercup that has the impertinence to grow in my path.

And meanwhile that small, uncomfortable voice of reason, or doubt, or common sense – I am not sure what it is exactly – whispers that she is right; I know nothing of Nicholas Congrevance and he should not be trusted.

He is certainly not the sort of man a woman should fall in love with.

But that is utter nonsense, and immaterial besides, for I have not fallen in love with him.

So there is no unpleasantness to be encountered. None at all.

Mr Nicholas Congrevance

I find Otterwell taking refuge in his library, another stifling-hot room. We have a short conversation in which I suggest he should apologise to the cast, in particular Mrs Gibbons and the two little boys.

'Certainly not!' He glares at me in outrage.

I help myself to his brandy, uninvited.

'Wonderful weather, is it not, Otterwell? It puts me in mind of Rome.'

Otterwell regards me with deep suspicion.

I continue. 'Ah, yes. Happy times, were they not? The best of society, the sunshine and picturesque scenery . . . Do you remember the day we spent at the Conte di Bardolini's villa? You must remember it, sir – that was where I discovered you and Bardolini's mistress on a balcony. You had your breeches around your ankles and *madama* bent over the balustrade with her skirts up, the better to admire the view.'

He gasps.

'Pretty, wasn't she? Did you make her scream like

a she-cat? No? Oh well, no matter.'

'Now listen here, Congrevance . . .'

'And Lady Otterwell was looking for you, as I remember. It was a good thing I was on hand to distract her.'

'You – what the devil are you telling me? Distract her how?'

'I showed her the paintings in Bardolini's collection, sir, and advised her on how to find a good laundress in Rome. Of course I doubt whether she would have minded your little adventure. I'm sure she'd find it most amusing if I told her.'

'Exactly what are you suggesting?'

I let him simmer in silence.

Eventually he lets out a great, aggrieved huff of air. 'I thought you were a gentleman, Congrevance.'

'So I am, sir – when I need to be.'

'Very well, very well. I'll make my apologies. And I trust you'll keep your silence about the Italian whore.'

We shake hands. I leave him to rehearse his apologies – doubtless he will compose them in abysmal verse – and wander through the downstairs of the house, wondering where Caroline is. It is time to resume the pursuit.

From an open window, I hear the voice of young Master Will, and see him and Caroline, hand in hand, wandering among the flower beds.

'. . . and then we shall go fishing again, shan't we, Lady Caro?'

'Of course, so long as we are all here. Will you be sad when the play is done?'

'I don't think so. Do you think I should go to look for Mama?'

'Yes, she'll probably be glad of your company.' She cuffs his shoulder in a friendly sort of way, points him towards one of the paths, and he runs away.

She stands looking after him, and then turns towards the house, meeting me as I intended. She looks particularly pretty, although slightly flushed with the heat, in a cotton gown and a wide straw hat, and with the scarf at her bosom coming adrift.

'Mr Congrevance, is our half-hour up yet?'

I bow. 'I don't know. I'd rather be out here with you, Lady Elmhurst, except that during the play I am able to take your hand five times, put my arm around your waist twice and kiss your hand three times.'

'Indeed. How like a man to keep a list. Did you count when we take our bow at the end? You will be able to hold my hand then.'

'Then that makes six in all, and I daresay I can kiss your hand again at that time without exciting too much attention. Thank you for reminding me.'

She stares in the direction Will has taken, looking thoughtful. 'I hope Otterwell keeps his temper for the rest of the day. I am afraid he might be particularly cruel to Will.'

I kick at the gravel of the path. 'Because he is a – a bastard, you mean.'

'Exactly. He's an earl's nephew too, but . . . Well, someone should teach Otterwell a lesson.'

'Don't worry. I think I have. You'll see him apologise when we are together next.'

'And that was your doing? How?'

'I blackmailed him.' It's strange, but quite often the truth is the most preposterous thing of all, and I expect Caroline to laugh in disbelief.

Instead she looks away, her lips pursed. What does she know of me? Immediately I wonder if Barton has been indiscreet.

'I'm jesting, of course,' I add with a smile, and take her hand.

'Of course, but I wonder . . . Congrevance, there is something I very much desire of you.'

I fear my mouth hangs open or I drool upon my neckcloth, for she takes her hand away and snaps, 'Not *that*, Congrevance.'

'Not that yet?'

She rolls her eyes. 'Pray wash your head in the fountain if it will help clear your mind, sir. It is this. Fanny and Darrowby—'

'Why,' I interrupt, 'must the whole world – or at least anyone other than the happy couple themselves – feel compelled to hold their hands every step of the way to the altar? Can we not leave them to their own devices now that she has accepted him?'

She grins, enchanting. 'I think *he* accepted *her*. But this is the problem . . .'

She explains to me the latest obstacle they have found to ruin their happiness, the future of Will.

'Well, for God's sake, why do they not talk to Linsley?'

'Fanny is afraid.'

'I don't think Fanny Gibbons is afraid of anything.'

'Sir, she fears she will lose her son.'

'Well, she won't lose him exactly, but—'

'But that is how it will feel to her.' She sidles close to me and lays a hand on my arm. 'I wish you would—'

'Ma'am, are you trying to seduce me?'

She gives a loud snort. 'Concentrate, if you please. I should like you to talk to Linsley.'

'But – but that's preposterous. I hardly know the man. Why me?'

'Because you are not involved in the matter.' She walks her fingers, forefinger and middle finger, up my arm, her touch melting my skin through my coat and shirt. 'Say you will, Congrevance. I shall be very . . . grateful.'

Good God, she is as duplicitous as I! How delicious!

'And how will this gratitude reveal itself?'

She smiles.

'I expect Fanny will be grateful too,' I say, in a speculative tone, purely to provoke her.

'And Mr Darrowby.' She flutters her lashes.

'Why, it will be a veritable . . . *orgy* . . . of gratitude.'

She stifles a giggle. 'Indeed. So you will do it?'

I gaze into her eyes and wait, that heart-stopping moment before a line that Fanny has taught us in the play. 'No.'

'Oh, fie, Congrevance!' For a moment I think she will cuff me, as she did young Will. 'You are such a tease.'

'So are you, Caroline. No, I'm sorry. I will not get involved in this matter. They must decide it between themselves. They're not children, you know, but rational beings.' Besides, I don't want to be further caught in the good-natured but interfering web that binds this group. God only knows what sort of plots are hatching regarding Caroline and myself.

She shrugs. 'Well, then, there is nothing for it . . . Oh, did you know, Congrevance, that Philomena is expecting again?'

'Yes, she and Linsley told me when we had our picnic on Puck's Hill. He thought she should not sit in the sun and paint.'

She frowns and a brief flash of disappointment crosses her face. 'She didn't tell me. Fanny told me.'

I don't quite understand the subtleties of this part of the conversation, but am quite happy to have her at my side – she seems to have forgotten that her hand lies on my arm, and she smells sweetly of rosewater.

She gazes into my eyes, but not with the playful amorousness of a few moments ago. There is something searching in her look; I hope to God she does not know me for what I am and what my intentions are.

'Congrevance?'

'Caroline?'

She unties her bonnet strings, the moment passed. 'I should like some lemonade. Let us go inside.'

Lady Caroline Elmhurst

The rehearsal resumes, and Otterwell, much to my surprise, takes James and Will aside and presents them with a basket of sweetmeats, patting the two boys on the head and behaving for all the world like an affectionate uncle. He makes a short, graceful speech in which he apologises for any bad feelings he may have caused, and hands the business of the rehearsal over to Fanny. I am not sure if he has spoken to her privately, or whether he has judged that a businesslike way of going about things will appeal to her.

Fanny seems completely recovered, save for a slight redness around the eyes. She is her usual brisk self, although I detect a certain coolness towards me, and no wonder. Well, she will thank me when I have an answer from Linsley about Will, and will be my friend again – I think.

We stop and start and everything goes wrong. We forget our lines, the painted backdrop falls with a great explosion of dust and we make our entrances from the wrong side of the stage. Late in the afternoon we stop for refreshments, and at that point we can hardly bear to talk to each other; we each skulk alone, daring anyone to approach, everyone sweaty and ill-tempered. Even Congrevance perspires with slightly less elegance than usual.

The little boys take the opportunity of stuffing themselves with sweetmeats, and Fanny mutters that they will make themselves sick, a prophecy James fulfils, necessitating yet another change of clothes and mopping of the stage.

I drag myself upstairs to change for dinner. My appetite is low, and I am hot and in no mood to tolerate Mary, who flits around the bedchamber singing. She sports a wilting nosegay.

'And how is Barton?' I ask.

She blushes and simpers. 'Quite the gentleman, milady. He—'

'Enough. Did you iron my gown? I need some clean stockings.'

She sulks for all of a minute before resuming

her song, some silly thing about a sailor returned from the sea to find his sweetheart, while I lie flat on the bed wishing I did not have to go back downstairs. I am sick of them all, and even flirting with Congrevance has lost its charm since my conversation with Fanny. And what if Congrevance does not declare himself, or, worse, turns out to have some terrible secret (an attic full of mad wives, an orphanage full of bastards: in short, a past more shameful than my own)? I have nowhere to go after the play, for Otterwell, having squeezed our acting skills from us, will politely cast us out. I shall have no choice but to go into squalid lodgings and wait for my creditors to catch up with me and throw me into debtors' prison.

A wash, a change of linen and a fresh gown cheer me a little; I should like nothing better than a good dinner with a lot of wine followed by some card games (which in my fantasy I would of course win), but alas, after dinner Fanny is to run through the copious notes she has made on our performance.

Tomorrow is our final rehearsal – in costume, with no interruptions, and with the servants' part of the play starring Otterwell's butler and Barton in his false beard. And after that, the next day, our performance in front of Otterwell's guests. According to him, it is the social event of the county. It is a daunting prospect, and at dinner all we can talk of is the play. Even those of us who did not take it seriously before, myself included, do so now.

Fanny's notes are humiliating in the extreme. Naturally I come in for a fair amount of criticism – smiling too much (still), not speaking out to the audience and so on. Even Otterwell receives some harsh words, but he smiles genially and takes notes. Altogether, we are roundly scolded for our transgressions and told to go to bed early, like a group of fractious children.

Although I was tired earlier, I now feel quite lively – I did manage to take several glasses of Otterwell's wine at dinner, and am not inclined to go to bed. I wonder if I should remind Congrevance of his offer to show me the maze, but remember that duty calls; if he will not speak to Linsley, then I shall do so. Besides, I must still play my cards carefully with Congrevance – why the devil does the man linger and procrastinate, even if it involves such delightful flirtation? I have made it clear enough, I believe, that I am available and it is up to the gentleman to make the next move.

As we prepare to leave the drawing room, I drop my fan as Linsley passes by. He picks it up and hands it to me, and I take the opportunity to whisper to him, 'Sir, I must speak with you.'

He looks startled.

'Meet me back here when all have gone.'

He nods. I linger as the others leave the room, and

then make my way to the doors that open on to the garden. The night air on the terrace is not as refreshing as I hoped, still humid and heavy.

Presently Linsley joins me. 'What mischief do you plan now, Caro? I can assure you I'll have no part in it.'

Not a promising beginning, but I must say what I have to. 'I wanted to talk to you about Fanny and Darrowby, and I am tired of everyone thinking so ill of me.' How remarkable – in the one sentence my voice descends into a whine and I have become the petulant, wilful creature of my short-lived *affaire* with Linsley.

'Hurry up, there's a good girl, Philomena is waiting for me.'

'Fanny is concerned that you will want Will to live with you and is wondering whether the engagement should continue.'

'The idiot woman,' he says, with a fair amount of kindness. 'Of course I want Will to be educated and have the advantages I can give him. I had thought of sending him to school, but he is still so young, and I think a tutor would do just as well. But as for claiming my rights under the law – now does she really think I am so hard-hearted that I would deprive the child of his mother?'

'So you will talk to her? After the play, of course. I think she is afraid to broach the subject with you.'

'Of course.' He clears his throat. 'It's very good of you to be so concerned for Fanny. I am glad you have all become friends.'

'Oh, me too,' I say, wondering exactly how friendly Fanny and I are now. 'Inigo, I am so glad I didn't marry you.'

'I too, although I don't remember asking you.'

'You didn't.'

We both laugh at this, in a way we could never have done during our liaison.

'Was I truly horrid?' I ask.

He considers for a moment. 'Absolutely. Shrill, demanding, voracious, unpredictable, expensive – all one could ask for in a mistress, in other words. Thank God we escaped each other.'

'And look what I escaped to – Elmhurst, who never loved me as I loved him.'

'Ah, Caro, don't be sad.' He puts his arm around my shoulders in a brief, friendly embrace, and for a moment I'm tempted to turn my head into his shoulder and weep; I, the woman who has cried for no one except Elmhurst, except now I feel like weeping for myself, what I have been, what I may become.

Philomena's irate voice makes us spring apart.

'You haven't changed a bit!' She stands there, fury in her face and in her hair, which has unfortunately sprung its moorings and stands around her face in a great cloud. I wonder which one of us she means.

'Must you pursue every man in sight, Lady Elmhurst?'

'Philomena, I assure you—'

She holds up one small, imperious hand. 'No more.'

Inigo steps forward. 'Philomena, my love, you know I would never—'

'No.' She glares at him and a tear runs down her cheek. 'No, I don't know. I don't know anything about you any more.' She runs back into the house.

'I'm sorry,' I say, a dreadfully inadequate apology.

'Oh, she's – it's her condition. I mean . . . Well, no, it isn't – what the devil was she to think? Forgive me, Caro, I must go to her.'

'Of course.'

He bows and follows his wife into the house.

I'm alone on the terrace – or I think I am, until a dark figure comes into view, and I nearly scream aloud.

It's Congrevance, a bottle cradled in one arm. I realise he is quite drunk and, from his ironic, weary smile, that he has seen the whole encounter between me, Inigo and Philomena.

'*Ill met by moonlight, fair Titania,*' he says.

'Indeed. Good night, sir.'

I pick my skirts up and run from him, back into the house, wishing I could undo all that has been done, or rather, all I have done today.

Mr Nicholas Congrevance

I'm drinking brandy before dinner, having purloined the decanter from Otterwell's library. One of his servants had filled it that afternoon, following my blackmail of his lordship. I am well on my way to emptying it.

Barton maintains a rigid silence, brushing my evening coat while I sprawl in a chair in my shirt-sleeves.

I'm the first to break down and speak. 'What did you tell her?'

'Who, sir?'

'Don't play the halfwit retainer with me. Lady Elmhurst's maid.'

'Ah.' *Swish, swish, swish* goes his brush.

'Very well. Answer my question, if you please.'

He lays the brush aside, twitches a sleeve back into place and holds the garment up for me. 'Truth to tell, sir, we don't talk much about you. Or Lady Elmhurst.'

I wave him and the coat away. 'It's too hot. I'll put it on before I go downstairs.'

He looks at me, and then at the brandy decanter in my hand. 'At this rate, sir, you'll be descending them stairs rather faster than you might like.'

'Hold your tongue.' I pour myself another glass of brandy.

'I heard it was a difficult rehearsal,' he says after a short pause in which he selects a neckcloth.

'Precisely why I don't want to talk about it.' My mind wanders around in a brandy-tinged maze for a while and settles on an earlier comment he made. 'I pay you to talk about me, Barton. To Mary or whatever her name is. Why the devil aren't you doing it?'

'I've done my part, sir. Now it's up to you.'

'Up to me?' I hold out my hand for the neckcloth. 'I'll tie that better drunk than you will sober. The emerald stickpin, if you please. Exactly what do you suggest?'

I stand and regard my wavering reflection in the mirror. I suspect it is I and not the glass that wavers. My hands act of their own accord, creasing, folding, tying.

Barton places the stickpin in the palm of my outstretched hand. 'In the old days – before the Contessa and Venice, that is – you'd have had the business done and we'd be on our way by now, or being set up somewhere nice where—'

'Everything is running according to plan, Barton. Trust me.' An odd request for one rogue to make to another; but we two rogues are allies, or at least I think we are. 'You wouldn't want to miss the play, would you?'

'Ah, the play, sir. Of course.' He gives a longing glance at the false beard, mounted on an old wig stand in my bedchamber for safe keeping. 'I see, sir. And the brandy . . . ?'

'All part of the plan, Barton. All part of the plan.' I jab the pin into the neckcloth.

'Coat, sir.' He holds it up. I shrug into it and straighten the sleeves while he pats and smoothes the shoulders.

'Much obliged, Barton.' I walk towards the door. Excellent. My gait is steady, if a trifle slower than usual.

'Sir?' He waves something black and shiny and bifurcated in my face.

'What is it now, Barton?'

'Shoes, sir.'

I gaze down at my stockinged feet. Yes, shoes. A gentleman wears shoes to dinner.

The mahogany surface of Otterwell's table undulates. Very odd.

Far away, I hear myself making eloquent comments about the play and our rehearsals. Why, no one would dream I was drunk. Other people pay attention to what I say, nod and respond.

One person has little to say. She sits on the opposite side of the table, a few places down, so I can glance at her as though addressing the whole table. If the table shifts and the candle flames weave and pulse in a diverting way, she is a constant, the North Star on which I set my sights.

Caroline. What the devil am I to do, what the devil am I doing?

More to the point, what is she doing to me? And why is she so inattentive?

Claret, that is the answer. More claret.

We gather for a short time in the drawing room for tea and Mrs Gibbons speaks about something, I am not sure what, but it generates some lively discussion.

Afterwards, I return to the dining room, where I had secreted a bottle behind a tapestry – an old trick, learned from when Barton and I fell on hard times. Very possibly we shall have to run through our entire repertoire of those tricks unless I can ensnare Caroline very soon.

I wander into the garden, where it is dusk and fireflies dance and swoop; and from the shadows I see Caroline in Linsley's arms.

I have failed utterly.

Of course she was his mistress once; I knew it from

the first time I saw them together. But she wants him back; she'll break pretty Mrs Linsley's heart – why, I cannot believe that Caroline, my Caroline, could be so callous to her friends. I see it all now, brandy and claret making the situation damnably clear.

Caroline is alone now. She rests her hands on the stone balustrade of the terrace and sighs.

She looks up and our gazes lock.

Ill met by moonlight, fair Titania.

The bottle slips from my fingers and crashes to the flagstones, claret spreading like blood.

And she runs into the house, leaving me alone in the night, where summer lightning flickers on the horizon and a few stars wheel crazily overhead. Were I to have a heart – but I do not – I think it might be broken.

Lady Caroline Elmhurst

'Downstairs,' Mary says the next morning with great drama, 'they all do say you are about to run off with Mr Linsley.'

'Oh, what nonsense.' I stand up and pace around the bedchamber, lines from the play running through my head. This evening we are to have our dress rehearsal and Otterwell has instructed us to rest or take what recreation we will during the day. 'And have you learned anything more from your friend Mr Barton?'

'Oh, we don't talk much about you, milady.'

Insolent slut. 'I trust he has not had his way with you, Mary, for I should have to sack you.'

'Why, milady!' Her eyes open wide in feigned shock. 'As if I would! I am a decent woman, milady. I should not give my honour away so lightly.'

In other words, they are at it like a pair of rabbits.

'I'm hungry,' I say, although for once I am not, but I might as well go downstairs and toy with some breakfast in a ladylike way for something to do. I have not slept well in the heat and my thoughts have made me wretched. I believed I had friends; to think I was hurt that Philomena did not tell me herself of her condition! I have offended Fanny, grieved Philomena, and fear a united front of hostility.

Sure enough, I enter the morning room, where the ladies are gathered, and see their heads swivel towards each other as they talk with great animation of people I do not know. As the conversation progresses, I am not sure they do either.

'I see the Sadlers are going to Scotland for the summer,' Fanny says, a newspaper in her hand. 'Why, their daughter is engaged at last.'

Philomena wrinkles her brow and pronounces, 'Yes, she is a very pretty girl – James, please take your fingers out of the jam.'

'Never heard of them,' says Mrs Riley. 'Unless you mean the Salters, whose daughter ran off with a poet and then tried to drown herself in her bath, but that was some thirty years ago.'

'Did she succeed?' Philomena asks.

'Good lord, no. She displaced so much water it caused a flood and water dripped into the drawing room. She was rather a stout girl.' This said with a sidelong glance at me. Me, stout! I have a big bosom, that is all – the rest of me is quite slender. I have quite the most handsome bosom of the assembled ladies, I am sure – I know, in fact, that the gentlemen would agree; why, Otterwell has not looked me in the face once since I arrived.

'No, no, that was not the Salters. Their daughter ran off with a dancing master and his best friend, a most effeminate sort of gentleman, and I believe all three set up house in Chester.' Lady Otterwell snatches the paper from Fanny. 'Oh good lord, look at the waistline on this gown; we shall all look frights. Where was this announcement, Fanny, about the Salters or whoever they are? To whom is she engaged?'

'On the right-hand page, below the advertisement for pills for diseases of Venus.' Fanny looks at me for the first time.

'No, you are mistaken,' says Lady Otterwell, peering at the paper. 'I see no such thing.'

Philomena looks up from wiping jam off her son. 'I think we should go out for a walk, ladies.'

They leave with great dignity.

I only just restrain myself from sticking out my tongue at their stiff, retreating backs.

I take some bread and butter and find the tea is lukewarm. After I ring the bell for a footman, eventually one wanders in, yawning and scratching at his wig. It is not so early, but probably they have been up for hours the night before rehearsing the play. I explain my predicament.

'Beg your pardon, milady, only the housekeeper and Lady Otterwell have keys for the tea caddy and we don't know where they are.'

So even the servants conspire against me!

'Nonsense!' I remove a hairpin and approach the tea caddy, which stands in gilt and mahogany splendour on the mantelpiece. After a few minutes' work, the lock is picked and the lid open.

The footman gapes at me.

'I learned to do it at school; it is a most useful skill. Now fetch me some hot water, if you please.'

When he does return with the water it is not boiling and I have to send him back. I suspect he has gone to boil the water on a fire a mile distant, he takes so long.

The amount of work I have had to do for a hot cup of tea is shocking!

I recognise the footman now – he is the one who held my parasol while I produced an execrable mess of paint when we picnicked. He now seems inclined to chat – I suspect he should be working elsewhere cleaning something unpleasant – and tells me that the gentlemen are out riding. At least I shall not have to face masculine disapproval just yet. I fiddle around with my breakfast and drink the rest of my tea.

It is going to be a long day. I fetch my hat and set out for a stroll in the gardens – that is, a stroll in the shade and a quick dash when I must go into the sun. I feel odd and out of sorts. For a moment I wonder whether it is lack of sleep and hunger, after my insubstantial breakfast, and then realise that what I feel is loneliness.

What a dreadful ninny I have become.

My wanderings take me into a cool, shady spot where there is a stone bench surrounded by moss and ferns. Had I thought of it, I would have brought a fashion paper or novel to read, but after sitting yawning for a time, I stretch out on the bench. Of course it will be impossible to fall asleep . . .

Mr Nicholas Congrevance

My head certainly needed clearing this morning and I find the ride with Otterwell and Linsley just the thing. Otterwell is in good spirits, playing the gracious host, pointing out features of his land that he is particularly proud of – a tenant's cottage converted into a miniature Parthenon, for instance.

'Splendid.' Linsley reins in his mare. 'I think, Otterwell, you may have a leak in the roof – see how it sags.'

'Nonsense, man!' Otterwell frowns. 'What do you think, Congrevance? It is to my own plan, you know.'

'Most artistic, sir, but the chimney looks about to come down.'

Otterwell raises his hat to a woman who hoes the garden, a child at her skirts. 'A good morning to you, Mrs Fell. And how is young Jack?'

'Good morning, my lord, sirs. Beg pardon, but I'm Mrs Fuller and this is my daughter Joan. And it's true what the gentlemen say about the roof and chimney, we've had that much damp in here, mushrooms grow in the dresser—'

'Very well, my good woman. I'll have the bailiff come out when he's not busy.' Otterwell's tone indicates his tenants have been inconsiderate enough to change names and gender purely to provoke him. He sets forward at a brisk trot.

The ride concludes with an invigorating gallop across a section of heath, brilliant with furze. A pair of kites circle overhead in the bright blue sky. We arrive back at the house and Linsley and Otterwell repair to the morning room for breakfast, while I take a stroll around the grounds. I had hoped the drink last night and the ride this morning might stop me thinking of Caroline.

It hasn't. I keep remembering last night, Caroline in Linsley's arms, their low, intimate whispers and laughter. What is wrong with me? I find myself, terrifyingly, wanting her to tell me it is all a terrible misunderstanding, or that I had a nightmare. I want her to smile at me, to kiss me; I want to pick her flowers, like that sentimental clod Barton does for his Mary. I haven't felt this way, distracted and unsure of myself with a woman, since I was sixteen, and that was a disaster I don't care to dwell upon. Oh yes, I believed myself then desperately in love—

What? *In love?*

It must be all the Shakespeare and sentiment and silliness and hot weather and exposed bosoms. I am not myself. Possibly I caught some mysterious malady from that Venetian canal and my brain is affected. This thought does not cheer me.

I wander among Otterwell's beautifully clipped yews and down a mossy path, at the end of which is a stone bench.

On that bench Caroline lies asleep. Her bonnet dangles from one hand, the other is under her cheek. She looks younger, defenceless and peaceful – so often she has a fierce sort of restlessness that exhilarates and arouses me. I have the urge to protect her – from adventurers such as myself, for instance.

I step forward. I remember how she feels in my arms, when she swooned at the inn; or when I quite unnecessarily tumbled her into the bracken (with the basest of intentions); or the chaste embraces of the play. I remember her laughing with young Will, her hat full of bait, and her kindness to him.

And, oh God, she may love Linsley still. Naturally we did not mention the subject on our ride – it would have been thoroughly ungentlemanly and I might have lapsed into sentimental ramblings and embarrassed myself.

A lock of hair has fallen over her cheek. Her bosom rises and falls.

I kneel at her side. 'Caroline,' I whisper. I smooth the lock of hair back.

She makes a sound that might, under other circumstances, be described as a grunt.

Her cheek is soft and smooth.

I should let her sleep. I should let her alone, but there is one thing I must ask her before I leave: does she love Linsley? (I must stay for the damned play, it is my duty as a gentleman.)

I should speak to her when she is awake and vertical, but the temptation to touch her and hold her one last time is too great – yes, indeed, I seem to have an arm around her and her lips inches from my own. Reason tells me that even if she did not harbour a partiality for Linsley, I have only made a fool of myself with her thus far; things have not progressed as they should. There must be other rich and willing widows in England who would be far less work – we shall go to Bath, or some other watering place, I and Barton. But before I go, I must find out for sure.

'Caroline,' I whisper again. Her scent makes me dizzy.

'Nick,' she murmurs.

She remembers my name! The name she refused to use before and which has not been used by anyone in years. I am absurdly happy. I will do anything, anything for this woman, run through fire for her sweet sake . . . 'Caroline, I love you.'

What? Where the devil did that come from? I start back in horror and she tumbles off the bench, landing on her bonnet – the one that has received rough treatment as a bait basket – in a flurry of lawn and petticoats, swearing mightily.

'What the devil are you doing, Congrevance?' She scrambles to her feet, pushing me away when I attempt to help her. 'Hell and damnation, I could have broken my neck. Are you a complete imbecile? What the hell are you about, creeping up on me and – and – *mauling* me so? Am I not safe anywhere here from fools and idiots and lechers who do nothing but look into my bosom?'

'Madam, I—'

'Oh yes you were. Do not deny it. I know you for what you are, Congrevance.' She pauses for breath.

'You – you do?' I am horrified. I have never been discovered so before.

She stamps her foot. 'Do not stand there like a fool staring at me so. Why the devil do you play so hot and cold with me?'

'I—'

'Do you think I am made of stone? You pursue every woman here and now I have no friends and—'

'And you are completely blameless, I suppose? You and Linsley—'

'You – you idiot, Congrevance!'

She launches herself at me. I fear for my life (she is not a small woman) while at the same time I realise that this is an amorous declaration, albeit of an unusual nature. She grips the shoulders of my coat like death; we overbalance, topple and fall on to the bench, she on top of me.

'Now what do you have to say for yourself?' she pants.

I, with the breath knocked out of me by her delightful bulk, can only gasp like a landed fish.

'Listen,' she hisses, answering my unasked question, 'I don't love Linsley. I have no interest in him. I was doing what you were not man enough to do. And you were most horribly drunk!'

'What do you mean?'

'I was asking him about Fanny and Will, you idiot.'

One part of my mind is giving thanks to something

(probably not the Almighty) that she has no idea of my nefarious plans, for she thinks me only a stupid, lecherous coward. But I am more interested in the fact that I am stretched flat beneath her and her eyes are hot – with anger, not desire, but I am willing to overlook that. I am completely helpless and enjoying myself immensely.

I groan.

'Oh, stop it!'

'Caroline, I believe I was injured in the fall.'

'Nonsense. Everything seems to be in prime condition.' She may mock me, but the wanton, deliberate way she presses against me tells me otherwise. 'Would you like me to get off you?'

'No. I want to stay here like this with you for ever.'

She frowns. 'Meals might be a problem.'

'Madam, I am attempting to declare my passion for you and you are concerned with being fed?'

'I think that with you, Congrevance, I should need to keep my strength up.'

I have rarely had a woman say such deliciously slutty things to me. I love her to distraction – no, I don't. I *lust after* her to distraction (and that just sounds foolish). 'Yes, you certainly would. However, I think, since I cannot move, that you should kiss me.'

'And I think, sir, you should ask me properly.'

'Kiss me, you shameless creature. If it pleases you, that is.'

'If it pleases me.' Her eyes no longer blaze. They are dreamy and soft, as soft as her lips on mine, and then I no longer see her eyes. I don't need sight, I don't need anything except this woman, her scent and warmth and roundness . . .

'Pray take your hands off my arse, Congrevance.'

I open my eyes. 'Tell me you love me.'

Her eyes narrow. 'Why?'

'Damn it, Caroline, let's go to bed—'

She hops off me with great speed and stretches out one foot, clad in a kid slipper. She prods me where women do not generally touch a gentleman with their foot, but quite gently. 'I think, sir, you forget yourself.'

'On the contrary, I am more than usually aware of myself, madam.'

'Indeed.' She bends (ah, heaven) to retrieve the unfortunate bonnet. 'I suggest we go back to the house separately. I have a reputation to maintain. Damn you, Congrevance, you trod on my bonnet – see the footprint?'

'My thoughts were elsewhere.' I stand too, and brush bits of moss from my coat.

'No matter. I'll give it to Mary. She'll need cheering up when Barton breaks her heart.'

Lady Caroline Elmhurst

Oh, the vile seducer!

How delicious he felt beneath me. And he invited me to go to bed in broad daylight! – that might have been a problem, although I daresay we could have wedged a piece of furniture against the door. I can only too easily imagine Mary blundering into the bedchamber with an armful of linen, chattering away and then bursting into giggles. Indeed, I find there is nothing to fan the flames of ardour like a little furniture-moving before the act; it is most arousing – why, I think as though Congrevance were privy to my thoughts. I can imagine the cock of his eyebrow, his half-smile, if I said that to him. And doubtless he would say something delightfully suggestive and absurd in return.

But I turned him down. I must be insane, for other than the difficulties of keeping the servants out, is not that what I intended from the beginning? And he declared himself in love with me, but why could I not say the words?

Sir, I am by no means indifferent to you.

Mr Congrevance, you may have noticed my distinct partiality for you.

I blush to tell you that I esteem you greatly, Congrevance.

Nick, I am so in love with you I think I shall die if

you do not remove your breeches this very instant.

Because to say *I love you* is so easy when you are in a close embrace and all you can think of is the gentleman's smell and taste and the feel of him (dear God). Too easy.

I pause and pretend to untangle a branch from my skirts. He stands there still, staring at me; even at this distance I can see that the perturbation in his breeches has not subsided (an excellent sign).

Shall I run back and fling myself into his arms? Absolutely not.

I am not a lovesick ninny like my maid. I am a sensible woman and I shall wait until Nicholas Congrevance has declared his intentions before I yield my honour (or, to be strictly truthful, what is left of it).

Our dress rehearsal is in truth a great disaster.

Mr Linsley, whom I encounter swearing mightily over the table where he keeps his properties, finds that they are disarranged and some missing. Puck, therefore, takes a large carrot from the kitchen to use as the flower whose juice causes instant passion in those into whose eyes it is squeezed. I regret that some of us find this obscenely amusing. Even Otterwell sniggers and quotes something about a flower shepherds do call by a grosser name – I presume it is Shakespeare. Unfortunately – or perhaps fortunately – Will and James, becoming hungry, eat the carrot, and then substitute a pineapple.

They eat that too, having persuaded one of the footmen to cut it up for them. Lady Otterwell, who wanted to eat the pineapple, is most angry, and in her bad temper one of her fairy wings falls off.

When Darrowby and Congrevance almost come to blows over Fanny, Darrowby's sword becomes stuck in its sheath. He becomes exceedingly red-faced as he tugs at it, and everyone on stage, even Fanny, laughs helplessly. This is but one of our many mishaps, but I do not think the way Fanny treads on my toes and changes our carefully rehearsed moves, leaving me to flounder helplessly, feeling like a fool, is an accident.

And so on, and so on. The play drags on interminably; by the end, we all yawn during the rude mechanicals' play, which I suspect is better acted than our attempts (Barton portrays a stalwart and bearded wall), and mutter our witty asides with a distinct lack of energy. A sudden drizzling sound from one side of the stage reveals that young Master James, invigorated by his carrot and pineapple (and with an exceedingly dirty, sticky face), has decided that Moonlight's dog shall do against one of the pillars of Theseus' palace something that comes naturally to a dog.

'James, you do not do that in the house and in front of the ladies!' Mr Linsley, who acts as our prompt, storms on to the stage, and plucks his son away with dire threats of punishment.

Moonlight's dog returns to the stage much chastened and tearful and insists on sitting on his mother's lap after he has said, or barked, rather, his few lines. Even little Will, our most professional of actors after his mother, forgets his lines in the epilogue and weeps. Philomena herself looks tired and subdued, dark shadows around her eyes. I suspect she and Linsley are still at odds with each other.

Finally it is over and we have a dinner we are nearly all too tired to eat. There is little lingering by the gentlemen over port in the dining room, or over tea in the drawing room. Fanny is remarkably cheerful, claiming that a bad dress rehearsal means a good performance, but I do not believe her.

I hear yawns and conversation as the others say their good nights and leave for bed.

I sit on a window seat, too tired to move. I shall stay here a little and then wake Mary, who has probably fallen asleep in a chair, but at the moment it is too much effort to move. I have opened the window to let in a little night air, but the air is sultry and heavy. Summer lightning flickers at the horizon, the threat of a storm still far away.

I remember last summer, nights like this when I sat at an open window, breathing in the night scents and waiting . . .

'You look tired.' To my surprise, it is Congrevance who settles beside me, interrupting my thoughts. 'Go to bed, Caro.'

No one has talked to me with such kindness and intimacy since my early days with Elmhurst, and generally such a comment was made to entice me into bed with him (not that I ever needed much encouragement). Possibly Congrevance has the same thought, but it is not uppermost in his voice. I wonder if this is the true man revealed.

'I shall.'

'What are you thinking about? You look sad.'

'Elmhurst died on a night much like this.'

He nods. I am grateful that he does not ask questions – surely he must know all by now; Lady Otterwell and the others must have fallen over themselves to heap infamy upon my head. But he says nothing, only takes my hand and squeezes it.

Then, 'You were right.'

'Right about what?' Usually women *are* right, when in dispute with men, except I can't think of anything I have done recently in which I could claim myself a moral victor.

'I should have spoken to Linsley. I shall. I will clear your name, Caroline.'

I shrug. 'It's kind of you, Congrevance, but this will blow over, I am sure.' Because, as I know, if it's not one thing, it's another, and trouble follows me around; much of it, of course, of my own making.

'Nevertheless, I will.' He looks at our entwined fingers. 'A boy like Will . . . Even with a loving father, there will come a time when the circumstances of his parentage will injure him.'

'You speak as though—'

'Not now.' He stands. 'Another time I shall tell you all. Come.'

I rise, my hand still in his. Congrevance, a bastard? I open my mouth to ask him, but his finger on my lips silences me.

Hand-in-hand, like a pair of children, we walk out of the drawing room and into the hallway, where moonlight spills silver across the oak floorboards and staircase. We don't need candles to light our way upstairs. The stairs creak lightly as we ascend; my gown rustles.

Is this a seduction?

He knows which is my bedchamber, and I his (what else are servants for?). We pause at the top of the staircase. The house settles into its night-time silence; the small creaks of ancient timbers, our breathing, the scratch of a mouse in the wainscoting.

We turn to each other, hands still clasped.

He raises our joined hands to his mouth and kisses my fingers.

I touch his face – the fine contours of bone and

skin, slightly rough beneath my fingers. His serious-
ness, his kindness and his confession of childhood
pain move me in a different way than his usual
flirtation. This is a man I could bed and love. This is a
man to whom I could spill my secrets, and who in turn
would share his with me.

It would be easy, so easy, to take those few steps
into his bedchamber. Just a few steps to the doorway
– and as if on cue, the door creaks slowly open and a
faint golden light spills on to the floor. Barton, waiting
for his master, stands with a lit candle in the doorway.

'Dismiss him for the night,' I whisper.

Mr Nicholas Congrevance

'I'm honoured, Caro. Deeply honoured. But . . .' I raise her hand to my lips again and the whole world flares into that patch of skin. 'Good night, my love.'

I let her go with much reluctance and bow, not even sure why I do not accept her offer. Some delicacy, or chivalry, or some notion of honour from long ago prevents me, as amorous as I feel.

She looks confused, blushes, stammers something and turns away in a rustle of silk. She disappears into the darkness, heading for her own bedchamber.

I turn to Barton and shove him back into my chamber. 'What the devil are you doing, playing peeping Tom?'

He puts his candle on the mantelpiece. 'I'd never have believed it.'

'Believed what?' But I know. I strip off my coat and

hand it to him – rather, I hold it out to him and he makes no move to take it.

I shrug and fling the coat on to the bed.

'You had her. You reeled her in. She would have let you take her on the damned stairs. She—'

Unbuttoning my waistcoat, I stop his spate of words. 'Enough. I've told you—'

'And you must think me a right fool. Sir.' That brief pause before 'sir' tells me all I need to know about Barton's state of mind.

'As you wish.' I drop my neckcloth on to the floor.

He ignores it. 'You've lost it. Lost your nerve like a horse that won't take a hedge. You ain't got a grand plan for this one. You're floundering like a fish out of water. You ain't good for anything.'

'I think I've heard enough, Barton.'

'She – or something, I don't know what, and I don't care over much – has made a eunuch out of you. Sir.'

'That's enough!' I shout, more loudly than I expected.

We stare at each other and I wonder if we are about to come to blows. He outweighs me by a good three stone although I have the longer reach. Both of us have clenched our fists.

He gives a short, unpleasant laugh. 'I only hit *men*. Sir.'

'Very well. You may leave. And don't come back. You may consider your employment with me at an end.' I cross the room to find my writing desk and open the secret drawer, my hands shaking. I know that what I am about to do to him is as insulting, if not more so, as his behaviour to me.

'I think this should cover any outstanding salary.' I toss the coin towards him.

He makes no effort to catch it.

We both watch the guinea roll in a few lazy circles before coming to rest, light from the candle dancing on the gold.

He doesn't move. I didn't expect him to; he's a proud man, Barton, in his way. One of us will leave this sorry mess with his pride intact, but it is not to be me.

He nods, once, and turns to leave. The door closes quietly behind him.

Dear God, I am a fool.

Then the door opens again. For one heart-stopping moment I wonder if it is Caroline – but no, it's Barton. Barton, come to beg my pardon?

Without looking at me, he crosses the room to where his false beard rests on the wig stand, clutches it to his chest and leaves again.

Once more the door closes behind him, leaving me with my thoughts, which are not pleasant ones.

*

The next day is that of our play. I find Will hanging around the garden, disconsolate. Like me, he seems uncertain of how to spend the day. We have many hours to fill until our performance at seven o'clock, which will be followed by Otterwell's ball and a supper for audience and the hungry players.

'What's the matter, Will?'

He turns tragedian's eyes on me. 'Mama says I cannot go fishing with Lady Caro, and Mama and Papa and Mrs Philomena are too busy to take me.'

'I'd be happy to take you, Will, but I should ask their permission first.'

'Oh, sir! Oh, sir, that would be splendid!'

We set off to find them, but backstage is deserted. Some sort of needlework project lies deserted, the needle stuck hastily into the cloth. A man's coat and a neckcloth are flung on to a chair.

'Woof.' A familiar bark, or voice, rather, greets us, as James runs into the room. He flings himself at his older brother. They begin to tussle together as small boys will.

Behind him is Mrs Linsley's lady's maid, a tall, handsome woman. I ask her where Mr and Mrs Linsley are.

'Oh, they're upstairs, sir.'

'Upstairs?'

'Yes, sir. Upstairs.'

'And they will be down . . . ?'

'I couldn't say, sir.'

175

'Ah. And how about Mrs Gibbons and Mr Darrowby?'

'They're resting before the play. Tiring work, it is.'

'I daresay.' I glance at the discarded coat and neckcloth. Had I played my cards right last night, Caroline and I could be resting upstairs even now, or at least making each other very tired. 'I was going to offer to take young Will fishing, but I don't want to do so without his parents' knowledge.'

'That's very kind of you, if I may say so, sir. I'll tell them, sir.'

'Papa and Mrs Linsley often retire in the afternoon,' says Will with great cheer. 'So do Grandmama and Admiral Riley. I suppose it is what happens when you are old.'

I am relieved to hear that the Linsleys have kissed and made up (and frankly jealous of Darrowby and Mrs Gibbons and full of admiration for the Admiral and his lady), but it means that I cannot speak to any of them to clear Caroline's name, as I promised. It will have to wait until the performance.

Will, something of an expert in finding rods and provisions, leads the way to the estate manager's office and the kitchen respectively – the latter a madhouse. It is vilely hot, cooks screaming and red-faced, sweaty staff running around on a floor slippery with offal and discarded vegetable trimmings.

When we get outside, it feels almost cool, for a few minutes at least.

Having collected some worms from a compost heap in the kitchen garden, we make our way to the lake where we swam a few days ago, and find a shady spot.

I wonder if Will knows of his mother's impending marriage, but it is he who brings the subject up in a rather roundabout way.

'I think the ending of the play is silly,' he says as he casts his line into the water.

'Why?'

'Everyone gets married.'

'Why is that silly? It's what people do.'

'I would have wanted them to stay in the wood and have more people wear asses' heads.'

'Well.' I watch my float bob on the water. 'I suppose that is the dream part of the play, and the getting married business is when people awake. And eventually you do have to wake up.'

'But everyone all at once,' Will grumbles. 'Are you and Lady Caro to marry, sir?'

No, indeed, I wear the ass's head. 'I don't believe I am to have the honour, Will.'

'She is quite pretty,' Will says. 'And she can fish and catch a cricket ball, which not many ladies can.'

'True.' She has other talents too, of which I have had but the merest intimation, but thoughts of her have been enough to keep me awake and amorous and unhappy most of the night. 'I hate to tell you this, Will, for it must get tedious to hear it repeated so often, but you will understand all this business of getting married when you are older.'

'That's what Mama says.' Will swipes at his face briefly.

'I had a stepmother when I was growing up.' For once, the truth, but I consider myself safe in telling Will of this; besides, he is a child and in distress. 'After my mother died, I went to live with my papa and some people I had never met before. He and my mother lived apart, as people sometimes do.'

'Your mama died?'

'Yes, when I just a little younger than you.'

'Was your stepmother cruel, like the ones in stories?'

'Not at all. She was very kind. But it was strange and lonely at first, going to a place I did not know, and finding my father had others who were important to him. I met my half-brother for the first time.'

At this point I am most grateful that a fish is good enough to succumb to Will's bait. He leaps to his feet, his face full of excitement. 'Oh, sir! I have a fish!'

Sure enough, he has a bite on his line, and with great pride reels in a carp some four inches long. Although he wants to take it to show to his mother and father, I persuade him to release the gasping, flapping thing back into the water.

It proves to be the first and only bite we get – it is no wonder, for I suspect the heat makes the fish stupid. The air shimmers heavy above the lake. Will yawns and falls asleep, curled up on my coat.

I lean back against the trunk of the willow we sit beneath and think of Caroline.

It seems I do little else these days.

And those damned earrings. I still have her confounded earrings.

Lady Caroline Elmhurst

To think that when I first arrived, the play was but a distraction, a triviality! Now, at this moment, before the velvet curtain draws back, it is the most important thing in the world; more important, almost, than Congrevance, who stands beside me and gives my hand a brief squeeze. He is a part of this new world I discovered, thanks to Otterwell and his play – a world where friendship and affection, and even love, are possible. I have seen Otterwell, pale beneath his actor's paint, pacing back and forth behind the stage, muttering and nervous, and this sign of weakness almost makes me think well of him.

I shall have friends again, for Congrevance shall make it so. I heard him approach Fanny Gibbons, who cut him off with a curt request to talk afterwards. This time, now, is when we must forget our petty affairs and adopt instead those of Athenian men and maidens and fairy folk.

The musicians who are to play at the ball perform a brief overture; Linsley, prompt book in hand, nods to the footmen who work the curtain; it swishes back to display a vast rustling crowd beyond the lamps at the edge of the stage. There is some scattered applause at the set, and, I think, for the actors, as Oberon strides majestically on to the stage to deliver his prologue.

And I – I am no longer myself. We are all transformed, other creatures, let loose in an inhospitable wood, the playthings of supernatural creatures, until order is restored and all is made well.

It's like a dream, a dance – knowing what to say and where to move, and I am assured that the man I am in love with, after misadventures and sadness, has my heart and I his.

Mr Nicholas Congrevance

I must tell her I am leaving the next day.

We exit the stage, our hands still clasped, and I realise I am sweating like a horse. Presumably Caroline is too, for she tosses aside the scarf that has, more or less, decently covered her shoulders and bosom. Around us our fellow actors jostle and laugh, drunk on the success of the play. Someone, Otterwell, I think, claps me on the shoulder and bellows, 'Well played, sir, Lady Elmhurst! Well played indeed!'

I ignore them. I see only her, her beauty made

exotic by her painted eyes and loosened hair, her hand hot in mine.

'Come. We'll get some air.' I am sure she knows what I intend, for I am certain she thinks the same.

We have learned the jumble of rooms behind the stage well, and know to take a dark, crooked passage that leads to an ancient door. Outside, wind stirs the tops of the trees, and lifts our draperies, ruffles our hair. It is considerably cooler and dark, not the dark of night – it is too early for that – but the dark of heavy clouds. Thunder rolls and mutters quite close.

She stops and raises her hands to the back of her neck to lift her mass of hair, with a sigh of pleasure. The nape of her neck is warm and fragrant, slightly damp under my lips.

'Damn you, Congrevance.' She turns in my arms and we kiss, clumsy, our mouths bumping rather than caressing.

Someone behind us clears their throat and then coughs in an obvious sort of way. It's one of Otterwell's footmen. 'Beg pardon, sir.'

'What is it?'

The servant tears his gaze from Caroline's bosom. 'A gentleman inside wishes to see you, Mr Congrevance.'

'Tell him you couldn't find me.' He nods and returns indoors.

I grab Caroline like a drowning man. I *am* a

drowning man. There's no denying it, I am in too deep, in something more terrible and wonderful – and much, much better tasting and smelling – than any Venetian canal.

She breaks her mouth from mine. She's out of breath, as indeed I am. 'Too near the house. He – they – they'll come looking for us. Not here.'

We start to walk – although indeed it is more than a stagger than a walk, with our frequent pauses to kiss and touch.

She leads me towards the maze. The wind now comes in powerful gusts, bringing the scent of rain with it.

I hesitate. I shouldn't do this.

She smiles, and says in that lovely husky voice, 'I explored it this afternoon, like Ariadne with a ball of twine. I wished you had been with me. I—'

'And am I to be the monster at the centre?'

'I hope so. Indeed, you may be as monstrous' – she glances down where the wind whips my draperies against me – 'as you please.'

I growl at her, and she shrieks, laughing, and darts inside.

I follow without a moment's hesitation, all my scruples gone. She has the lead on me – I see her draperies flutter around a corner and run to catch up with her. The dark yew hedges give little light, but I can hear the crunch of her feet on the gravel. I take a turn and stop. She isn't there, and panic rips through me, halting me.

'To your left.' I take the turn and she stands before me, hands on hips, but before I can touch her she springs forward and dashes around another corner. I lunge to catch her, and my hand closes on the hem of her gown, pulling it from her shoulder for one brief moment before she laughs and wrenches it back.

She runs fast with the speed and grace of a goddess, remaining just out of my reach, and then suddenly we're at the still, silent heart of the maze, only a few paces wide. The gravel beneath my feet gives way to flagstones and the thyme planted between them gusts sweet in the air. She stands next to a plinth, on which a statue rests; the living woman in drapery mirrors the marble goddess, hand outstretched.

I take her hand and press it to my lips, falling to my knees before her and burying my head in her draperies. I inhale her scent and warmth. Her hand comes to rest on my hair.

'You caught me,' she whispers. There is something about this still, green centre – a tiny patch of grass, vivid against the darker green of the yews and dotted with daisies, surrounds the plinth – that invites hushed voices.

'No. You have caught me.' I turn my lips to her hand and bite her finger. Gently, quite gently. I do not know how long I can be so with her, for I wish to consume her, devour her like the monster I am.

'Ah. And what shall I do with you?'

'Whatever you wish, my love.' Does that endearment slip too easily from my lips? I don't know. I don't know anything, now – the world could be flat, the earth move around the sun, dragons could lurk around us – all that is certain is that she and I are together.

She sinks to her knees so we are joined face to face.

And at this point, everything goes wrong. First, after a fumble of what seems like several frantic hours with the drawstring of my drawers, both of us swearing horribly, I forget there are two sets of skirts to contend with. I am only thankful I am not wearing hideous pink tights, not that I think too clearly at this point.

Yards and yards of damned skirts – how can this be when Caroline's gown seemed so flimsy? I comment aloud, in my frustration, that it's like tupping a laundry.

'Most flattering. Ouch! Wait, you fool.'

Much writhing, sweating, swearing. She wriggles around and I wonder whether she simulates ecstasy or – oh God, it's like the first time ever, wonderful and surprising, musky and sweet—

Very much like the first time, in fact.

Christ, how embarrassing, over before we've scarce begun.

She slaps my shoulder. 'Get *off* me.'

She does not sound friendly, or satisfied (how could she?), or loving, or anything other than annoyed.

I remove myself from our mingled skirts. 'I beg your pardon. I—'

'Damned stone under me,' she mutters, raising her hips in a way that makes me suddenly ablaze again with lust. She produces a piece of gravel that evidently had been trapped under her arse. 'I tried to tell you, but of course you weren't listening. That was awful,' she adds. 'Quite the worst I've ever had. And don't you dare think we're going to do it again, because we're not.'

'I love you,' I offer, and regret it as she glares at me. 'I'm sorry, I don't usually—'

'Oh, of course not.' She puts herself to rights – damnation, I hardly had a glance at that magnificent bosom – and glares at my nakedness, shaming me to cover myself up.

'Caro, I leave here tomorrow, very early in the morning.' Why, damn it, why did I choose this moment to tell her?

She becomes quite still. 'Wh – where do you go?'

Her face is pale and thunder rumbles close, very close. The first spots of rain, dark and heavy as pennies, appear on the flagstones.

Her eyes fill and overflow. Caroline, weeping? Oh God, I cannot, will not make her sad. But I can make her angry; I would far rather she think of me with hatred than with a broken heart. I want her to keep her pride, if I can.

I rise and tighten the belt of my tunic. 'My destination is none of your business. Frankly, Lady Elmhurst, I'm bored. The play was amusing enough in its way, as were you. But now I've tasted your somewhat overblown charms – I must congratulate you on your chaste reserve, I really expected a faster surrender, from what the other gentlemen told me—'

She jumps to her feet and slaps my face. 'You *bastard!*'

And she runs from me, briefly illuminated by a great crack of lightning, and thunder rolls as she disappears in the darkness of the maze.

Rain spatters heavily around me. She may hate me, but I have probably broken her heart anyway. I cannot put out of my mind the expression on her face as I insulted her. Rainwater trickles into my eyes and down my face – I can barely breathe, and I wonder if I am destined to wander this maze lost in pain and shame for eternity. No, that would be too light a punishment for what I have done. *Turn right* – a voice of reason suddenly cuts in. *Keep turning right and you'll get out.*

And a tedious business it is, but I emerge into the gardens with the rain now almost over. The storm has moved on and the sky lightens, although lightning forks on the horizon.

My sandals squelch as I walk back to the house. I attempt to make plans. I should pack my belongings and leave. Bath, yes, that would make sense. I can be there in a couple of days, maybe sooner.

I head for the side door of the house, the one Caroline and I used when we left together.

It swings open. The man who tried to murder me ten years ago stands there, silhouetted against the light. I come to a stop and we stare at each other.

'Nick?' he says. His voice cracks. 'Nick?'

And he flings himself at me.

Mr Nicholas Congrevance

My half-brother the Duke of Thirlwell weeps and hiccups on my shoulder. 'I – I – thought you were dead. Damn you, Nick. Damn you to hell and back. Damn you.'

'For God's sake, Simon . . .' I pat his back, attempting to calm him and wishing I felt more moved by his appearance. To tell the truth, it seems like another episode in a bad, fitful dream that for a very short time (say, ten seconds) was erotic and the rest of the time consisted of getting soaked to the skin and being lost in a maze wearing skirts.

'You're all wet.' He steps back, still grasping my shoulders.

'It was raining.'

'Yes, yes, I know. We watched it from the ballroom, quite a storm. But what the devil are you doing here? Where have you been?'

'Outside.'

'Before that. It's been ten years, Nick. Why are you here at Otterwell's? I could scarce believe it when I saw you in the play. I almost swooned.' He fishes a handkerchief from his coat pocket and blows his nose. I'd recognise Simon's nose-blowing anywhere; it has a particularly annoying upward squeak to it, unchanged in the past decade. He has changed, though, as of course have I – he's taller, broader than the gangling fifteen year old I knew ten years ago. We still look something alike, having shared the same papa.

'I've been abroad. I'll explain. Let me get out of these damned skirts.'

I push past him – *beg pardon, your grace*, I think, but don't say it – and lead the way to the gentlemen's tiring rooms. There I strip off the skirts. I'm soaked to the skin.

'Who the devil whipped you?'

My usual answer is that it was when I was discovered in a harem in disguise (absolute nonsense, of course; any sultan worth his salt would have removed more than a few strips of skin from my back), but I am too weary and heartsick to engage in deception. 'It was when I was a sailor.'

'A sailor?'

I drop my shirt over my head. 'I was press-ganged. Don't worry, I deserted as soon as I could.'

He frowns. 'You mean you're in danger of being hanged?'

'No, a sailor called Simon Allondale is.'

'That's *my* name,' he says so indignantly I almost laugh.

I take a cloth, dip it into a bowl of salve and rub at my eyes to remove the black. Now I'm thinking furiously as to what I should do.

'Why didn't you write to me to tell me you were safe?'

'After you pushed me off a cliff?'

'An outcrop.' He glares at me.

'A tall outcrop.'

'Very well, a tall outcrop. Fairly tall. I – I'm so sorry, Nick. Forgive me. I ran for help but you'd gone when we came back. I made the men search for you for days . . .'

I remember the fall, waking with a dreadful headache and one eye sealed shut with blood so I feared I was blind; another bad dream where I got a lift with a carter to Newcastle, dazed with shock and pain. I remember the discovery that what little money I had with me had been stolen, and innocently thinking that the jovial man in the naval uniform would help me instead of throwing me and a dozen other unfortunates into the bowels of a ship.

What I can't remember now is what our quarrel, and subsequent fight, was really about. I remember it started with Simon's half-joking request that I address him as *your grace*, and my refusal to do so. So I ask him.

'Why, it was over Molly.'

'Molly?'

'Molly Salthwaite. She married shortly after you – you left, and her first child was born only a few months later. I always thought I could see a likeness there and I hoped it was so. I asked her to name the child Nicholas, but it was a girl, so—'

'Wait. Molly? Molly, the milkmaid with the huge bosom? You thought I—'

'You said you were.'

'But . . . I was sixteen, Simon. Of course I'd say so, particularly if it would annoy you.'

He sighs. 'I was dreadfully in love with her. She'd handle the teats in a – a suggestive way while she was milking and wink at me.'

'She used to do that to me too. It drove me half mad.'

'And you didn't . . . ?'

'No, never. I stumbled over my own feet and could scarce remember my own name whenever I saw her.'

'Oh God.' He blows his nose again. 'I'm so sorry. But Nick, what have you been doing? Why did you not write? I always hoped you were alive, but I didn't know.'

Ah. There's the question. I squint into a mirror and comb my hair with my fingers.

He knows I'm playing for time. He waits, with that annoying, virtuous expression on his face, the young Duke caring for his own. And the trouble with Simon is that he is a decent fellow, and he can't help it if he irritates the devil out of nearly everyone.

He says, 'Old Ruby died last month. We buried her with the other dogs, in the shade under the horse chestnuts.'

'Ruby?'

'She was close to fifteen, Nick. She had a good long life. She—'

I slump into a chair, head in hands, and weep, tears running through my fingers, helpless with grief over a dog I'd hardly thought of in the last decade. I remember Ruby's muzzle working its way into the palm of my hand as she walked with me, her joy when she ran to retrieve sticks, her unabashed adoration. Part of my mind realises that Simon, somehow during these years, has learned a little of the guile that I possess in abundance; blood will tell, I suppose. He knew exactly how to unman me and did not hesitate to unleash his weapon.

And I'm weeping for Ruby and myself, and my half-brother, and our father, and Caroline, while Simon pats me on the shoulder and croons, 'There, there,' in a particularly idiotic way until I shake him off.

'You bastard. Your grace.' Barton couldn't have done better.

He grins. 'No, you're the bastard. Why didn't you write to me?'

I take the handkerchief he offers me – a very fine lawn, with a T and a coronet embroidered on it – and blow my nose in a way that, with his efforts earlier, renders it unusable.

'Well, Simon. At first I was too poor and too angry. Then, when I could afford to do so, I was still angry. And then embarrassed because it had been so long. I did, however, write to Pickering.'

'You wrote to my land agent but not to me?'

I shrug. 'I always liked Pickering, and I was his apprentice.'

Simon's face reddens. 'Damn him, he should have told me.'

'Why?'

I know he's longing to reply that it was Pickering's duty, as a subordinate and servant, to tell him, but he clamps his mouth shut. He sits on a rickety chair next to mine and tips melted wax from a guttering candle so it may burn a little longer.

'His rheumatism is getting quite bad,' he says eventually, in an offhand manner. 'He's been thinking of retiring and going to live with his sister.'

'He didn't say.'

Simon, owner of many sheep, leans forward and fingers the sleeve of my coat. 'Hmm. Wool with silk? Very nice. I'm glad you've done so well for yourself.

What profession did you choose after your, er, naval career?'

'It's rather difficult to explain. By the by, I should offer my congratulations on your marriage to Miss Julia Longbenton.' Pickering has kept me informed of his grace's activities, and I'm anxious to change the subject.

Simon, saintly though he may be, is no fool. 'Are you in trouble, Nick?'

We've stopped sparring at each other, more or less, and besides, he'll drag the truth from me sooner or later. 'Yes. I've seduced a gentlewoman and broken her heart. I love her to distraction but I'm afraid she'll only think I'm after her money.'

'Oh, dear me.' He wrinkles his brow and actually wrings his hands. 'Maybe I can help. Who is she? Is she here?'

I tell him.

He becomes so still I wonder if he's turned to stone. 'How long have you been back in England?'

'About three weeks.'

'Then you haven't heard that Lady Caroline Elmhurst is on the run from creditors. She doesn't have a penny to her name, and word has it that she's on the lookout for a new protector. Her last lover, a military gentleman, left her deeply in debt. She is a notoriously . . .' He pauses for the right word. '. . . indiscreet person.'

I can only gape at him in astonishment. 'But her maid told my man that—'

'Well, of course she wouldn't want you to know. Obviously she was after your money.'

This is far worse than I could have imagined.

My brother continues, 'You have had a very lucky escape, Nick.'

'On the contrary, she has had a lucky escape from me.'

'You mean . . .' You can almost see my brother thinking. I always won from him at cards, so transparent was his face.

I hang my head and mutter, 'I thought she was rich, and although I was after her money initially, I love her. I led her to believe I was wealthy, but I have hardly any money. I've broken her heart and insulted her greatly. I don't know what to do.'

'You fool,' my brother pronounces. 'Who else knows of this unsavoury liaison between you and Lady Elmhurst?'

'Mr and Mrs Linsley, Mrs Gibbons and Mr Darrowby, at least. I'm not sure about Otterwell, but he's not a friend, and—'

My brother stands, strides to the door and shouts for a footman. The Duke of Thirlwell is about to take charge of one of his responsibilities – myself – and I don't care for it one bit.

Lady Caroline Elmhurst

I see it all now. One long pattern of seduction, and I was fool enough to believe him and his protestations of love. Thank God I shall never see him again.

I shall never see him again.

I think I shall die, I am so desperately unhappy.

I creep back into the house, my wet drapery clinging to me in an obscene fashion, and fortunately meet no one on the way back to my bedchamber. Mary doesn't rise when I drip my way into the room – she is huddled on a chair, weeping.

I stand as wet as a drowned rat, and realise she doesn't even know I'm there.

I touch her shoulder. 'Mary, what's the matter?'

She jumps, startled, and rises to her feet, tears streaming down her face. 'He's gone, milady. Barton. He told me – told me he was leaving Mr Congrevance's service and he couldn't take me with him, though I wanted to go with him, but he said it was over, and – oh milady, I love him so.' She heaves with sobs.

I don't have the heart to give her the bracing sarcasm she so badly needs. I put my arms around her, thinking that she cannot make me any wetter than I am, and let her howl upon my shoulder.

After a while she stops and wipes her nose on her sleeve. 'Don't you cry too, milady.'

'I'm not. I never cry.'

She opens her hand and shows me what she formerly had clenched in her fist – not, as I would have thought, a flower or trinket from Barton, but a small packet. 'He said I should give you this, milady, and not to trust his master, for he's a bad'un.'

I unfold the paper. Inside are my earrings, the ones Congrevance won from me at cards.

And the two of us descend into a soggy female morass of grief, no longer mistress and maid, but two stupid, gullible women who have loved men who didn't love us back.

Mr Nicholas Congrevance

I suppose it is one of the advantages of being a duke that you can take over your host's household, for within a very short time Simon has assembled my fellow actors in Otterwell's library, and has commandeered a vast amount of food and drink from the ball. Had he lived in medieval times, Simon would amass an army, and I suppose that is what he is doing now; besides, my half-brother always had a taste for the dramatic.

He dismisses the footmen, fusses over chairs and who shall sit where – I prefer to stand, feeling that I am on trial – and then calls us to order. I still don't know what he's about, and am touched and surprised when he introduces me as his long-lost half-brother with a great deal of affection – possibly more than I feel for him at the moment. Dry clothes and some of Otterwell's brandy have improved my mood greatly, but I suspect the worst is to come.

'So were you really a spy in Europe?' Darrowby asks.

'Among other things, yes, although it was quite tedious work.'

'And the other things?' Simon actually steeples his fingers.

I take a deep breath. 'Dancing master, music master, footman, tutor, fencing master, valet, cabinet-maker, doctor, priest—'

'You became a Roman Catholic?' Simon jumps to his feet, horror on his face.

'Well, no. Not as such. Someone needed a child christened and I obliged for the parents' sake.' I continue with my list. 'Fortune-teller – I wasn't very good – ratcatcher—'

'Cicisbeo.'

We all turn to stare at Mrs Riley, who for some reason decided to join us although Simon did his best to dissuade her.

She cackles. 'Aye, were I a rich woman and not married to the Admiral, I might have taken you on. You'd have given me value for money, I wager. I knew it from the first time we met.'

I keep my mouth shut as the room explodes into a frenzy of supposition and accusations.

My brother leans towards me and whispers, 'Nick, you mean women paid you to—'

'More or less,' I whisper back. 'They usually offered me, well, gifts, and it wouldn't have been polite to refuse, and—'

'You were a *male harlot*!'

That makes me extraordinarily uncomfortable, although he doesn't sound nearly as shocked as at the possibility of my turning Papist – merely titillated. 'I didn't think of myself that way. I mean, yes, I went to bed with them but I talked to them as well. You'd be surprised how many women have never had a conversation with their husbands. I nearly always liked them, too.'

'How much did they pay you?'

I am spared having to present my brother with a bill of fare by a comment from the sweet, virtuous, pregnant Mrs Linsley, made to Mrs Gibbons but audible to the whole company. 'Heavens, he must be exceedingly good in bed.'

Linsley, already scarlet at his mother's admission, leaps to his feet, his chair clattering over on to the floor. 'If you've touched my wife, Congrevance—'

'Of course he has not, sir,' cries my brother, who is thoroughly enjoying himself. 'Have you, Nick? Sit down, Linsley, pray calm yourself. No, I regret he has eyes – and other parts, too – only for Lady Elmhurst.'

I, aghast that my brother should attempt a mildly

indecent witticism, interrupt him. 'I must speak out in Lady Elmhurst's defence as I promised her I would. She does not seek Mr Linsley as her lover and is a more honourable woman than you suppose. You have wronged her.'

A silence falls on the room.

Linsley stands. 'I wish to say that whatever transpired in the past between me and Caroline, it is over long ago. She has no designs on me, or I on her.'

Philomena takes his hand and smiles.

Linsley continues, 'Caroline has her faults, but she is loyal and honest.'

'I never really believed that horrible rumour about Elmhurst,' Mrs Gibbons says.

'What rumour?' I must know the worst about her.

They tell me about the duel Elmhurst fought, suspecting Caroline's flirtation with another man to be something more, and how his wound, at first a trifling matter, festered and eventually killed him. A vile rumour started that someone eased his agony as he died a slow and painful death. Caroline was at his bedside until the bitter end.

'That was last summer,' Linsley says. 'And ever since, accusations have been made, from a pillow over his face to an increased dose of laudanum.'

'And I say she's a brave woman, whatever she did.' I remember Caroline's sadness as she sat by the window, just two nights ago, a lifetime ago; the only time she mentioned her husband to me.

'And of course society said she was a fortune-hunter, marrying Bludge, her first husband, quite a bit older than her, and very rich,' Mrs Riley says. 'I don't believe she killed him, though.'

'Only with connubial delight. I heard that Bludge shuffled off his mortal coil under rather intimate circumstances with her,' Linsley says. 'Doubtless he died happy.'

His wife slaps him, but in a friendly sort of way. 'I like her,' she says. 'I thought she was vulgar and fast when I knew her in London, but she is much improved.'

'So,' says my brother with great glee. 'What's to do next?'

'What's to do?' I wish heartily that he would mind his own business.

'Doubtless Lady Elmhurst's creditors will catch up with her and throw her into debtors' prison,' my brother continues. 'I heard a figure of several thousand guineas bandied around. She is entirely alone in the world, for her family cut her off years ago. What do you intend to do, Nick?'

I was right; I am on trial. Possibilities flash through my mind. A wager at cards or on a horse – unreliable; an *affaire* with a wealthy woman – untactful; a loan – but not from my unpleasantly smirking brother; a job – but as what?

'You need honest employment,' Simon says as though lecturing an indigent tenant, but I suppose that's how he sees me. 'And as the retirement of my land agent is imminent, and you trained – or began to train – in that profession before you went abroad, I shall consider you for the position.'

'An excellent decision,' Linsley says. 'Congrevance has a good eye for land, your grace.'

'But it won't keep Caroline out of debtors' prison,' I say.

'My father, the late Duke, left you a small bequest, Nick. I invested it for you because I . . . I didn't know what to do with it, to be honest. I believe it's worth a few thousand now. I am willing to make you an advance on that money to pay Lady Elmhurst's debts.'

'I have money?' All this time, raking around Europe, I have had an inheritance. If only I'd known. I really should have written to Simon, fool that I was. I grit my teeth. 'How very generous of you, your grace, to lend me my own money.'

'And there's a house on the estate. I'll rent it to you for a modest amount – we can speak of that later. It needs a new roof, however.'

'You'll charge me rent on a roofless hovel?'

He gives a ducal wave. 'Details, Nick. Details. Now, will Caroline have you? For you must make an honest woman of her, Nick. I can't have you living in sin and setting a bad example to the tenants.'

In the pause that follows all eyes are upon me and my brother taps his foot waiting for my response. I have the floor.

'Your grace, ladies and gentlemen. Apparently you expect me to ally myself with a woman who is notorious for her indiscretions, her gambling and her general profligacy; moreover, you expect a lady who is accustomed to life in fashionable London to live in a roofless house in a field full of sheep.'

'Nonsense, Congrevance!' says Mrs Riley. 'Why, but a moment ago you were defending the lady to us.'

'So I was, ma'am. I was obliged to do so, but possibly I consider my obligation at an end.'

My brother ignores me. 'It's a perfectly decent house. You remember the one – Pickering used to live in it before his family grew up and went away. I'll throw in an allowance for firewood, too. She'll love it. It's very fashionable to retire to a cottage to contemplate the glories of nature.'

'Most tempting, your grace. And you suggest I should use my inheritance to bail the lady out of the debtors' prison in which she so rightly belongs.'

Simon smiles and, damn him, steeples his hands again, an effect spoiled by the chicken leg he holds. 'The legacy was to be released at my discretion, I'm afraid. It's the way Papa set things up.'

'Oh, surely Caroline will have you, Nick,' says Mrs Linsley. 'She is in love with you – anyone could tell that.'

'It is your duty and obligation, sir,' says my brother, very frosty and aristocratic, despite the chicken leg. 'You admit you seduced her, and she is a gentle-woman. She has no brother or male relative to protect her. Besides, I wouldn't think,' he says, starting on another chicken leg, 'that a male harlot could afford to be too fussy about the sort of woman he'd marry.'

'I am not a . . .' I fling my hands up in the air. 'Don't you see? It's too late. She wouldn't have me. I insulted her grossly, thinking it was better she should feel anger towards me than grief, for I could offer her nothing. I cannot go hat in hand to her now. I truly believe we'd kill each other, and she'd rather go to debtors' prison than let me near her.'

'It would not be an auspicious start to a marriage, your grace,' says Darrowby. 'These matters should be resolved first.' I remember that he has proposed marriage to a woman who has borne another man's child, and is still remarkably well-disposed towards the child's father.

'Caroline has a great deal of pride,' Linsley says, a remark that earns him a frosty glare from his wife.

'Well, well,' says my brother. 'We shall have to come up with another plan.'

And he does.

It is so ludicrous, senseless and stupid a plan that I feel I am back in my nightmare again. Yet everyone crows with delight and is delighted to be part of the deception, and assures me that all will be well, and the necessary separation can only do Caroline and me good.

And, as my brother points out, it will give me time to put a roof on the house in which she and I shall enjoy married bliss among the Northumberland sheep.

'There's one thing more,' I say to him. 'If you lay one finger upon her, I'll make a eunuch of you. And then I'll kill you.'

'Just as I thought,' says Mrs Linsley, who overhears this fond brotherly exchange. 'You're in love, Congrevance. How delightful!'

THE FALSE PROPOSITION –
A Play in One Scene

The would-be protector played by His Grace the Duke of Thirlwell

The mistress-to-be played by Mrs Gibbons (late of Sadler's Wells, etc.)

As himself, Mr Nicholas Congrevance (late of disgraceful carryings-on on the Continent)

Scene – Otterwell's library, late that night.

THIRWELL: Come now, Nick, I thought you were the great seducer, yet you have been of no help whatsoever.

CONGREVANCE *(sighs heavily):* Not so, brother. She has undone me, unmanned me. Oh, very well. Let us begin, then. You come upon her walking in the garden.

Enter Mrs Gibbons, smiling and smelling imaginary flowers.

THIRLWELL: Good morning, ma'am. I am a duke but I shall allow you to address me as Thirlwell.

CONGREVANCE: Stop! That will not work, brother. She does not respond well to condescension.

THIRLWELL *(deeply offended)*: But I *am* a duke, Nick.

CONGREVANCE: Again, if you please. Your grace.

THIRLWELL: Good morning, ma'am. Why, you are as pretty as those flowers.

MRS GIBBONS: Thank you, sir. *(She curtsies.)*

CONGREVANCE: She would not respond so.

MRS GIBBONS: You are correct, sir. *(Addressing the Duke.)* Who the devil are you?

CONGREVANCE: No, no. It will not do. Simon, please try again.

THIRLWELL: What a pleasant day! That reminds me, I must find a mistress to ease my lonely hours in London. Why, ma'am, forgive me, I am thinking aloud. I am a duke and exceedingly rich, by the way.

CONGREVANCE: Well, it is to the point, I suppose, if lacking in subtlety.

MRS GIBBONS: Why not congratulate the lady on her acting last night, your grace?

THIRLWELL: Oh, capital, Mrs Gibbons, capital. Ma'am, I much admired your bosom last night.

CONGREVANCE: Her acting, you numbskull.

THIRLWELL: I much admired your acting last night, ma'am. Did you wear stays?

CONGREVANCE: For God's sake! *(Exit, slamming the door.)*

THIRLWELL: I am afraid my brother is unhappy.

MRS GIBBONS: A moment, sir. *(Exit, following Congrevance.)*

Thirlwell examines one of the porcelain ornaments upon the mantel and in so doing knocks another off. He looks around guiltily and pushes the pieces beneath the carpet. Mrs Gibbons and Congrevance enter.

MRS GIBBONS: Sir, be easy and natural, and all will be well. Shall we try again?

Lady Caroline Elmhurst

On the first morning of the day after my life has been ruined it rains steadily and I walk up and down Otterwell's long gallery trying to decide what I should do. Mary has cried all night and I have packed her off to iron my gowns – they don't need it, but she needs something to keep her busy. It's very early in the morning, and after the late night, my fellow guests are still abed.

I don't wish to see them and I am sure they do not wish to see me, for they are no longer my friends.

My choices are not attractive:

1. Throwing myself upon the mercy of my sister. I daresay I shall become accustomed to her smugness and the tedium of country life. Her husband's parishioners would come to love me as I visited them on their sickbeds, forcing unpleasant foodstuffs and piety upon them. At least I would

learn the names of my nieces and nephews.

2. Under an assumed name, I could become a governess. Of course this would necessitate the purchase of at least two Quakerish sorts of gowns (which I cannot afford) and an intensive study of everything I have forgotten from my own rather haphazard education.

3. Setting myself up in a genteel, impoverished sort of way doing embroidery, making silk flowers and painting china and so on. Not that anyone would offer me such work, once they knew who I was, and my skills with paintbrush and needle leave much to be desired.

4. Flinging myself into a river, my pockets loaded with stones. Absolutely not – it would give far too much self-righteous satisfaction to too many.

5. Escaping to India, where my brother lives, or to the Continent, where I have heard one can live exceedingly cheaply, but getting there may be a problem.

6. Healing my broken heart, and hopefully my finances, in the arms of Another.

Up and down the long gallery I pace, my shoes making scarce a sound on the aged wooden floor, and the eyes in the portraits seem to follow me, accusing me of all sorts of wrongdoing. Rain trickles down the windows.

At the far end I see one of the footmen gesture towards me, and two gentlemen approach. I suppose they must be guests from last night – I never did make an appearance at Otterwell's ball and missed supper entirely. But as they approach I see they are not gentlemen – they look like clerks or tradesmen of some sort.

How could I have forgotten that small detail that complicates all of my unhappy options – why, number seven in my list is to go to debtors' prison. Oh, quite definitely they are here on business and hold a warrant for my arrest.

'Lady Elmhurst?' They stop a few feet away from me and bow. The one who addresses me is the taller and stouter of the two.

'Oh, you are mistaken, sir. I am not she. I believe she may have left the house early this morning.'

They look at each other. 'It's her,' the shorter, thinner one says with a regrettable lack of grammar.

They take a step towards me. Mr Tall and Stout says, 'I regret we must take you away, as this paper says, unless you can pay your debts, milady.'

There's little use in denying who I am – they must have experience with people such as myself. Besides, the footman has told them my identity, but I decide to try one more time. 'It's remarkable how often the lady and I are mistaken for each other at a distance, sirs. I am sorry to disappoint you.'

'Come along, Lady Elmhurst – we don't want to make a fuss, now, do we?'

If there is one thing I have never feared it is making a fuss, but they are not to know. I turn, gather my skirts and run as fast as I can, heading for the other end of the gallery. I pause briefly to overturn a side table and a pair of chairs to slow them down, but although they swear and stumble, I can hear their footfalls thud behind me. I'm nearly at the end now, and can either run into the garden, which I know so well now, or—

I cannon into a gentleman who appears from a doorway and land sprawling on the floor, out of breath.

The two sheriffs bound heavily towards me. 'Lady Elmhurst, I am arresting you—'

'Gentlemen, what the devil are you about?'

'Out of our way, sir, if you please.' Mr Short and Skinny lunges towards me, and I gather my skirts around my ankles and skid with little dignity across the floor away from him.

'You are addressing the Duke of Thirlwell, my good man.'

They both stop short then, and engage in some obsequious forelock-tugging.

For the first time I get a look at my deliverer – or at least, my delayer – and my heart nearly stops.

It's Congrevance.

No, it isn't. What a fool I am. To be sure, he has

similar colouring – but with blue eyes, not those beautiful grey ones – and is not so tall and lean and graceful. Like all gentlemen of high rank, he is dressed in a down-at-heel way for the country, in a threadbare riding coat and scuffed boots. He rubs his hands together as if enjoying himself, then offers me one so I may rise.

'I trust you're not hurt, ma'am.'

I assure him I am not and curtsy.

'Now, what is the trouble, gentlemen?'

'Beg your pardon, your grace, but we must arrest Lady Elmhurst for her debts.'

'Good heavens!' he exclaims. 'What a dreadful thing, indeed.'

'Oh, it is but a simple understanding, your grace,' I say. 'Why, I was just about to fetch the trifling sum I owe to pay off these good gentlemen. If you'll excuse me, your grace, sirs, I shall fetch the money and pay you directly. It is upstairs in my bedchamber.'

The two sheriffs laugh. 'They told us you were a cunning one, Lady Elmhurst. We'll send for your maid, shall we?'

The Duke meanwhile watches this exchange with a broad smile on his face. 'Why, Lady Elmhurst, you do not look like a hardened criminal.'

'Oh, sirs.' I produce a handkerchief and sniffle into it. 'May I – may I not step into Lord Otterwell's chapel and pray for strength to endure my ordeal?'

'No, Lady Elmhurst, you can pray all you want in prison.'

'A moment.' The Duke plucks the warrant from the sheriff's hand. He beckons to the footman who lingers in the doorway watching the scene, to my mortification, and murmurs of refreshments.

I see it is the same footman who assisted me in breaking into Lady Otterwell's tea caddy. 'Sorry, milady,' he mutters as he passes me. 'I didn't know who they were, otherwise I would have sent them away.'

'It's not your fault. Pray do not concern yourself.'

Mr Short and Skinny, seeing this brief conversation, steps forward and grips my arm.

'Unhand me, you blackguard!' I shriek quite loudly.

'You'll not corrupt the servants, Lady Elmhurst. You' – addressing the footman – 'go about your business as his grace told you to.'

The footman nods and leaves, and my captor (the effrontery!) leads me to the small group of chairs around the table, now righted, that I knocked over in the pursuit. There we sit and wait until footmen arrive with tea. It is all quite civilised; at least I am not clapped into chains just yet.

The Duke sends a footman off on another errand and continues to peruse the warrant.

'Dear, dear,' he comments. 'You are indeed in Queer Street, Lady Elmhurst.'

I do not answer.

All three men look at me and then at the teapot. Thinking how extraordinary it is that even under these circumstances a lady is expected to pour, as though men's hands somehow cannot grasp the handle of a teapot, I do so. The fools – what if I choose to hurl the teapot, a formidable weapon of porcelain and near boiling water, at their heads?

A gentleman appears with writing materials, and it is quite obvious from his demeanour that he is some sort of personal servant to the Duke, although not in livery. He, his master and Mr Tall and Stout withdraw a short distance away. They have a conversation I strain to overhear, while Mr Short and Skinny keeps his eyes fixed upon me, doubtless expecting me to dive through the window.

'There is no need to stare at my bosom so, sir. I assure you I have no weapon hidden there.'

He blushes bright red and spills tea on the table, to my great pleasure.

The three men return. It is evident that some sort of arrangement has been made. Thirlwell's servant, or rather his secretary, sits and draws up a document – although I try, I cannot read what it says, for it is at the opposite side of the table and on a portable writing desk. Thirlwell signs, and stamps it with his signet ring.

There is more obsequiousness, bowing and so on,

to the Duke. The two sheriffs give me a cursory sort of bow and depart.

'I take it, your grace, that you have assumed my debt. Why?'

'Walk with me if you will, Lady Elmhurst.' He offers his arm and nods to his secretary, who stands aside.

'I'm not thanking you yet, your grace, because I have learned that acts of generosity are rarely unconditional.'

'Dear me, such cynicism. Well, you see, I am away from my estate at the moment because I have some pressing business at the British Museum. There are some recently acquired items there I wish to study . . .'

He drones on for a while – obviously this is his passion, ancient fusty things – and I make the right sort of encouraging sounds and wait for him to get to the point. I've heard – who has not? – of the famously rural and scholarly Duke of Thirlwell, who spends his infrequent time in London in the House (rumour has it he is awake most of the time so others may sleep undisturbed) or investigating antiquities.

Now apparently the Duke has decided he will have a third occupation in London – or, to be precise, a second, since Parliament is in recess. That occupation is my person. I have never heard that he is in the habit of keeping a mistress in London, where he seems to live as a monk. I believe there is some sort of rural Duchess at his country seat, doubtless a horse-faced paragon of virtue who divides her time between brewing concoctions in the stillroom and performing good works.

The gentleman even has a secretary standing by to draw up a contract. But one thing concerns me . . .

'Your grace.' I interrupt a lengthy blather on what colours were used on Greek statues (what nonsense! Why should anyone care, even if it was so?). 'Are you sure you act alone on this matter?'

He stops so suddenly I almost trip over. 'I beg your pardon, ma'am?'

'Surely, sir, you must admit it is an extraordinary coincidence that as I am pursued by the law, you appear as though by divine providence?' I add, just to see if I can disturb him further, 'I am sure I do not know what I can do to repay you, sir. I have no income, I fear. Do you, perhaps, need a governess?'

For one worrisome moment I fear he will think I am offering to take a riding whip to his backside (something I have not encountered yet, although I hear it is a common preference among gentlemen).

'Oh, good heavens, ma'am, no. My nursery is empty, I regret to say.' He clears his throat. 'There are certain – needs a gentleman has. I am sure you understand, ma'am. While in London, away from the comforts of my house, I seek . . . *congenial female company.*' The last said with great emphasis and so much head-nodding he blurs.

'I should be delighted to act as your hostess, your grace. Do you have an elderly female relative, perhaps, who could chaperone me in your London house?'

He loosens his high collar. 'You misunderstand me, ma'am. I entertain little in London. I am thinking of a more intimate connection. In short, ma'am, in my bed.' This last in a whisper.

'I beg your pardon. I didn't quite catch that last part.'

'In my bed,' he hisses, now bright red.

'Your grace?' I cup my ear as a deaf great-aunt might do.

'*In my bed!*' he bellows, and his voice echoes and rings in the ancient room.

'Well, why didn't you just say so?' We resume walking and I watch with fascination as the blush fades from his fair skin, remaining for a little while longer on the tips of his rather prominent ears. 'Do you perhaps have a wager with some other gentleman that you cannot bag yourself a London mistress?'

'No. Well, that is to say . . . Why, ma'am, you are remarkably astute. That is indeed . . . almost . . .' He nods again, so vigorously I fear he will injure his neck. 'But tell me, how did you guess? I do hope I have not offended you. I should tell you that I find your face and form entirely exquisite.'

'Thank you, your grace. How much money rides on this wager?'

'Ah. I . . . my secretary, Beck, will know. The exact amount escapes me at the moment.'

'And what if I refuse your offer?'

He stops again, and wrinkles his brow. 'But . . . my dear Lady Elmhurst, I . . . If you are a woman of honour, surely you must repay your debts.'

'Normally a gentleman does not ask a woman of honour to repay her debts in bed.'

'True, ma'am, true, but I believe you to be above these trifling conventions of society. Besides, your circumstances are somewhat unusual. I assure you I shall extend to you the utmost courtesy and generosity.'

Unusual? Hardly, for most women of quality have little control over such things as money and whose bed they shall share, unless they choose celibacy. It is the way of the world. I cannot pretend I writhe with shame and guilt or wish to rend my garments; neither can I bring myself to proclaim that I am virtuous, pure and would rather die than become a courtesan. I was well on the way to becoming a fallen woman when I allowed Colonel Rotherhithe to pay my rent, if not before.

Certainly, allowing Congrevance untold liberties – the consummation of which was such a grave disappointment – was not the action of a woman of virtue.

I turn to the Duke, who has the same sort of eagerness on his face that young Will and James have on seeing a dish of sugar plums.

'Sir, I accept your offer. I think it only right to tell you I am in love with another gentleman, but as I do not expect ever to see him again, I believe there will be no awkwardness.'

'Oh, thank you, ma'am. Capital, capital. I do appreciate your candour.' He beams as though I have given him the best news in the world and actually shakes my hand. 'And now – yes, I do believe Beck has finished drawing a document up for us; shall we . . . ?'

What an odd gentleman he is.

We return to the table, where I scan the document Beck has prepared, although the letters blur and dance before my eyes. I sit staring at it, not even sure what I have let myself in for, or for how long. There is mention of a house in Hampstead and an allowance (not overgenerous in my opinion) and servants. (Hampstead! What on earth shall I do there, other than the time spent on my back? Although I do not quite phrase the question that way, the Duke explains that it is convenient to the road north.) I insist that Mary shall remain in my employment with a substantial raise in her pay to forty guineas a year, to be backdated to the beginning of the last quarter, with any money owed by me to be paid also by Thirlwell; the Duke agrees with an alacrity that suggests he is as eager as I to get the document signed, although for different reasons, and Beck writes in the additional terms.

We both sign, with Beck as our witness; it is done.

'We'll leave this afternoon,' Thirlwell says. 'Beck shall go ahead and make sure the . . . ah, the sheets are aired and so on – I mean, he'll make sure the house is in good order. I trust that's convenient, ma'am.'

'Perfectly. Thank you, your grace.' After all, I have no wish to stay in this house, where almost every room, excepting my bedchamber, holds memories of Congrevance. No, even my bedchamber, for I spent a great deal of time imagining him there, until our disastrous encounter in the maze stripped away my illusions.

But I can't help remembering, however hard I try, how I first met Congrevance and decided he was the man for my purposes, and my thoughts then:

. . . although I cannot deny the attraction I feel to Congrevance, it would not do to sell myself short. How would I feel if, for instance, I missed a duke?

Lady Caroline Elmhurst

'Thirty pieces of silver!'

'Don't be a fool, Mary. Besides, you're accepting them too. And don't grumble under your breath. You know very well I can hear you, and it is most irritating.'

We stop bickering as the footmen, who have loaded our luggage into Thirlwell's coach, enter the house, shaking rain from their umbrellas.

I have no money for vails, as is customary when leaving a house. But I recognise the footman I know a little, and hold out my hand to him, thanking him for his kindness. He shakes my hand and wishes me luck, and I realise I don't even know his name. Mary, the great snob, snorts with disgust at my familiarity – naturally, as a lady's maid, she considers herself far above footmen.

My host, Otterwell, fawns over Thirlwell – I wonder if he will offer to lie down in the puddles between the front door and the coach so his grace's feet remain dry. Otterwell allows me only a smirk, a careless attempt at a bow and a farewell leer into my bosom.

I thank Lady Otterwell for her hospitality, and how grateful I have been for the kind, nay, *extreme* condescension of Lord Otterwell, particularly the help he gave me, just the two of us alone, in improving my acting. I am most gratified to see the lady turn upon her husband, spitting abuse (and in front of the footmen!), as we leave the house.

'You really shouldn't, milady,' Mary says. She is in a dreadfully improving mood today, doubtless repenting of the sins she has committed with Barton, but I'd rather have her complaining and criticising than weeping. Her eyes are quite red still. She, I and the Duke arrange ourselves in the carriage – I am indeed glad that Thirlwell and I are not alone, as he might be tempted to claim his property en route. At least I gain a little breathing space this way.

Thirlwell produces a book and reads; Mary finds something to embroider – a handkerchief, I believe, no hint of personal linen or saucy stockings. I look out of the window, at the rain trickling down the glass and the sodden fields and dripping trees, and try not to dwell on my broken heart. It is unlike me to be a great blubbering fool (as I was last night with Mary), but my tears wait like creditors outside a front door; an unpoetic conceit, to be sure.

At least I am wretched in luxurious comfort, enjoying the pleasure of good springs and velvet and leather. But wretched I am, thinking of how deceived I was in Congrevance; how I loved him, love him still, fool that I am; and I thought he loved me until those cruel final words that still pain me like a raw wound. I cannot work out if I should feel better or worse had our consummation in the maze taken me to heights of bliss, or however one wishes to describe that experience – possibly ten minutes more might have helped. But to have neither quality nor quantity; well, I expected better, particularly from the quality of his kisses.

There was a stone beneath me that has left quite a bruise on my arse. The bruise will fade; I wonder how long it will take my broken heart to mend. I do not think it will. But a courtesan, I believe, does better without a whole heart.

I regret, too, that I have lost my friends. There can be no possibility that anyone in polite society will consort with me now I am officially a fallen woman. I should so like to hear about Philomena's baby, and how Will and Tom and Fanny do. I hope Tom and Fanny marry soon, before something else goes wrong.

We stop for refreshment at an inn, and I must say it is quite pleasant to have the staff bow and scrape when they notice the coat of arms on the carriage door – they have to be polite to me, too, since I am in the

Duke's company and do not have the word *whore* branded on my forehead.

It is there, at the inn, in a private parlour we are shown to, that I discover I cannot possibly be pregnant. Mary, grumbling mightily, has to have our luggage taken from the top of the carriage so she may seek out rags and pins. I regret that I negotiated more wages for the bad-tempered creature; besides, the two of us are as regular as clockwork, like a pair of village pumps together, and it may well save her petticoat.

I am delighted that I have an excuse to keep the Duke out of my bed for the next few days. But the knowledge that I am not to have Congrevance's child – although I am sure I would have viewed impending motherhood with the greatest of horror and alarm, particularly knowing the worst of the father – makes me burst into tears once more.

Mary hovers over me, offering me a handkerchief, and she actually looks alarmed. 'It's not like you, milady.'

'I have a belly ache,' I snuffle. 'Fetch me some brandy.'

If I cannot be happy, I shall be drunk, and then I shall sleep for the couple of hours remaining in our journey. Why not? The Duke has been quite content with his nose stuck in a book, and this offends me somewhat. I would think, under the circumstances, he might be inclined to a little flirtation, or possibly even some conversation. I should have shown some interest in his damned Greek statues. Possibly I shall have to do so in future, but what can you say? They are there. They are old. Some have limbs broken off, and some, specifically the males, have little to boast of.

I shall not think about Congrevance, who in contrast . . .

I am sure that had Congrevance and I ever embarked upon a conversation about ancient broken things, it would have been scintillating, but in truth most of our conversations were a sort of mask for how and when we intended to seduce each other. What we didn't say, therefore, was far more interesting, and besides, he talked little of himself. So why did I feel that I knew this man?

Because he wanted me to feel so. He planned to seduce me to relieve his boredom – he knew how to play the hand he was dealt. And how expertly he fooled me. I remember that quiet walk in the woods, the feel of his cheek against my lips – enough.

I hold out my glass again.

Mary sniffs and fills it.

'He won't like it if you're drunk.'

'He won't know.'

'Sometimes you snore when you're drunk, milady.'

'You horrible liar.'

'Ladies, are you ready to depart?' Thirlwell calls through the closed parlour door. As Mary and I emerge, he offers me his arm with much gallant twinkling, and I think with a mild sort of pleasure that my particular condition will wipe the smile off his face later tonight.

I manage a grimace, mostly inspired by the brandy, that may pass for a smile, and the well-sprung motion of the carriage makes me drowsy. As I fall asleep, I hope I don't snore, or, worse, drool.

'Lady Elmhurst?'

I wake to see the beaming face of the Duke of Thirlwell just inches from my own – even in his expensive carriage there is very little room, and he has bent forward to wake me.

'We have arrived, ma'am.'

'You know, Thirlwell, you may as well call me by my Christian name. It is rather absurd not to do so.'

'If you insist – Caroline.'

I am not in a position to insist on anything, but I alight from the carriage. I feel out of sorts and I have a slight headache. It's still light; we have drawn up in front of a modest row of brick houses, and the one nearest us has the door open and a couple, the man in livery, standing on the doorstep.

They are introduced as Mr and Mrs Tyson, the entire staff of the house, apart from a boy who comes in during the daytime. She ushers me and Mary into the house, murmuring of tea and how she hopes the rooms are aired well enough and other domestic matters. Tyson meanwhile hauls luggage inside.

We are shown into a modest parlour. It is altogether a very unassuming house for a duke, but I imagine it is just one of several properties he owns.

Mary goes to unpack, and after Mrs Tyson serves tea, curtsies and leaves us, the Duke and I are alone for the first time.

Once again I assume the womanly duty of pouring tea and search around, as befuddled as I am, for a topic of conversation.

'It is no longer raining,' I offer.

'Ah. It's been quite dry here for some days, I believe.'

I break the deathly silence that falls. 'I regret I shall be indisposed for a few days, your grace.'

'You will be?' He looks quite alarmed. 'Shall we send for the doctor?'

He's obviously spent too long with ancient statues. 'No, sir. Not indisposed in that way. I mean it is my . . .' I search for an appropriate phrase. 'My female time.'

'Oh. Oh, that.'

Do I imagine things, or does his face show a sudden flash of relief?

He rubs his hands together, a favourite gesture and one that already makes me flinch after less than a day in his company. 'Well, never mind. I've ordered you an early dinner; I expect you'd like to rest after the journey.'

'You're not staying, your grace?'

'No, ma'am. Caroline, I mean. I have a – some other business in town I should attend to. I shall return in a few days, and meanwhile . . .' He gazes at the other end of the room, where a pianoforte stands. 'Ah, good. I see Beck has rented an instrument as I requested. I trust it proves satisfactory.'

'You're very good, sir.' I walk over to it and bang out a few notes, hoping I look more enthusiastic than I feel. 'Oh, quite a superior tone. How splendid.'

I notice also, at this end of the room that looks out over a small garden, that there is an easel and a set of paints and brushes, tablets of paper and so on. A small bookcase holds some rather serious-looking literature bound in opulent gilded leather. Good God, it is like an expensive academy for young ladies, and I thought I was descending into the very pit of impropriety. It is bad enough to have become a whore, but to be expected to practise the accomplishments of polite society as well seems to be remarkably unfair.

'I shall be away for much of the time,' my future protector says, 'so I trust you will keep yourself pleasantly occupied. And there are some very pretty walks around here also.'

'Thank you.' He really is trying quite hard to be congenial, but the knowledge that after a few days I shall be thanking him on my back (or on my knees or whatever his grace prefers) makes me less than grateful.

'Well!' He puts his teacup on to the table. 'I don't want to keep the horses standing for too long. I'll send word when you may expect me. Please send for Beck – the Tysons know how to reach him – should there be anything you require.'

He fidgets, produces a handkerchief and blows his nose with a peculiar squeaking sound. That, and the hand-rubbing, could drive me mad in a matter of a few hours.

I curtsy, he bows, and then he leaves, reminding me that the next day is Sunday and I should make sure to attend worship (another obligation I was hoping to evade. Is there truly no peace for the wicked?). It is dreadfully polite and awkward. I must be his first mistress, that must be it – and he still has to prove to his friends, or with whomever he has placed his bet, that he has made a conquest. How exactly will he do so? Invite a gaggle of languid dandies to take tea and inspect the bedsheets?

I am not sure I believe his explanation, anyway. For some reason the Duke of Thirlwell is determined to take a mistress he does not really want, and I am compelled to take a protector I do not really want.

What a sorry state of affairs.

Letter from the Duchess of Thirlwell to the Duke of Thirlwell

My dearest and best Woolly Ram,

I am quite desolated without you but hope your Particular Business in town progresses well. How I long to see your sketches of fine antiquities that amuse me so greatly. I particularly like the male ones, although they are not nearly as *Masculine* as you.

Congrevance arrived yesterday, much weary after his long journey by the mail coach – shame upon you that you could not provide him with a superior form of transport. I was much surprised at his Foreign Polish – oh dear, that sounds like furniture – and I took the liberty of inviting him and Mr Pickering and the Revd and Mrs Fellwinkle to dine; also my Aunt Brillstone was there, so I was very well chaperoned. He (Congrevance) looks a little like you, but I think you are more handsome. The tenants are very excited, by the way, that Congrevance has returned, and I think it a most romantic story.

We had a pretty good dinner – mutton and trout and a stuffed marrow and a salad, and then cheese and nuts and a peach ice, sadly with the last of the ice; I am sorry, my dear, for

I know how much you like such things. We asked Congrevance to tell us stories of foreign parts, and he was vastly entertaining, but I see a melancholy in him. Aunt Brillstone was in fine spirits; she told me she would have her skirts up for him in a heartbeat and I confess I blushed, this being almost in the gentleman's hearing.

But Lady Caroline Elmhurst! I am much shocked. Is she as beautiful and reckless as everyone says? I hope she is not too charming.

Congrevance has the spare bed at Pickering's while he works on his house, which is in a sorry state, and he and the men have been hard at work repairing your dry-stone walls. I gave him some salve for his blisters and, by the way, he repaired the wobble in the dining-room table, that the butler said could not be done. For a gentleman – I suppose that is what he is – he is remarkably good with his hands.

I met him only a couple of times when we were all children; I remember how people were shocked that the old Earl should bring his bastard into his house, and they whispered that his mother was French and nearly got her head cut off. My dear, you never told me we had her portrait – he showed it to me; it is the one of a lady as a nymph or some such that hangs in the drawing room next to the one of the ugly dogs. She was very pretty in a foreign sort of way. I am glad that you and Congrevance are once again the greatest of friends.

And now my candle is almost burned down and it remains only to tell you that your Little Lambkin misses her Great Ram most sorely and longs once more to bury her hands in his fleece and caress his great curved horn *[at this point the letter becomes very personal and of no consequence]*

Letter from Mr Nicholas Congrevance to his half-brother the Duke of Thirlwell

Brother,

Your dry-stone walls are a disgrace, for Pickering has been too rheumatic to climb the hills, but slowly we make progress.

The Duchess is an angel you do not deserve; I do not think I have met a sweeter woman, although her Aunt Brillstone seems most peculiar. When I dined at the house, the lady insisted on showing us after dinner how the minuet was danced at the assembly rooms in her youth, fell on to the sofa and broke wind like a monstrous female trumpet before falling asleep. The astonishing thing is that she drank only water at dinner. Your Duchess only smiled and rearranged her aunt's skirts so we did not have to view her garters or more.

You need more ice. I shall look into obtaining some, but meanwhile the ice house needs a thorough draining and cleansing.

Yes, I keep busy.

Tell me how Caroline does and remember what happens to you and your line if you take advantage of the situation.

I remain, sir, your most loving brother, etc.

Nicholas Congrevance

Letter from the Duke of Thirwell to his half-brother Mr Nicholas Congrevance

My dear brother,

The Duchess writes that she finds you handsome and charming, and I should be obliged if you do not become overly familiar with her. My affairs in London progress well; I am happy to report that Lady Elmhurst is currently indisposed in a Female Way (I am sure you know of what I speak; it is an extraordinary messy business indeed, quite unlike ewes) and so I have had no reason to visit her. I daresay I shall have to put in an appearance soon, for I am afraid a woman of her reputation and tastes may get into trouble – by which I mean gambling and low company and so on. I am happy to report that she still yearns and sighs heavily for you and drank herself into a stupor on our journey.

I was somewhat alarmed to discover that although I suspect her education is sadly lacking (she stared at the books in the house as though they were vermin), she is not without some native intelligence. From the first, she voiced her suspicions that my motivation for taking a mistress was not what it might seem; I had to invent, or rather, she did, a preposterous story about a wager.

Pray put a roof on your house soon.

Your loving brother,

Thirlwell

Lady Caroline Elmhurst

The day has come, or rather the night has come, and with it comes Thirlwell, to take his ducal delight.

Beck arrived this morning to tell me that his grace will dine with me tonight, the fifth day as the Duke's official mistress, and I can put the moment off no longer. I must do my duty, repay my debt, and it is with a heavy heart that I descend to the kitchen to talk to Mrs Tyson about dinner.

I interrupt the lady taking her ease at the kitchen table, a cup of tea by her side, feet up, shoes off and deep in perusal of a fashion magazine.

'Oh, milady. I beg your pardon.' She stands up, attempting to push her feet into her shoes and hide the magazine behind some bowls on the table.

'What were you reading?'

'*La Belle Assemblee*, ma'am.'

I gaze at the magazine, as a starving woman might at food. I have tried to read some of the books upstairs; there is one, however, by a female author, entitled *Prejudice and Pride* or some such, that is quite good.

'May I borrow it, Mrs Tyson? When you are finished with it, that is.'

'Why, of course, milady. It's several months old, though.'

'No matter. Thank you. Now, the Duke dines here tonight and we should talk about the menu.' I am relieved that oysters and asparagus are not in season; it is odd that although some foods are as extolled as aphrodisiacs, very few are recommended for quenching desire.

We talk of food for a while in the pleasant atmosphere of the kitchen, with its well-scrubbed flagstone floor, the scent of smoke and food, and copper pans and blue and white china arranged on a dresser. A cat and her kittens lie before the fire – and that reminds me, how shall I avoid pregnancy? It is a pity indeed that there is no instruction book for courtesans, in the same style as the book Mrs Tyson produces, which has recipes and information on cleaning things and other aspects of household management.

We decide on roast duck and a beef pie and vegetables for the first remove, and a gooseberry fool and Aylesbury cakes for the second, foods the Duke enjoys, according to Mrs Tyson. Mr Tyson will choose the wines, also knowing his grace's tastes. I am all too aware that I shall be the delicacy that concludes the feast.

'And Mrs Tyson, if you will be so kind, please put fresh sheets on my bed.' There. I've said it. I shall do my duty.

'Oh. I don't think that will be necessary— Why, of course, milady. Yes indeed, milady, right away.' She looks as embarrassed as I feel.

'Have you been in the Duke's employment long?' I wish to know, of course, if the Duke has ever had a mistress before, and this seems a good introductory question.

'Why, I was the old Duke's housekeeper, milady. When Mr Tyson and I married, the young Duke sent us to look after this house, for we wanted our own establishment, and he wanted a place near London.'

'To keep his mistresses?'

Now that sounds absurd, as though he has a house bursting with women of ill repute, as others may keep rabbits, although I am sure a lot of gentlemen would find the idea attractive.

'Oh no, milady. No, his grace is more interested in his old statues and his livestock.'

As I suspected.

'Not like the old Duke, his father,' she says with a knowing look.

I make an encouraging sound, for I still have a taste for unseemly gossip, even if I am now a subject for it myself.

'Now the old Duke, he kept a mistress, a French lady, not some ten miles from his house, and when she died, he brought their son into the household. A sweet child he was, and the old Countess was pleased to have a companion for her son, for the two were only a year apart in age. 'Twas a pity indeed that— What is it, George?'

The servant, a child who reminds me of Will Gibbons, for he is only a little older, bows. 'Please, milady, Mrs Tyson, there's a grand lady to see milady and she said she'd wait in the garden. And may I show the boy who came with her the kittens?'

I can't think who could possibly be calling on me, with my new reputation as a courtesan – indeed, no one knows where I am. It can only be someone to whom I owe money, but curiosity, as well as manners, compels me to receive my guest.

To my astonishment, it's Mrs Riley. A heap of weeds lies at her feet as she examines a rose bush with a fierce expression on her face. When I appear, she straightens and pushes her grandson Will forward to make his bow. He runs to me and throws his arms around me, much to my surprise, and I bend to kiss him.

'Lady Caro, I am so glad to see you. I am in London visiting my grandmama and we have been to the Tower to see the wild animals and all manner of wonderful things. I wish you had been with us.'

'I'm glad to see you too, Will.'

'Will you come with me and George – he is my new friend – to see the kittens?'

I am amused to see that once again Will has decided that a complete stranger should be his friend, just as he did with me.

'No, Will,' his grandmama says. 'Lady Elmhurst and I wish to talk.' She beckons to George. 'Fetch me a bucket of water with soap and a good handful of red pepper in it; that will take care of these greenflies, hideous things, and Lady Elmhurst and I will take tea in the garden.'

The two boys run off together.

'Mrs Riley, I trust you are in good health? I am of course very pleased to see you, but you should know that I am ruined.' I am dying to know why she is here after I left Otterwell's house in disgrace; double disgrace, one should say – an adulterous embrace with Linsley followed by becoming a duke's lightskirt.

'Oh, I am too old to bother with such things. Besides, I have been ruined at least twice in my life.'

She hands me a trowel. 'See if you can do something with those weeds.'

The last thing I expected was to receive a visit from the high-and-mighty Mrs Riley and become her undergardener, but I am quite pleased to see her and Will. It is also more pleasurable than I would have thought to dig up weeds – Mrs Riley tut-tuts at one point and snatches away something that looks like a weed to me but is apparently not. Meanwhile she, despising garden implements, pulls weeds from the earth with her bare hands and beats the soil from their roots on her skirts.

George and Will arrive with the bucket of soapy water Mrs Riley requested, and she allows them to tip it over the rose bush, much to their delight.

I am longing to ask after the Linsleys and whether Mrs Gibbons and Darrowby have found yet another excuse not to wed, but she anticipates me. 'Will is staying with me for a few weeks while his mother is on her wedding trip. They married by special licence two days ago in my drawing room, none of this dreadful vulgarity in a church. Inigo gave her away, which I considered indelicate, and I regret he wept throughout. I was never so embarrassed in my life.'

'I'm glad to hear they married. And how is the Admiral?'

'Very well. He cried too. I felt as though I were

surrounded by watering cans. What sentimental fools men are.' She brushes dirt from her hands. 'Ah, the children have brought us tea. How delightful. Let us repair to the shade.'

Mr Tyson, who accompanies the boys, arranges a pair of Windsor chairs and a small table under an apple tree for us, and we sit. The boys run off to fetch the kittens and settle in a sunny spot, with the mother cat keeping an anxious eye on her offspring.

'Mrs Riley, I am delighted to see you and Will, but how did you know where I was?'

She gives the teapot a vigorous stir. 'Oh, I make it my business to be informed. And how do you do with the Duke?'

'Tolerably well, ma'am. He dines here tonight and I'd be delighted to invite you to stay for dinner.' I should be indeed. I would love to have a chaperone – two, if you count Will – so his grace cannot lunge for me across the table.

'We're already engaged, thank you.' Odd, that she does not find my invitation unusual. 'To get to the point, Lady Elmhurst, I am here as an emissary. We – that is, the Linsleys, the Darrowbys and myself – feel that we misjudged you. There was some unpleasant-ness regarding you and Inigo, who has a regrettable informality in his manners, and it was interpreted as . . . well, you know. Thank God he has stopped keeping mistresses; not that he could ever afford to do so properly, as you well know. In short, ma'am, we misjudged you. We wish to offer our apologies and extend an olive branch.'

'Oh. Thank you.' I gaze stupidly at my tea as tears of relief and happiness threaten. 'I am more grateful than I can say. I—'

'If it is agreeable, Mrs Linsley would like to call on you.'

'I should be honoured, if she is certain her reputation will not suffer.'

Mrs Riley laughs. 'Do not concern yourself. The *ton* has bred scandal about Inigo, Philomena and Mrs Gibbons for years. Now tell me of Congrevance. Was he satisfactory between the sheets?'

I surprise us both by bursting into tears.

'My dear Caro!' She fusses over me, offering a handkerchief and a vinaigrette. 'I did not mean to upset you, indeed. My apologies. I am perhaps too plain spoken.'

I gulp tea. 'I beg your pardon. I am not usually given to weeping. Congrevance was a grave disappointment.'

'Indeed? I am surprised. I would have thought from – well, from his general appearance and air, that he would have been a most competent lover.'

'Competent for less than a minute by my reckoning, ma'am.'

'Well!' She shakes her head in disbelief and then

smiles. 'You should be complimented, Caro. A man like Congrevance would not lose control so easily, you may count on it. He must have been overcome with passion.'

'It's little comfort to me now.'

'I suppose not.' She pats my hand. 'But tell me, Caro, you are not with child, are you?'

I shake my head, but an unpleasant suspicion creeps into my mind concerning Mary, who has been dour and unhappy ever since we left Otterwell's. The only complaints of belly aches or headaches have been mine, with no reciprocal grumbling from her. Surely it must be too soon to tell, but . . . and that raises the question of how I shall avoid the same problem in the future.

I don't want to insult Mrs Riley, but she has admitted that she has been the subject of scandal herself, and she is of an earlier, and somewhat more lax, generation. So I ask her with as much delicacy as I can muster.

'Oh, I don't think you have anything to worry about there,' she says, and gathers her reticule.

'Ma'am, exactly what do you mean?' Is the Duke gelded? Does he favour unnatural practices, and if so, how have I never heard any such gossip?

'Believe me, Caro, everything will work out well in the end,' is her cryptic reply. 'Heavens, look at the time. I must take that child home and wash him before we dine. He gathers dirt like a cheese rolling down a hill.'

We retrieve Will; he and George have been thwarted by the mother cat, who has taken her offspring back to the kitchen. They now entertain themselves in pulling carrots and picking beans from the garden, eating half as many as they collect. I kiss Will farewell – in truth, he is quite filthy, but so am I from grubbing in the garden, and his grandmother is not much better, with long streaks of dirt on her gown and her hair coming down.

I trudge upstairs and find Mary fast asleep on my bed, which only confirms my suspicions of her condition. I know it is probably ridiculously early, but my sister claimed she knew from the moment of conception and was unwell but a week following.

'I beg your pardon, milady.' She wakes up and stretches. 'I was helping Mrs Tyson with the sheets and I don't know what came over me.'

'It must be the warm weather.' Yes, of course. That must be it. 'Send for hot water, Mary. I'd best bathe.'

In for a penny, in for a pound. Somehow I have decided, and I'm not quite sure when this happened, that if I'm to be the Duke's mistress, I shall be the best he has ever had – entertaining, charming and endlessly inventive in the sensual arts. I select my finest gown and my least-darned stockings. I suppose I should have shopped for some new ones, but at least I have some pretty garters to wear.

Mary and the Tysons haul hot water upstairs for me and fill a tin bathtub. I abandon myself to the pleasure of hot water and lavender-scented soap, and Mary scrubbing my back.

A horrible thought occurs to me. 'Mary, what about my hair?'

'We'll wash it of course, milady.'

'No, no. Not that hair. *That* hair.'

'*That* hair? Oh, lud, milady, do you mean we should – it wouldn't be *nice*, milady.'

But I'm not nice any more, and somehow – well, it must be from certain obscene prints that Elmhurst was good enough to share with me – I am convinced that his grace should find me as bald as an egg beneath my skirts.

'Yes, we should remove it. Will – will it hurt, do you think, Mary?'

'Ooh, I expect so, milady. I've never done it, but I believe you use boiled sugar and rags, at least that's what I've heard.'

It hurts already, just thinking about it, and I believe it may take some level of expertise. I am not too keen on Mary learning the skill on my person (hot sugar syrup!). I clamp my knees together in a self-protective gesture.

'We should have asked his grace's manservant if that is what the Duke prefers.'

'Yes, milady.' She giggles, but a drop of what can only be a tear falls on to my shoulders. I must add *manservant* to the list of words that make Mary cry, in addition to earrings, flowers, ironing, ribbons, cucumbers (I do not enquire too closely into the last item) – it goes on and on.

'Maybe you could practise on yourself.'

'No one's likely to see, milady.' A heavy sigh, another tear. 'Besides, I don't think it's decent for a woman of my station, begging your ladyship's pardon.'

Bathing done, I dress in a clean shift, petticoat and my prettiest pair of stays, and my best (or least worse) stockings. Mary laces, arranges and smoothes in silence. I believe another fit of disapproval has overtaken her. I rub lotion on to my face, wondering whether I should attempt to paint my eyes with lampblack and redden my lips, or attempt a worldly elegance. I smother myself in perfume.

Then I have to wait for my hair to dry so I do not leave wet patches all over my silk gown, but to my great pleasure Mrs Tyson sends up her copy of *La Belle Assemblee*. It turns out to be a very pleasant afternoon. In fact, if all I had to do were to slop around in a state of undress and pick at some food with my fingers, spilling it all over my magazine, with maybe a few glasses of wine, I couldn't be happier. But tonight I am to become Thirlwell's mistress.

I ignore the quivers of nervousness until they intensify so that I cannot ignore them. A quarter-hour before Thirlwell's arrival, as Mary arranges my hair, I lose my nerve.

'I can't do this!'

'Yes you can, milady. You must, otherwise we'll be out on the streets.'

'Fetch me some brandy.'

Mary leaves the bedchamber and returns with a scant half-inch of brandy in a glass.

'Is that all?'

'You'd best keep your wits about you.'

'Oh God.'

'You must put your gown on, milady. Come, get up.'

I groan and let her drop my gown over my head. Heavens, I show a lot of bosom. For sure I must not bend over, for I'll fall right out.

I hear the sound of the front door opening and the voices of Thirlwell and Tyson.

'Go on, milady.' Mary gives me a shove – the arrogance of the girl – towards the bedchamber door.

'Mary, listen – after dinner, when we have retired to the drawing room, I want you to come in every quarter of an hour. You can listen to the clock in the hall. Make any excuse you like. Bring me my fan. Bring—'

'What if it only takes fourteen minutes? Besides, I don't want to see the Duke undressed.'

'Neither do I, Mary. That's the point. I don't know. Just do as I say.' I am convinced he will spring on me when I am pouring tea and there are no servants around.

'Which earrings would you like to wear, milady?' Oh lord, she is crying again.

'Not those ones!' I smack Elmhurst's earrings from her hand, and they fall to the floor. 'My pearls. No, the paste ones.'

'Maybe he'll give you a new pair.' Mary retrieves the earrings from the floor with a tragic air and blows dust from them. 'You could do with some new silk stockings, too.'

'I know.'

'You could give him a hint, milady.' This is fine advice from the woman who has received only wilted flowers and (possibly) a growing belly from her lover. Besides, she knows I'll give her my old silk stockings, which are marginally better than the ones she wears and continually darns.

I take a deep breath, as Fanny Gibbons taught us to do before going on stage. Mary is right; my womanly charms are all that stand between me and the streets, and I remember my earlier determination to be the most fascinating and desirable woman of the demi-monde.

I descend the stairs and enter the dining room.

The Duke rubs his hands and beams at me with extraordinary affability. He looks quite presentable in a black coat and breeches, but has undergone a haircut that leaves him with a tuft standing straight up from the crown of his head.

'My goodness!' he declares. 'Pray, madam, do you like sheep?'

Lady Caroline Elmhurst

Do I like sheep?

For sure, I thought for one dreadful moment this was Thirlwell's favoured perversion, and that an unfortunate animal would be produced for his grace's pleasure. I prayed it would not be a ram that would require my participation.

I had thought Thirlwell's passion old statues. I was wrong. His grace likes, nay loves, adores, idolises sheep.

All sorts of sheep – and there are many. Lambs, ewes and rams I knew about, and my knowledge is expanded all through dinner.

I interrupt his flow of words. 'A moment, sir. I thought you were talking of sheep, yet you apparently also like pigs?'

He waves his fork at me. 'No, no, my dear Caroline. It is *hogg*, with two Gs – it is what we call a sheep of nine months to a year and a half. Now, as I was saying . . .'

I struggle to make sense of what he says. 'So a sheep may be a glimmer, a hogg and a teg, all at the same time?'

'Very good! Yes, so long as it is female. Or it may be an old-season lamb. On the other hand, if it is a male castrated late, that is, after six months, it is a stag.' And off he goes again, and even when he talks of rams (or, as I learn, *tups*, for the word means the same) he does not turn to bawdy innuendo, but is still as earnest and pedantic as ever.

I am mightily bored.

I dressed in my best and even considered unnatural and painful applications of molten sugar for this sheep-obsessed booby?

I nod and smile.

He progresses on to breeds of sheep.

'Now, the Swaledale is a particularly good sort of sheep. You'll recognise them by their curly horns and black faces, and both meat and wool are very good. I do find the wool somewhat coarse in texture, although it has a good bind and fills the hand . . .'

Unfortunately this makes me think of Congrevance. I have drunk just enough wine to make me at ease, and appreciate the delicious food and the play of lamplight upon silver and china. Were I alone with the right gentleman, I could quite easily feel amorous.

'On the other hand, Caro, I think you'll agree that the Cheviot has a most superior wool – the breed is well suited to our rough hills, and because, as I mentioned, the sheep have no wool on face or legs, they are less likely to develop footrot or wool blindness. You may not believe this, Caro . . .' He leans forward and gazes into my eyes. 'But sheep are most delicate creatures, prone to all sorts of ills.'

'Indeed.' If I have more wine I shall fall asleep. My smile feels more like a grimace at this point, and were his grace to hurl himself across the table and plunge his face into my bosom it would be a relief.

My apparent interest spurs him on to talk more of sheep illnesses, many of which have disgusting names. I am quite glad we have finished eating. He is deep in a vivid description of something revolting called flystrike when he falters to a stop and stares at me.

The reason is quite simple. I have kicked off my slipper and now run my stockinged foot up his leg beneath the table. I smile innocently at him. Thank God he has shut up.

He reaches down, pushes my foot away and continues with a somewhat frantic air, '. . . and then there's pizzle rot, which I hate to see in my rams. The, ah, affected part is—'

'Shall I retire to the drawing room?'

'Indeed, yes, a capital idea.' He springs to his feet, looking exceedingly nervous.

'I'll leave you to your port, sir.' Thus neatly giving

myself a breathing space I leave the dining room and proceed upstairs to the drawing room.

There I sink on to a sofa and contemplate my imminent fate.

The clock strikes one quarter past the hour and Mary creeps in. She looks around the room, wild-eyed, as though expecting to see his grace emerge rampant from behind the furniture. 'Your fan, milady.'

'Very good, but he is not here yet. Try again later.'

The Duke spends almost half an hour with his port, and my palms grow quite damp with sweat. Finally he enters, somewhat red in the face and, from his unsteadiness, foxed.

'Pray, sit, your grace.' I attempt a seductive coo.

He flops on to the other end of the sofa and gazes at me. I am not sure of his expression – is he nervous, repulsed, confused, amorous? I wait for him to make some sort of gesture that will indicate his intentions.

He produces a handkerchief and blows his nose in his annoying way.

As the Duke clears his throat as though about to say something, Tyson enters with the tray of tea things.

'Sugar? Milk?' I spend rather a lot of time fussing around with pouring Thirlwell tea. 'Why, what pretty cups and saucers. They cannot be English, or are they?'

'French, ma'am, I believe.'

He grasps the teacup and saucer in one large hand and clears his throat.

Mary taps on the door and enters. 'Your fan, milady. You forgot it.'

'Why, thank you. Do you think you could find my vinaigrette?'

The minutes tick by, or at least I assume they do, since there is no clock in the room. After several years, or so it seems, the Duke clears his throat again.

'Your grace?'

He places his cup and saucer on a small table at the end of the sofa. 'I should like you to demonstrate your accomplishments.'

Oh, good heavens. He does not move, and to me it is obvious what he expects. I ease myself from the sofa – these stays do not allow a great deal of movement at the waist – and shuffle towards him on my knees.

As I approach, he clamps his knees together, clutches them with his hands and gasps, 'At the pianoforte, ma'am.'

I swear I blush. Why the devil could he not say what he wanted? At this point all I want is to get the business over and done with.

Another tap at the door, and Mary enters, yawning, with my vinaigrette. I thank her and tell her that is all I shall require until I come to bed.

She frowns and mouths something at me, pointing over her shoulder at the hallway and the clock.

'Oh, for goodness' sake, Mary, go upstairs and stay there.'

'Very well, milady.' She flounces out and bangs the door closed behind her.

I spend some time bent at the waist (or as much as I can in these damned stays) looking through a collection of music. I consider this an open invitation to a gentleman to approach and grab – certainly, it has been most effective in the past – but nothing happens.

I have even practised a little, although my playing is as bad as ever, but I do not believe the Duke's interest in me is entirely musical. So I spend some time fussing around at the pianoforte, making sure that the candelabra shows me to the best effect (the music on the stand is barely visible, but it does not matter). I remove my bracelets very slowly, letting them slide over my fingers. I fuss with my hair, particularly a loose lock that keeps falling into the bodice of my dress, and giggle a little; oh dear, what a dreadful nuisance. I sit, arranging the folds of my gown so that my limbs are shown to the best advantage.

I have chosen a sonata by Haydn that I have always found quite boring, but since it is one of the first pieces I learned, my performance is not quite so dreadful as the rest of my limited repertoire. As I play, I become aware of another sound.

Now, I am quite used to sniggers, conversation or

even rude comments when I play. It is rarely that my playing induces sleep – there are too many mistakes and hesitations for it to be sufficiently restful. But I hear behind me the unmistakable sound of a snore. I raise my hands from the keys.

Thirlwell is fast asleep.

So much for my seductive arts or even my ladylike accomplishments. I have only become a sort of unmusical Orpheus, although I think the amount of drink the gentleman consumed has much to do with it.

I play a fairly loud chord, and then another louder and more untuneful one.

He does not stir.

I approach him, grasp his knee and shake it. 'Your grace?'

Given his shyness before, I expect him to leap to protect his virtue, but he sleeps on.

'Sir, wake up!'

I cross to the fireplace and bang the coal shovel against the grate. No good. The Duke continues to sleep.

I consider what I should do. Frankly, I am annoyed. I have spent most of the evening trying to gauge the gentleman's intentions and doing my best, under extremely trying circumstances, to repay my debt. And now it looks as if my efforts have been in vain, and I shall have to start all over again next time.

In something of a bad temper, I leave the room and

call down the stairs to the servants' quarters. I wonder if I should disarrange my hair and clothing to look as though I have been thoroughly ravaged by his grace – but really, why should I bother to preserve his male dignity?

'His grace has fallen asleep,' I tell Tyson.

'Indeed, ma'am. I'll call his carriage.'

Thirlwell's coachman, a large, burly man who looks at my bosom and winks – I give him a frosty glare – eases the unconscious Duke over his shoulder and removes him from the house.

I tell Tyson the dinner was excellent and go upstairs to bed. I have to wake Mary up to unlace my stays, and she is so stupid and sleepy I send her away and finish getting ready for bed on my own. Next time I shall wear the short stays; it will make life infinitely simpler.

Letter from Mr Nicholas Congrevance to his half-brother the Duke of Thirlwell

My dear brother,

An extraordinary thing has happened. You may remember I spoke to you of Barton, my former manservant, who departed from my service in great anger. He left Otterwell's before I did, taking with him a pair of earrings that belonged to Caroline, which I had won at cards; I regret he also left behind a broken-hearted woman, Caroline's maid Mary. Now he has once again appeared.

A circus of sorts arrived in the village a couple of days ago. The parish authorities were most nervous, anticipating all sorts of dreadful consequences such as a crop of bastards nine months hence and general corruption, so I put on my best coat and rode down to the village as your grace's representative. (Since I have spent most of my time on that damned roof when it is not raining, I am burned as dark as a gypsy myself and do not cut as impressive a figure as you might wish.)

It was a drab collection of wagons and people in dirty costumes. Under the sun of Italy they would have looked picturesque; here in the dour north they looked merely grubby. As a preview to the day's show, a dancing bear was performing on the village common. Its keeper was none other than Barton, wearing his false beard. You may remember him as the Wall in the play. He has an inordinate fondness for the beard.

Also, now, apparently for the bear, which has become a sort of brother to him. They are fairly alike in build and countenance and the animal is as gentle as a kitten under his command. I took them to the alehouse and the bear drank us both under the table and was kind enough to share its fleas.

The upshot is that I have hired him again, at the moment with no pay, and as Barton was afraid the animal would pine for him, the estate now has its own bear. I traded the animal for a quantity of mutton and vegetables from the gardens and four jewelled stickpins I received from obliging ladies in my former profession. I have also arranged for the bear, whose name is Daisy (it is a male, but Barton is sentimental about flowers), to receive a gallon of ale every day. Its only contribution to the estate so far is the destruction and consumption of wasps' nests. Barton believes Daisy can be trained to herd sheep; I have my doubts. Barton takes him on a leash to accustom them to his presence, but so far they scatter in panic. I suspect the creature has poor eyesight and operates predominantly by scent, for mostly it seems unaware of them. I insist in any case it be muzzled.

Barton has taken upon himself the task of digging manure into what will be my garden, while Daisy sleeps nearby. I had wanted him to assist me with the roof, but the bear insists upon accompanying us and Barton is afraid its extreme affection may cause a fall. The bear's devotion does not bode well for any sort of intimate connection Barton may plan with Mary. She may well lie down with Barton and get up with the bear's fleas.

Before I address the pressing subject of manure collection and spreading on the estate, may I remind your grace of what I will do to your person should you lay a finger, let alone any other part, upon Caroline.

That said, let us speak now of dung *[the letter becomes concerned with agricultural matters and is of no further interest]*

Letter from Nicholas Congrevance to Lady Caroline Elmhurst (never sent)

My love,

I am so jealous of my brother I think I may well try to kill him next time I see him. I know it is a most awkward situation and I trust he has revealed all to you now. But the fact that he may call upon you any time, talk to you, even look at you – although I do not want him looking at you more than is necessary for common courtesy – makes me rage with jealousy and anger and regret.

I was a fool. More, a selfish fool. Had I told you I loved you – although I did, I recollect, but you were astute enough to doubt my regard – and proposed marriage to you, what would have been your response? Moreover, if I had told you I had lied about my wealth (and if you, Caro, had told me of your distressing financial situation; the blame is not all mine), what then? We could have left for the Continent to escape your creditors, and I could have found a reasonably respectable occupation (as a teacher of languages, for instance). We would have been poor; I like to think we would have been happy.

I dare to think you might still take me as your husband. I beg that you will. I may have been dishonest before, but now I must tell you the truth. You will marry – if you wish to – a man who is little more than a poor labourer, until my brother is pleased to release some money to me from the bequest that our father the late Duke made me. I am fortunate in that I do have at least this last evidence of my father's regard – I loved him greatly, by the way, as I do my brother, even though I find him the most provoking man that ever lived. He has a generous heart beneath his peculiar ways.

What concerns me most in our situation is

that you will feel that this marriage is forced upon you, and I beg you not to let your pride stand in the way. I would not have you starve; neither would I have you live without love. My love, to be specific.

I wish also to tell you, should this matter weigh as much upon your mind as it does mine, that in Intimate Congress I have been known to last ~~forty-five minutes up to an hour once an entire morning two hours as much time as required~~ a considerable and respectable (or unrespectable) amount of time. ~~I have never received a complaint, and bear in mind, ma'am, I performed in a professional capacity.~~ Without unnecessary obscenity or boastfulness I believe I can and shall love you in all ways and always as you deserve and desire.

Although, my lovely Caro, I do wish some, nay, *much* necessary and unnecessary obscenity with you, and thank God I have a roof to occupy me, for I truly believe I should go mad *[the letter ends here]*.

Lady Caroline Elmhurst

'**M**y dear Philomena, you have saved my life!'

I clutch the fashion magazines and silk stockings she has bestowed upon me, and I have never been so glad to see anyone in my life before.

'Oh, it's nothing. Mrs Riley said you might be a little down in the dumps, so I thought of what would cheer me up and brought it to you.' She turns to Will and James, who have accompanied her. 'Now, boys, you may go to visit the kittens, and Will, do not let your brother eat or drink too much.'

As the boys are escorted from the drawing room by George, she turns to me with a smile. 'I am so glad we are all friends again. I am dreadfully sorry I misjudged you so. Now, how do you get on with Thirlwell?'

I am rather shocked at such a question and consider carefully how to answer. If, for instance, I had been asked that question in my early days with Elmhurst, I could have given an inventory of which rooms, how many times, and which pieces of furniture had been broken as a result. I remember a regrettable incident with a harp and the ruin of some particularly expensive velvet curtains.

I clear my throat. 'He is most generous and gentlemanly.'

'Yes, he is a kind man despite his eccentricities.' She peers at the book I have laid face down on the table. 'What are you reading? Why, *Pride and Prejudice*. It is very good, is it not? I think Linsley is so like Mr Darcy.'

I privately thought he was rather more like Mr Wickham when I knew him, but I do not wish to disillusion her. I decide to change the subject and ask her when her baby is due.

She obliges with a long monologue of how pleased she is about the arrival of the baby in November. Although her own mother and Mrs Riley want her to give birth in London with a fashionable accoucheur, she much prefers to give birth in the country. There is someone called Goody Prunewell on their estate who is indispensable in these matters. I shudder, thinking of a hag who has not washed in a decade.

'Frankly, Caroline, my mother talks too much, although I love her dearly, and Mrs Riley is – she means well, but you know how overbearing she can be. I should much prefer to be at home with Inigo.'

Inigo as a man-midwife? What a hideous thought. I enquire after her health.

'Oh, I am quite well now, although I was so sleepy at first I could scarce keep my eyes open. And weeping like a waterspout about nothing. It was dreadful, although I felt better by the time we were at Otterwell's.' She sees my expression. 'Oh, Caro. Surely not. Was it . . .'

My dismay is because I see Mary in this description, not myself. I assure her that I do not expect to bring a bastard into the world, but do not voice my fear that a ducal bastard may be a problem later.

I am most grateful that she does not pursue the topic, and I suggest that we take a walk. Will has brought his kite and we can take advantage of the Heath, but a few steps from the house. I am glad of the exercise and company.

Young George is allowed time off from his kitchen duties to accompany us, and the three boys cheer as the kite bobs high in the sky. It is a clear day with a brisk wind that blows away the London smoke, affording us a fine view of the city.

Philomena chatters away quite agreeably and asks my opinion on her bonnet. I assure her it is most elegant.

'You do seem out of sorts,' she says suddenly, 'and although Hampstead is considered a most salubrious spot, I think a change of air would do you good.'

'I have no plans to travel at the moment.' I sound rather curt, but too often I feel like a prisoner in my pretty little house in this pretty little village.

'Oh, but Thirlwell has invited us to Northumberland later this month.'

I am quite relieved to hear this, as it means I shall not be expected to entertain his grace, but she continues, 'And we shall all travel together and meet the Darrowbys there. I long to see Fanny again, and Caro, her wedding clothes are quite the thing; I am sure you will admire them.'

'You mean *I* am to be one of the party?'

'Of course!' she cries. 'I am sure it will be delightful.'

'But – the Duke, I believe he has a Duchess?'

'Yes, a most charming lady. You will—' She claps her hand to her mouth. 'Oh dear. I have spoken out of turn. Has not Thirlwell . . . Pay no attention to me, Caroline; for sure, my condition makes a dullard of me.'

'Philomena, maybe you could pay me the compliment of not treating me like a fool, and telling me exactly what is going on. I suspect a great conspiracy is afoot, and I am at the centre of it.'

She looks at me. 'I'm a dreadful liar, I know, and I shall not insult you by presenting you with an untruth. I can say no more. Believe me, we all wish you well.'

'I trust this has nothing to do with Congrevance,' I snap. 'I shall be very angry if that is the case, for I assure you I want nothing more to do with him. You forget too, ma'am, that I am Thirwell's mistress and thoroughly bought and paid for.'

I turn my back on her and walk away, feeling churlish and ill-used. The only possible reason Thirlwell might have for taking me up north to the bosom of his family is to test my newly acquired knowledge of sheep – that I doubt; or to engage me in some sort of amorous play with his duchess. That, too, given the gentleman's behaviour so far, seems unlikely.

Cries of distress reach my ears, and I see that the boys are losing control of the kite, which is looking fit to plummet earthwards. I run towards them, shouting to them to reel it in, and run, run! I snatch up little James, who cannot keep up with the older boys, and our efforts send the kite aloft once more, as we come to a stop, laughing and breathless.

'Would you like a go, Lady Caro?'

'Oh yes, Will, I would indeed.' I have not flown a kite in years. I have forgotten the pure exhilaration, the joy, as the kite tugs and kicks like a living creature and dances against the blue of the sky.

I laugh aloud. I have forgotten what it is to be happy.

*

I finish *Pride and Prejudice* and start on *Sense and Sensibility*; good lord, what a silly pair of dull girls, one so correct (she certainly deserves that tiresome clergyman) and the other forever spouting poetry. It reminds me of the other girls on the marriage mart when first I came out in society, which I suppose must be a tribute to the authoress. Yet I keep reading, for although I feared Marianne would marry that ancient military relic, who is obviously destined for Elinor, I am glad when Willoughby appears.

Beck visits to announce that his grace will dine again with me. This time, I decide, I shall play the seductress; surely then his grace will find it entirely inappropriate for me to travel to his estate. Possibly screaming very loudly in simulated ecstasy will persuade him that his *affaire* will not be so discreet beneath the ducal roof (unless he owns a huge house; I shall have to ask Mrs Tyson). But then if I scream loudly in this house, Mary, if she is awake, may rush down the stairs to rescue me.

Not that I find the Duke desirable. Far from it. I doubt very much that he could make me scream. But he has rescued me from debtors' prison and I owe the gentleman. It is my duty to give him value for money, and since I am sure no sheep are involved, I can discover his preferences. I know too that gentlemen after the act are in a state of extreme stupidity when they will agree to almost anything. At the appropriate moment I have decided that I shall remind his grace of my allowance and point out to him the extreme impropriety of taking his mistress to his country house. I am close enough to London; perhaps it is time to make some sort of entrée into society again.

I have by no means discarded the possibility of some sort of conspiracy; it is only that I cannot fathom what they have in mind.

So it is once again, primped, perfumed, wearing a gown that displays most of my bosom and with a vacuous smile, that I present myself to the Duke in the dining room. That is, I enter and curtsy – nothing so vulgar as arranging myself on the table splayed between the oysters and the asparagus as I did once for Elmhurst (needless to say, we dined alone that night).

If anything, he seems more nervous than before. During the first remove alone he knocks over a wine glass, breaks the butter dish and has to call for two more knives as his cutlery disappears beneath the table.

I ask him if he has received news from his estate on how his sheep do, and I fear he will bolt from the room, as terrified as he appears. He mutters an incomprehensible reply.

Eventually – as we eat a particularly delicious blackberry pie, he clears his throat and treats himself to one of his musical nose-blows. 'I must beg your pardon, Caroline, for exposing you to my – my inebriation, on my last visit.'

What a fool, I think, as a glob of blackberry and cream drips from his spoon on to the ruffle of his shirt; and how unfortunate for his valet, as everyone knows blackberry stains are impossible to remove. 'It is no matter, sir. I assure you I hardly noticed.'

'You did not? But I—'

'Well, *afterwards* you fell asleep, that is true. It is perfectly natural. Some gentlemen – particularly those blessed with *strong appetite* – need to gather their strength.' What abominable rubbish, but my emphasised words do the trick.

He looks at me with absolute horror.

'I shall leave you to your port, sir.' I rise. 'Pray, do not linger too long.'

He rises too, tipping over his water glass and sending his dessert plate on to the floor with a clatter. Tyson opens the door – I swear he winks at me – and it has no sooner closed than it opens again and the Duke runs towards me.

'Caroline, tell me the truth. I did not – oh heavens, tell me I did not take advantage of you . . .'

I smile sweetly and pluck his napkin from his waistcoat. 'You fell asleep, sir.'

We enter the drawing room and the Duke drops on to the sofa, looking so wretched I finally relent.

'Thirlwell, I was teasing you, for heaven's sake. It

is the truth – you fell asleep while I was playing the pianoforte because you had drunk too much port.'

'And I did not . . .'

'No, you did nothing. But I am your mistress; what on earth is the matter with you? Although I suppose you should like to be awake when we—'

Fortunately at that moment Tyson enters with the tea tray.

I pour, splashing tea and leaves into the saucers, and fairly shoving a cupful at the Duke. 'For God's sake, why don't you tell me what you are about?'

'What do you mean, ma'am? I beg your pardon if I have done something to upset you – I mean, other than my regrettable lack of manners in falling asleep the other night.'

'You obviously don't want a mistress. So you'd better tell me why you are pretending you do.'

There is a tap at the door and Mary enters, a laundry list in her hand. 'A letter arrived for you, milady.'

'No, it did not. Go away.'

She does.

Thirlwell looks at me, brow creased. 'Why did your maid—'

'It doesn't matter. Now, if you please, explain yourself.'

He sighs and places his teacup out of harm's way. 'Well, as I explained before, there is a wager—'

'Nonsense.'

We glare at each other like a pair of bulls, or as Thirlwell would most likely prefer, a pair of rams. It is time to try a different approach. He is a dreadful liar, which means he probably expects only the truth from others. He is surely ill at ease being harangued by a woman (even if he deserves it), for he expects women to flutter around in a pathetic, female sort of way and concur with male opinion.

I produce a handkerchief from my bosom and dab at my eyes.

'Oh, sir.' I allow a tremulous quiver to affect my voice. 'This is very upsetting.'

'My dear Caroline . . .' He actually pats my hand. Excellent.

'I do beg your pardon, sir.'

'No, no. It is I who should beg yours.'

I refill his teacup, allowing my hand to shake. 'I have behaved in a most unwomanly fashion.'

'Do not concern yourself.'

I notice that he does not rush to contradict me.

'Perhaps I should play the pianoforte for a little. I am sure it would calm me.'

'An excellent notion. Pray proceed.'

Of course, playing the pianoforte is something he associates with female docility. Place me in front of an instrument, an easel or an embroidery frame, and I shall become a simpering idiot.

Eyes downcast, I seat myself at the instrument and begin the sonata that sent him to sleep so effectively before, playing softly in the hopes that my frequent wrong notes will be hidden.

Good. He is actually smiling as he listens, and although I know it cannot possibly be my playing – more likely it is satisfaction that I am behaving as a woman should – I know he has let his guard down.

'So,' I say in my most dulcet tones as I pause between movements, 'how is Mr Nicholas Congrevance?'

He sits bolt upright. 'I beg your pardon?'

'You do know the gentleman, do you not?'

He recovers faster than I would have thought. 'Why, you're mistaken, ma'am, although the name is familiar. Was not that the name of one of the gentlemen in the play?' A credible attempt at a lie for someone who is mostly honest, I think.

'Oh, how foolish of me!' I let a girlish giggle escape. 'I am quite confused. Why, I must be the one who overindulged in wine tonight.'

Absurd as this is, he accepts it, and his rigid stance relaxes just a little. I continue to play, but inside I seethe with rage.

You despicable sheep-lover, I'll show you Caroline Elmhurst is not to be trifled with.

I finish the piece, and he applauds as I rise and

curtsy. I have to move fast as he is about to stand, ever
the gentleman, while I am on my feet. I bound over to
the sofa and hurl myself into his lap, landing astride so
he cannot tip me off too easily.

'Your grace – Simon – I can resist you no longer!'

Letter from Nicholas Congrevance to his half-brother the Duke of Thirlwell

Brother,

I cannot believe what I read.

You have not told her the truth yet? I am all
astonishment. This is what we agreed, you
incompetent oaf, your grace. What the devil
have you been about all this time?

It is to your credit that I trust you, your
grace. At least I try to. Allow me to amend that
– I trust your morals, but certainly not your
judgement.

To remind you of the arrangement: you were
to tell her as soon as she was settled in the
house that we are half-brothers, and that you
have no intention of becoming her lover, but
offer yourself as a friend only.

The rest was up to me at our meeting here.
As I told you, I did not expect you to explain my
former occupation or any other shameful aspect

of my behaviour. How in God's name do you think she will react now, thinking you and our mutual acquaintances have made a fool of her? I hope to God she has flayed you with that acid tongue. Be assured she will do so in the future.

Please tell me that somehow you have persuaded her to come to Northumberland, although how you shall do so I have no idea and can offer no suggestions.

I remain, your grace,
Your most obd't srv't,
Nicholas Congrevance

Letter from Nicholas Congrevance to the Duke of Thirlwell

Briefly, brother, this is far worse than I anticipated.

Your newest idea is worse than the original. Yes, I am aware that Barton and his beard will be invaluable, or would be if I were to agree to this insane plan. May I point out to your grace that women may enjoy being heroically rescued from brigands and such in popular novels, but the men they regard as heroes in real life do not land them in situations where they require a rescue.

Similarly, Caroline is more than capable of rescuing herself, except from creditors.

Since you seem incapable of acting rationally and asking the lady to accompany you to Northumberland, but are intent upon relying on theatrical subterfuge (I suggest you offer your talents to Lord Otterwell for his next theatricals), I do have a suggestion for removing her from the house. You will have to find alternative accommodations for the servants, for it will render the place uninhabitable for a few days. It is a simple process involving the house's cesspit, and here are my instructions *[odiferous details of no interest to the reader follow]*.

20

Lady Caroline Elmhurst

'It's not proper.' Mary, lips pursed, shakes out a petticoat.

'I'm his mistress.'

'No you're not. It's not decent.'

'You mean that if you entered a room and found me on the lap of a gentleman whose mistress I was, it would be decent? I must start somewhere, you silly girl.'

To my surprise, she giggles. 'The look on his face, milady.'

I remember the Duke's pop-eyed, red-faced terror. I laughed then, too, helpless with mirth by the time he had tipped me from his lap and was heading for the door at an undignified gallop. He'd almost bowled Mary over in his haste.

But I remember how he turned to face me at the last moment, and his frozen expression reminded me that he was a duke; a powerful man related to royalty and descended from many generations who held life-and-death power over commoners like myself.

The Duke was in those few minutes an impressive figure of a man as he said with quiet menace, 'You do me wrong, ma'am.'

And that was it. He left.

'Do you think he'll be back, milady?'

'Oh, I expect so. You know what men and their wounded dignity are.' I wonder how long we have before he turns us out, and what Mary and I shall do. Just as the Duke has power over his tenants and household, I am responsible for Mary. She has stuck with me through thick and thin – mostly thin, and probably because there was a slight chance that I might pay her.

This is the morning of the sixth day since, and we have heard from neither his grace nor Beck.

There's a tap at the door, Mrs Tyson with hot water for me, and I climb out of bed. A faint odour hangs about her – I do not like to comment on it, for it is most unpleasant. Perhaps she trod in something.

Mary hovers with a hairbrush at the ready. 'What shall you do today, milady?'

'Oh, I thought I'd take a walk after breakfast, and then I suppose I should practise the pianoforte. I wonder if anyone will call.'

'Morning dress, then, milady, and a spencer for later. You should hurry, for it looks like rain.'

When I am dressed we go down the stairs and I become aware of a smell – a very unpleasant smell indeed, like the one that clung to Mrs Tyson. I pause at the landing outside the drawing room.

'Mary, do you smell that?'

She nods.

The smell is noticeably stronger as we descend the final flight of stairs, and Mary and I both scream as a rat darts along the passage, zigzagging as they do when they are on unfamiliar ground. The door to the servants' quarters flies open, releasing a great gust of stink, and a dog, not much bigger than the rat, hurls itself in pursuit.

'Good boy, Jack! Get him!' someone cries from downstairs.

Before I know it, I am standing on a chair in the dining room, clutching my skirts to my legs, while the dog, shaking the rat by its neck, growls and snarls.

Mary, meanwhile, has rushed to the sash window and pushed it open, so that she may vomit outside.

A figure, draped in white – I swear it must be a corpse and bearing with it the putrefaction of the grave – emerges from the open door. But it is Tyson, with a piece of cloth draped over his face and wearing a long linen apron.

'Beg your pardon, milady,' he says. 'We have a bit of a blockage.'

'A bit of a blockage?' The smell is so bad I can scarcely breathe.

Mary, wan and wobbly, creeps to my side. 'Is – is it dead?'

'Yes, miss. I'm afraid Jack is the only one who'll have any breakfast this morning . . .'

Mary dashes back to the window.

'This is intolerable!' I cry. 'Can you send for Beck?'

'I have done so, milady, but I fear we'll have to dig into the pit, and the rats—'

'Oh God!' I cover my mouth with a corner of the tablecloth. 'Will there be more rats?'

'There will likely be a few, milady, and they're bound to run upstairs, for they can get beneath doors just as that one did. But Jack won't mind, will you, you good dog! It's grand sport for him, milady.'

I am delighted that one of us is enjoying himself.

Jack picks up his breakfast in his mouth and retires to a corner.

Mrs Tyson, also with her face covered, joins us, her skirts tucked up, and wearing old-fashioned pattens; there must be a veritable flood downstairs.

'A dreadful thing indeed, milady,' she says. 'And now the fire is out.'

She moves towards the front door as someone knocks, and I pray it is someone – even the Duke – who can rescue us.

It is the capable and well-trained Beck, who raises

a handkerchief to his nostrils and bows. He does not seem particularly surprised that I am standing on a chair, Mary is vomiting out of the window and a dog in the corner is consuming a rat.

'Milady, his grace wishes you to leave as soon as it is convenient.'

'Oh, thank goodness.'

'Mrs Tyson will help you pack your belongings.'

'No, no, we shall manage quite well on our own.' I am afraid that Mrs Tyson, who has been in the thick of the stink, may transfer it to our clothes.

I extricate Mary from the window and lead her upstairs. She is quite ill and weak, so I make her lie on the bed, with a wet cloth on her forehead, while I throw my belongings into trunks and bags, knowing they will be horribly wrinkled. After a while, Mary is recovered enough to totter upstairs to her bed-chamber and retrieve her own things.

And so we leave the Hampstead house; I barely have time to say our farewells to the Tysons, and then we are outside in the blessed fresh air. I shake out my skirts in case they hold any lingering odour and help Mary into the carriage.

'Where is his grace?' I ask Beck.

'He went ahead yesterday, milady, in the best carriage.'

So this luxurious vehicle, also with a coat of arms on the door and furnished inside in leather and velvet, is his second best; even Bludge did not own two such carriages. Despite myself, I am impressed.

'I suppose we are bound for Northumberland,' I say.

'Indeed, ma'am, you are most astute.'

It seems I have underestimated the Duke of Thirlwell.

There is one thing only that prevents me from opening the door of this superior vehicle and seeking liberty – to be precise, one person. Mary has given up all pretence of sitting and lies with her head in my lap, her face pale and sweaty with a greenish tint. I have no doubt now that she carries that rogue Barton's child.

And to be completely honest, there are a set of lesser reasons that make an escape impractical: what I have to sell – that is, the clothes on my back and my pearl earrings, for I doubt I could flee with any more of my belongings – would not support me for long. I wish to confront Thirlwell with this latest outrage. Above all, I want to see exactly what his grace has in mind for me next, and how involved my alleged friends, the Linsleys and the Rileys, are in the matter.

And although I can hardly bear to admit it, I know Congrevance is tangled in this somehow and I long to see him one more time. I allow myself to dream that somehow I can forgive him.

I am such a fool. He must know I'm Thirlwell's

mistress (or allegedly so); if he were kindly inclined towards me at all, could *he* forgive *me*?

After several stops to change horses, we arrive at a pleasant inn where I am shown into a private room. I am glad to see the table is set for dinner (I am not so indignant or lovelorn that my appetite is lost), and to my great pleasure, Philomena Linsley rises from a chair to give me a hearty kiss.

'Where is he?' I mutter. I am not sure of which one I speak.

'Oh, Thirlwell has gone ahead, you need have no fear, and Beck goes to catch up with his master.'

So I am being handed on to a different set of gaolers, albeit friendly ones, who I am in truth very glad to see.

Philomena glances at Mary, whom I have deposited on another chair. 'Your maid looks very unwell.'

'She is.'

'Travel sickness can be a most unpleasant thing. I'm surprised, for I'd expect Thirlwell's carriage to be better sprung.' She sends for her maid Kate and her travelling medicine cabinet, and we embark on a discussion of what might suit Mary best, deciding on a dose of ginger and camomile.

Kate takes Mary upstairs, ostensibly to unpack what we need for the night, but I suspect Kate will do the work while Mary sleeps. After a while, the rest of the party, Linsley, his sons and Admiral and Mrs Riley, arrive from an expedition in the surrounding countryside. Will rushes to my side, enquiring after his friend George and the cat and kittens, and James, somewhat muddy, presents his mother with a bunch of drooping buttercups.

'We have been to see a ruined castle, Lady Caro,' Will says. 'I wish you could have come with us, but there will be other interesting sights, Papa says. And I shall see Mama when we arrive at Lord Thirlwell's house.'

Mrs Riley cross-questions me about the condition of the cuttings we planted in the garden on her last visit two days before. I have to admit that the garden was the last thing on my mind as we left the house.

James, who has progressed beyond barking, sits for a time on my lap and tells me at great length about a pig they met on their walk. A very friendly young pig, it seems, who showed much interest in them.

'And then—' Will says, interrupting him.

'Let your brother tell the story,' says Linsley.

'And then the piggy ate Will's button.'

Sure enough, Will shows us his coat with the button missing.

'We'll have our revenge,' Linsley murmurs to me. 'I believe we are to have roast pork for dinner tonight.'

'And are you brave enough to tell me more of this great conspiracy you and Thirlwell have cooked up?'

'Why, Caro, I'm not a clever enough fellow for that sort of thing. I'm just a simple country gentleman.' He winks at me and shakes out a newspaper. 'Besides, it would upset Philomena, and I can't have that happen in her delicate condition.'

'Well, Lady Elmhurst!' Admiral Riley takes a seat next to me. 'We have excellent weather for travel, and two fine carriages between us, for Mrs Riley's son the Earl of Terrant was good enough to lend us his while he and his family travel on the Continent. We may exchange places often so we do not tire of each other.'

I wonder how they will manage to keep their stories straight with such an arrangement, but my pleasure in seeing them all overcomes my reservations, and shortly good food and a tolerable wine distract me.

After dinner we play cards, before most of the party, tired from travel and their walk, retire to bed. I'm sharing a bed with Mary, who is so fast asleep she doesn't notice me or the light from my candle. I am shocked to discover (for I remembered to bring *Sense and Sensibility*) that Willoughby is a thorough rascal.

And so the trip continues, a jaunt through the countryside, stopping to visit picturesque ruins, and once, detouring from the Great North Road to visit an aged uncle of the Admiral. The uncle, a picturesque ruin in his own right, calls us all by the names of people long dead and frequently orders Will to climb up the rigging. The children are fascinated when at dinner, the uncle uses his false teeth, having first removed them, as a hammer to crack nuts on the table. Will offers to help, and is allowed to crack nuts for us all by this entertaining method.

The hours and days pass as we make our leisurely progress northward. The small adventures of travel and a holiday – good and indifferent inns, meetings with strangers, unfamiliar food and dishes and discussions of places we visit along the way – occupy us.

I am still concerned about Mary, who spends much of her time drooping and pale, and occasionally we have to ask our driver to stop if she is feeling particularly unwell. I wish she would confide in me, but I know she is afraid I will sack her; indeed I should be expected to. I decide I must ask Thirlwell to settle a sum of money on her so she can support herself and the child.

Meanwhile the winks, sly smiles and cryptic comments I receive in answer to my questions about Thirlwell's intentions are about to drive me mad. Now and again I mention Congrevance and am presented with an appalling, studied carefulness; much pursing of lips, propping of chins on fingertips, or wrinkled brows accompanies an inane comment such as: 'Who? Oh, Congrevance. Yes, indeed. I believe – or so I was told – he went to . . .' Any number of cities or countries are cited.

I am sure Fanny Gibbons, who trained us as actors, would be shocked.

The countryside grows wilder and hillier, the roads rougher, and heather scents the air. We are now in Northumberland, and I suspect some ridiculously coincidental meeting will be arranged between me and Congrevance; or at least between me and Thirlwell so he may explain himself.

It is no surprise when, on our second morning in the county, the day we are supposed to arrive at Thirlwell's house, his second best carriage grinds to a halt a few yards from its original position in the court-yard of the inn where we spent the previous night.

Linsley and the Admiral and our coachmen descend to have a masculine discussion of the problem. There is much concerned nodding and bending to inspect axles; carriage wheels are kicked. A few of the inn's grooms and manservants wander over to join in.

'Why, what can be the matter?' Philomena asks with wide-eyed innocence. She, the two boys and her maid travel with us in the Terrants' carriage, and I am glad, since I am sure she knows of Mary's condition but is too discreet to mention it.

I roll my eyes and simper. 'Oh, I am sure the gentlemen will make all well, Philomena. Pray do not concern yourself.'

She smothers a giggle.

As the masculine deliberation continues, we – or at

least I – lose patience and descend. Mrs Riley has now joined the men and appears to be lecturing some of the scruffier grooms on their appearance.

'Why, Lady Elmhurst,' she says. 'Here's a pretty pickle! And look at this fellow – I should not think his neck has been washed in a quarter-year.'

The groom in question shuffles his feet and grins, as though receiving a compliment.

'Under the pump with you!' Mrs Riley dispatches him and turns to us. 'Will and James, pray stand and touch nothing; you must not get dirty and shame us in front of the Duke. Well, sirs, what's to do?'

Much head-shaking and incomprehensible mumbles – the accent of the people in these parts is almost Scotch, and thoroughly unintelligible to my ears.

The coachman is good enough to translate. 'We'll need repairs to the fore axle and offside front wheel, ma'am. 'Twill take at least two days to mend, for the blacksmith in the village has a broken arm, they say, and his sister-in-law's neighbour's son will come over today from the next village to help; but it will take him the best part of a day to get here, and—'

'Never mind,' says Mrs Riley. 'Admiral, what do you think we should do?'

More of the infernal lip-pursing, etc., as they all pretend to make a decision that was agreed upon long ago.

Of course we cannot all cram into Terrant's carriage – why, even for the beginning of the journey, before Mary and I joined them with a second carriage, it was a tight fit, with the children sitting on laps and Linsley in front with the driver. No, no, fitting the nine of us into one carriage is impossible.

'Shall we send word to Thirlwell that we are delayed?' I suggest, eagerly anticipating the reasons why this ordinary and sensible solution will be turned down.

A veritable storm of head-shaking ensues.

'Indeed, no, Lady Elmhurst, it cannot be done,' the Admiral says.

'Why not? There are horses, and these idlers.' I gesture to the grooms and other servants belonging to the inn, who have begun a game of dice in a sunny corner of the courtyard. The cobblestones, I imagine, make for some interesting results.

'Beg pardon, milady, but his grace is most particular about his horses,' says Thirlwell's coachman. He gives a longing look towards the dice game. A couple of maidservants and a few large stone bottles have now joined them, and there is some flirting and much merriment.

'Then a horse from the inn?'

Naturally all the inn's horses are spoken for, lame or suffering from mysterious ailments, or some such.

Wishing to cut to the chase, and to see the

expression on their faces, I say, 'Why, I have the best idea. Why do not I take the other carriage and go ahead to meet his grace? We are great friends now, and I so wish to thank him for his hospitality. Besides, I am sure he has a blacksmith on his estate whom he could send over to help.'

Dead silence. A few embarrassed glances later, there is a chorus of agreement.

I look around for Mary, who seems to have disappeared. Ah, there she is, poor girl, discreetly losing her breakfast in a corner of the courtyard.

Mrs Riley frowns. 'You know, Caro, I believe your maid may be—'

'Yes, she is unwell and she had better come with me.'

I do not want to leave her here at the mercy of Mrs Riley, who will surely bully her, even in a kind way, into a confession; besides, the ginger and camomile are in the carriage.

So Mary and I set off in Terrant's carriage, she pale and lying down on one seat, while I await whatever ridiculousness will reunite me with Congrevance, not even sure whether I want to see him again. But my palms grow quite damp with sweat and I cannot help wondering how I look today, and how he will look, and what his manner will be. (Idiot that I am.)

What if he is contrite and loving and tells me he did not mean those dreadful words he spoke? Or he could be surly and unwilling, forced by Thirlwell and the others to make an honest woman of me. That would be dreadful. I only hope Barton is still with his master, for surely Mary must marry now; and I believe Barton, in returning the earrings, must be an honest man.

We are in the middle of nowhere, hills covered in bracken and heather, with huge rocks scattered here and there, splotched with orange and green lichen, and deserted except for sheep. It's very quiet. A curlew calls overhead, and now and again I hear the bleat of a sheep (or possibly a lamb, glimmer, hogg, teg, ram, ewe, stag, etc.).

The carriage jolts to a stop and I hear a murmured conversation between our coachman and postilion.

I pull the window down. 'What's the matter, sirs?'

'Milady, stay in the carriage if you please!'

Mary looks out of the window and screams.

I join her and see why. There is a large, dark furry blob on the road in front of us.

A *bear?*

Yes, it's a bear, sitting on its haunches, and as I watch, it lifts one large paw, armed with long yellow talons, to scratch its ribs. It swivels its head and snuffs the air.

Perhaps it has escaped from a circus, for it wears a collar. Even in the depths of Northumberland I believe bears do not run wild.

The horses shift and snort. They are not pleased at the presence of the bear.

I hear the thud of hoofs, and men on horseback, masked and bristling with weapons – blunderbusses and some other ancient rusty guns – swarm around the carriage.

Mary and I scream (I, I must admit, while trying to stifle laughter) as one of our attackers waves a blunderbuss at our driver, yelling at him to 'Stand and deliver!' in the dreadful local accent.

First bears and now *banditti* in the English countryside! It is just like a horrid novel.

21

Lady Caroline Elmhurst

'Oh God! They'll kill us.' Mary clutches my sleeve. 'Milady, I'm sorry, I'm with child.'

What an odd time to tell me. 'I know. Don't worry.' I lower my voice to a whisper. 'Don't be afraid. I'll take care of you. I don't think they're really highwaymen.'

But at that moment a shot is fired outside, and Mary and I shrink against the seat.

There's much yelling and shouting, and the door of the coach swings open. One of the ruffians, his face obscured by his hat, steps inside, waving a pistol.

At that moment, the coach gives an almighty jerk – I discover afterwards that the horses decided the bear was thoroughly untrustworthy – and my assailant lifts one leg to brace himself against the seat. Afforded this excellent opportunity to grab and twist, I do so, and the bandit falls backwards out of the coach with a strangled howl of pain. His pistol clatters to the floor.

I grab the weapon as the other door flies open to

reveal a bearded ruffian; a ruffian with a very familiar beard.

'Barton!' I cry, lowering the pistol. 'What the devil are you doing here?'

'Mary, my love!' He ignores me and snatches Mary in his arms.

'Careful—'

My warning comes too late. Mary vomits on to his waistcoat.

'There, there, my little flower,' Barton croons, mopping her up with his coat. 'Beg pardon, milady. Don't worry, milady, that pistol is not loaded.'

I toss it aside, thoroughly annoyed. 'You must marry her immediately. Where is your master?'

Barton looks up. 'He came in the other door, milady, or at least, I thought he did, to rescue you.'

Oh no.

Chiding myself – surely I should have recognised him, by what I held briefly in my hand if nothing else – I open the door, noticing that the carriage sits at an odd angle.

Mary screams again, and I turn to see the bear attempting to squeeze itself inside. The creature has a powerful odour.

'Good boy, Daisy!' Barton says. 'Don't you worry, my love, he's as gentle as a little lamb; he wants only to be your friend, don't you, Daisy?'

I open the other door and peer out.

Lying in the mud is a familiar figure, curled up, hands clutched at his groin. I recognise that long, elegant thigh, the tumble of tawny hair, now that his hat has fallen away.

I jump down beside him.

Mr Nicholas Congrevance

Absorbed as I am in my pain, I know it is she who jumps into the mud with a splash and a curse. My eyes are tight shut. I want to look at her, but fear that any movement will add to the dreadful pain and possibly make me vomit.

She kicks me fairly hard in the ribs.

'What the devil are you doing, Congrevance?' She kicks me again. 'And that's for my "somewhat overblown charms", you whoreson.'

Well, I didn't expect her to cradle my head on her bosom and shower me with kisses after nearly castrating me. Neither had my brother led me to believe that women attacked by brigands turn on their rescuers, but I daresay I look as ruffianly as the rest. I spit out some mud. I daren't move, but I believe I can speak now.

'Sorry,' I croak.

'Bastard,' she spits at me.

I swear I shall kill my brother for this.

'Mr Congrevance, sir?' It's Jeb, one of the men

from the estate who my brother recruited for this ridiculous venture. 'Have some of this, sir, it will do you good. Milady, please do not kick him again, he's hurt.'

She swears and stamps her foot – I know because the mud splashes in my face.

I sit, very cautiously, and take a swig from the flask. It is some vile sort of home-brewed spirit that courses a fiery tide down my gullet and threatens to return.

Jeb stares after Caroline with horror as she stamps off to sit on a boulder at the side of the road. 'Is she the one, sir?'

I nod.

He mutters something under his breath, shaking his head – I make out the words *poor* and *bastard*.

Barton jumps from the carriage and turns to help Mary down. She's pale and in tears, but has a radiant smile on her face.

'We're getting married, sir,' he says and places one big hand on her midriff with surprising tenderness. 'She's having a baby!'

'My felicitations.'

Daisy squeezes himself out of the carriage after them and lumbers over to the side of the road.

Caroline gives the bear a furious glare, and I don't know whether it's just coincidence, but the creature backs away to Barton's side.

Mary reaches out a timid hand and strokes the bear's head. It makes a low, rumbling sound of enjoyment.

The coachman approaches me. 'Beg your pardon, sir, we have a broken wheel. When the bear scared the horses, we bumped against a rock at the side of the road.'

'Oh, very well done,' Caroline says. 'By the way, Congrevance, the Duke has been tupping me for weeks now. He's much better than you are in bed.' She ties her bonnet with a determined air and shakes out her rumpled skirts. 'Bigger, too. *Much* bigger; I believe you know to what I refer. Good afternoon, gentlemen.'

She marches down the road.

'Needs a good whipping, if you ask me,' Jeb says, staring after her in horror.

'I wouldn't even dare try. Thank you, gentlemen. Barton, Jeb, help them with the carriage and horses. The rest of you, get back to work, if you please.'

They grin, raising their weapons, and wish me luck as I follow her down the road.

'Go away.'

'Where do you think you're going, Caro?'

'Away from you.'

'This road leads to the Duke's house. You'll get there in a few hours, I should think. I'll follow you to make sure you're safe.'

'Oh, indeed, yes. From *banditti* and bears, I suppose.'

'I'm sorry it went wrong. I was rescuing you, you see, and—'

'Hold your tongue, Congrevance.'

My lovely Caroline. Despite my pain, I am overwhelmed with happiness to be close to her again. I run a few steps so I can walk side-by-side with her. She gives me the same look she gave the bear, but I am not so easily deterred.

'You look thin.' The bosom is as magnificent as ever, but I do not think it tactful to say so.

'I can't think why. I've been eating like a pig. Not much else to do, though – it's quite boring being a duke's mistress.'

'Except when bouncing upon his oversized ducal member, I suppose.' A thought strikes me. 'You're not with child, by any chance, are you?'

She turns her head to glare at me. 'No, thank God, but Mary is, and that rogue must marry her. You or the Duke had best settle some money on him.'

'I'll see to it.'

The road turns a corner, and a vista of hills and crags opens up, glowing in the afternoon sun.

She stops and regards the view with surprise and pleasure.

I can look only at her.

Lady Caroline Elmhurst

He stands and stares at me while I try to decide what to do as I pretend to enjoy the view; to be quite honest, it is a splendid view, or would be, if I were not so angry.

And I really want to look at him again. He has wiped most of the mud from his hair and face; he is still as lean and beautiful as ever, his hair lightened a little from being outside, I suppose. His cheekbones are sharper than I remember; his mouth just as luscious, if a little chapped.

I want to feel those chapped lips on mine, on my skin. All over me.

'Why did you do it, Congrevance? Why did you say those terrible things to me?'

'I . . . had rather you hated me than grieve for me.' He stares at his hands. They are bare and scratched and somewhat dirty. I don't think he's been playing cards or flirting in drawing rooms recently (but if he has, I shall kill him).

'That's remarkably stupid. It did not occur to you that you might well have caused me to do both?'

'I know.' He looks at me. 'There's a short cut we can take to Thirlwell's house. Your half-boots are very pretty, but I doubt they'll last the road.'

'Don't change the subject!'

'I beg your pardon.' He bows, as elegantly as ever, despite his shabby appearance.

I swallow. 'You're thinner, too.'

He gives me that crooked smile, the one that then, and even now, makes something twist inside me.

I look away, angry with him and myself. A chill wind springs up, ruffling the heather that stretches away around us. The shadows of clouds shift along the hillsides; colours change, brighten and fade. A hawk hangs motionless in the air, before plummeting downwards so fast it disappears from view.

'Who is Thirlwell to you, anyway?' I ask.

'My half-brother.'

So that explains the resemblance between them.

'This way,' Congrevance says. He takes my hand in his and leads me down a steep slope. My feet slip on loose stones and heather, and I am obliged to clutch his arm, bumping against his side.

'But why did you do it? Why did you go away?'

'It wasn't because I was tired of you or had no regard for you. Not by any means. It was because I had no money and because of what . . . what I'd done before I met you.'

'You had no money?' I keep hold of his hand as we pick up a small path that winds between huge boulders.

'Hardly any.'

'Well, neither did I. I was horribly in debt. So what did you do before you met me? Were you a spy?'

'For a time. It's very boring work and no one ever tells you the reason why you're doing what you have to do. But the truth is, Caroline, that I . . . well, women paid me to . . .'

'To what?'

Mr Nicholas Congrevance

I tell her in a short, if obscene, phrase.

Her shoulders shake, her face hidden by her bonnet.

Oh God, I have made her cry.

'Caroline.' I clutch her hand. 'I know it was a despicable thing to do. I . . .'

She turns her face to me and I see she's laughing. I don't know whether I should feel relieved or insulted.

'They *paid* you?'

'Yes.'

She leans against a boulder and howls with laughter. 'You mean . . . I hope you did better with them than you did with me, for I would not have paid you a shilling. Oh God, Congrevance, that is the funniest thing I ever heard.'

'Indeed, ma'am.'

'So, how did you do it?' She starts walking again.

What on earth does she mean?

'How did you find your . . . victims?'

I trudge alongside her, not daring to look at her face. 'I usually kept an eye open for a bored married woman or a rich widow—'

'Like me?'

'Yes. Like you. You'd be surprised how many wealthy women are bored and looking for adventure, particularly with someone exotic, a foreigner.'

'Really? How would you persuade them?' She stops and looks me in the face, for the first time, I think, since I burst in upon her carriage. 'Show me.'

'Show you . . . what exactly?'

'What you would say. What you would do.'

I remember my pathetic attempts to seduce her with my usual nonsense about nursing a broken heart; how I could not sustain the illusion.

She taps her foot. 'Congrevance, I am *waiting*.'

'Yes, yes. I know.' I look around. 'Oh God.'

'What's wrong?'

'I think we have lost the path.'

'What path?'

'Well, it's not much of a path, but there should be a cairn – that's a pile of stones – behind and ahead of us to mark the way, and I think we've descended too low, and—'

'You are such a fool.' She cocks her head. 'Is that a stream? I'm thirsty.'

We follow the sound of the flowing water and find a tiny waterfall maybe a foot high that tumbles into a black pool. Creamy blossoms from a rowan tree, rooted in a split boulder above, cascade into the water.

'The country folk around here believe rowans are the fairies' trees,' I offer, as I attempt to clean the mud dried stiff on my face.

'I trust they won't begrudge us refreshment.' She raises her cupped hands to her mouth and then to mine. I drink icy water and kiss the palms of her hands, and with a brief, light touch she trails her fingers over my face.

'I love you,' I say, startled and aroused.

'I think you say that when you're trying to avoid something, as you are now. I want to know, Congrevance.'

'Caroline, don't you think you've humiliated me enough? I'm little more than my brother's indentured servant, you've probably destroyed any chances I have of begetting children, you've humiliated me in front of my men, you've—'

'Humiliation? I beg your pardon, sir, you know nothing of it. Nothing! I have been betrayed and lied to and forced into becoming another man's mistress, or at least been made to think so; and then your idiotic attempts at banditry – what was the point of that?'

'It was my brother's idea. He thought that it might increase your regard for me if I appeared as a hero to rescue you, but you didn't give me a chance to explain myself. As for yourself, ma'am, you're no innocent. You became – or thought you were becoming – my brother's mistress with very little moral struggle—'

'As you planned! You're a fool, Congrevance.' She stands and runs downhill beside the stream, sure-footed and graceful, and disappears into the thicket of trees that line this narrow valley. I have never seen this place before in my life. What I should do is to climb back up the way we came and search for the path, but I cannot leave Caroline behind; not now, not ever.

I push my way between the close-growing trees. It's quiet in here, dim and cool, much moss underfoot, and very little light coming through the branches.

I stand and listen. All is silent, save for the quiet murmur of the stream.

'Caroline! Where are you? Be careful; my grandfather, the old Earl, liked to set mantraps in woods like these.'

'Nonsense. They'd be rusted through by now.' Her voice is nearer than I would have expected.

'Where are you?'

'Here. Stuck.' With some difficulty, my coat tearing on a branch, I find her trapped by brambles, eating blackberries with great tranquillity. She has a purple smudge at the side of her mouth I long to kiss; her hair is half down; she is the most beautiful creature in the world.

'Did you leave any for me?' I ask as I bend to disentangle her skirts.

She slips a fruit, warm from her hand, into mine.

'Only one?'

'That's all you deserve for not doing as I ask.'

I take her hand and attempt to lead her out of the trees, but I cannot work out which way we should go. The stream that would lead us out, if only we could find it, burbles quietly, but I cannot tell where it is. Branches rip at our hair and clothes and roots trip us. Out of breath and out of patience, at last we find ourselves in a small open space. Some sunlight filters through the branches above, and there is enough space to stand upright.

'Well, Congrevance?' She sits on a boulder, hands folded, a bright, expectant look on her face, as if at the play, or waiting for some delightful entertainment to begin.

I shake my head. 'Very well. I would assume a – an identity other than my own; something foreign and exotic. Or at least foreign to the ladies.'

She nods.

'And then I'd seduce them – or at least show I intended to seduce them – and quite often they'd offer me an apartment or jewels or some other gift. Or I'd lead them to think that I was in financial difficulties and they'd offer a loan – they were always rich women. I liked some of them. I think most of them knew what I was about.' I fall silent. I remember how I planned to do this with Caroline, and how my usual subterfuges and flattering lies failed.

'Show me. Pretend you are seducing me.'

I sink to my knees in front of her and take her hand. I am about to do what I have never done before: tell a woman the truth about myself.

'My name is Nicholas Congrevance. I am the bastard half-brother of the Duke of Thirlwell, whom I believe you have met, ma'am.' I slide her redingote she wears for travel, a long, close-fitting coat, from her shoulders, and peel it from her arms.

'I have, sir. I noticed the family resemblance immediately.' She unbuttons my coat.

'My mother was French, the old Duke's mistress. I was raised as his son's companion after she died, and all went well until our father died quite suddenly in a riding accident when I was sixteen and my brother, a year younger, inherited the title. I resented my brother's new status, and we quarrelled over a woman. A milkmaid.' I draw the fichu from the neck of her gown.

'I do not wish to hear of other women.' She pouts and takes her hands from my waistcoat.

'She made excellent butter, but she was not as lovely as you. She did not have this beautiful, creamy skin, or such wonderful shoulders.' I reach to unfasten her gown, kissing her neck and shoulders.

'Ah. So you quarrelled?' Her fingers return to my waistcoat and I shrug it and my coat off.

'Yes, and I left the country after we fought. My brother thought I was dead. But many years later – careful, Caro, don't throttle me with my neckcloth – I met a wonderful woman who fainted into my arms at an inn, and it was only then that I fell in love again.'

'Oh! How dare you talk of another woman!' She clutches her descending gown to her bosom.

'I wronged this woman quite dreadfully, and my brother, with whom I became reconciled, was determined to make an honest man of me and an honest woman of her. He offered me the position I was to have had as his land agent, and I wore my fingers to the bone putting a roof on a house for her.'

I prise her hands from the gown, kissing each fingertip, and then start on the delightful task of unlacing her stays – short, side-lacing for ease when travelling, easy enough to remove as she rips a button from my shirt.

'And now, my brother, who has squandered most of an inheritance my father left me on paying off his mistress's debts—'

'That was your money? I thought Thirlwell—' She pulls my shirt over my head.

'No, it was mine. All these years, and I never knew I had money here. Alas, he holds the purse strings and refuses to release what is left, although he promises to do so any day. I regret I find myself somewhat short . . .'

Her hands busy themselves with my breeches. She giggles. 'Short? You do not mean, I believe, a *small* legacy?'

'Somewhat large, with time, I think, ma'am. I could not possibly impose . . .'

'Quite larger. Oh, sir, please do impose yourself upon me, I beg you.'

'It is my pleasure, ma'am.'

And so it is; hers too. Time is kind to us, slowing to a heartbeat, a breath, as we learn each other's ways and sounds and tastes.

Well pleased, I open my eyes to see, through a strand of her hair, a path that leads plainly out of the wood, and now I know exactly where we are.

Dressing takes a little longer than it should, and the wood transforms around us into a friendly, noisy place, as birds flutter and whistle, and the trees rustle in a soft breeze.

Hand in hand, we walk out of the woods.

'That was quite acceptable, Congrevance. I shall recommend you to my friends.'

'Much obliged, ma'am, but I am to be married soon.'

308

'Wait.' The play-acting is over. 'You expect me to marry you?'

Lady Caroline Elmhurst

The look on his face is altogether comic.

He stutters, 'But – but – I've thoroughly compromised you. Of course we must marry. My brother won't let us live in sin on his land; he's afraid it's a bad example to set the tenants. Besides, I have a house for us. I have a *salary*. I have a *position*. I have *responsibilities*.'

Poor Nick. Poor Nick, with his battered hands and ragged coat and scuffed boots, forcing out the words *salary, position* and *responsibilities* as though they were shameful things.

He continues, 'It's a far cry from London and society, of course, but my brother often has congenial company, and there are assembly rooms in the town, and . . .'

He runs out of words, apparently, resorting to a somewhat Italianate flourish of his hands and a thoroughly Gallic shrug. 'Damn you, Caroline, I love you to distraction!'

Sheep scatter into the heather as he strides ahead.

'You must be mad!' I shout back at him. 'Why should I marry you? You've done nothing but deceive me since we first met.'

'What?' He stops and turns to face me. 'On the contrary, Caro, I've done nothing but show you myself. It terrified me. The thought of marrying you terrifies me. But you're stuck with me because I love you and you love me.'

I make my way through the heather towards him. The stuff has a tendency to trip me up. I could trip and fall into his arms.

'Are you sure?' I ask.

'Sure of what?'

'Love.'

I can say no more. And in truth, there is nowhere I wish to run, nowhere for me to end up but with him. The cabal of concerned friends who plot and plan our happy ending have done their work. It is up to us, for there is no one else now. We have emerged from the woods and the dreams and nightmares and must now tumble headlong into marriage.

I reach my hand out to him.

little black dress

**brings you fantastic new books like these
every month - find out more at
www.littleblackdressbooks.com**

**Why not link up with other devoted Little Black
Dress fans on our Facebook group? Simply type
Little Black Dress Books into Facebook to join up.**

**And if you want to be the first
to hear the latest news on all things
Little Black Dress, just send the details below to
littleblackdressmarketing@headline.co.uk
and we'll sign you up to our lovely email
newsletter (and we promise that we won't share
your information with anybody else!).***

Name: ——————————————————————————

Email Address: ————————————————————

Date of Birth: ——————————————————————

Region/Country: —————————————————————

What's your favourite Little Black Dress book?

——————————————————————————————

How many Little Black Dress books have you read?———

*You can be removed from the mailing list at any time

Pick up a *little black dress* – it's a girl thing.

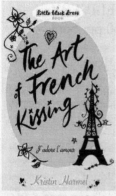

978 0 7553 3828 3

THE ART OF FRENCH KISSING
Kristin Harmel
PB £4.99

When Emma lands her dream job in Paris, she starts to master the art of French kissing: one date, one kiss and on to the next delectable Frenchman. But what happens if you meet someone you want to kiss more than once . . .

A très chic tale of Paris, paparazzi and the pursuit of the perfect kiss

THE CHALET GIRL
Kate Lace
PB £4.99

Being a chalet girl is definitely not all snowy pistes, sexy ski-instructors and a sensational après-ski nightlife, as Millie Braythorpe knows only too well. Then handsome troublemaker Luke comes to stay at her chalet and love rages, but can he be trusted or will her Alpine romance end in wipeout?

978 0 7553 3831 3

You can buy any of these other
Little Black Dress titles from your
bookshop or *direct from the publisher*.

FREE P&P AND UK DELIVERY
(Overseas and Ireland £3.50 per book)

TO ORDER SIMPLY CALL THIS NUMBER

01235 400 414

or visit our website: www.headline.co.uk

Prices and availability subject to change without notice.